THE HIT

and

THE LONG NIGHT

Julian Mayfield

THE HIT
and
THE LONG NIGHT

with a new foreword
by PHILLIP M. RICHARDS

Northeastern University Press
BOSTON

Northeastern University Press edition 1989

The Hit © 1957 by Julian Mayfield
The Long Night © 1958 by Julian Mayfield
Reprinted by arrangement with the estate of Julian Mayfield

Quotation used as epigraph and on pages 36, 115, and 131 of *The Long Night* from *The Divine Horsemen* by Maya Deren. Copyright 1953 by Maya Deren.

Library of Congress Cataloging-in-Publication Data

Mayfield, Julian, 1928–
  The hit : and, The long night.
  (The Northeastern library of Black literature)
  Reprint (1st work). Originally published: New York : Vanguard Press, 1957.
  Reprint (2nd work). Originally published: New York : Vanguard Press, 1958.
  1. Harlem (New York, N.Y.)—Fiction. 2. Afro-Americans—New York (N.Y.)—Fiction. 3. New York (N.Y.)—Fiction. I. Title. II. Title: Long night. III. Series: Northeastern library of Black literature.
PS3563.A9566H58 1989   813'.54   89-16360
ISBN 1-55553-065-6 (alk paper)

Printed and bound by Edwards Brothers, Inc., Ann Arbor, Michigan. The paper is Glatfelter Offset, an acid-free sheet.

MANUFACTURED IN THE UNITED STATES OF AMERICA
93 92 91 90 89   5 4 3 2 1

FOREWORD TO THE 1989 EDITION

The Hit and *The Long Night* were products of an extraordinary career that spanned politics and the arts. Born in Greer, South Carolina, in 1928, Julian Mayfield grew up in Washington, D.C., where he was educated at Dunbar High School. Following discharge from the Army in 1947, he attended Lincoln University, then moved to New York, where he began a career as an actor, playwright, producer, and director. Mayfield wrote three novels in the fifties and early sixties: *The Hit* (1957), *The Long Night* (1958), and *The Grand Parade* (1961). After a brief involvement in the Civil Rights movement at the beginning of the sixties, he went to Ghana, where from 1961 to 1966 he was an advisor to the Nkrumah government and a journalist. After returning to America he played the lead in the Paramount motion picture *Uptight*, which he coauthored with Ruby Dee and Jules Dassin. From 1971 to 1974 he was engaged in advising the regime of Forbes Burnham in Guyana. Throughout the sixties and the seventies, he published a number of increasingly nationalistic articles on black affairs in *Commentary*, the *New Republic*, *Freedomways*, and *Negro Digest*. By the time of his death in 1984, he had taught at New York University, Cornell, Howard, and the University of Maryland.

Mayfield's considerable powers of observation and commentary are evident in his first two novels, *The Hit* and *The Long Night*, striking period pieces that capture the life of urban blacks in the early fifties. The fictional world of both books turns around a cruel paradox: at a time when American society seems to offer unlimited possibilities for personal advancement, these possibilities are not made available to most blacks. Meditating on how blacks might find fulfillment in such a world, Mayfield's fiction suggests that self-knowledge within the marginal realm of the ghetto is ultimately more rewarding than a deluded striving for a place in the American mainstream.

By the time he had completed these first two novels, Mayfield had had ample occasion to reflect on the theme of marginality. He had entered the arts at a time when there were few opportunities for blacks. As a young man in New York, his desire for artistic expression and his political commitments drew him to a number of leftist political and artistic organizations, including the Jefferson School for Social Research, the Committee for the Negro in the Arts, People's Drama, and the newspaper *Freedom*, for which he, John Henrik Clarke, Harold Cruse, and Lorraine Hansberry were floating editors. During the late forties and early fifties, Mayfield lived and worked on the periphery of the established worlds of theater and literature.[1]

Mayfield quickly established himself as both an actor and a playwright within the world of small theaters in the New York City area. There he joined such figures as Sidney Poitier and Ossie Davis, who were also trying to make places for themselves in drama. After a brief success on Broadway in the 1950 production of *Lost in the Stars*, he returned to the small theaters, acting in such plays as William Branch's *A Medal for Willie*. Later he wrote *A World Full of Men* and *417*, two plays that were also produced in small theaters in the early fifties.[2]

Mayfield developed as a novelist in the Harlem Writers Guild, which in the early fifties under John O. Killens had become a sounding board for black authors seeking to refine their craft. The Guild drew from the black New York literary and political communities that Mayfield knew well; among early participants were Rosa Guy, John Henrik Clarke, Sylvester Leaks, Paule Marshall, Lonnie Elder, and Louise Meriwether, in addition to Killens. Langston Hughes, a longstanding literary presence in Harlem, was an honorary member. In the course of their meetings, Guild members subjected each other's writing to frank and often brutal criticism. From this rigorous scrutiny emerged a number of works including *Youngblood* by John O. Killens, *Brown Girl, Brownstones* by Paule Marshall, *Purlie Victorious* by Ossie Davis, and Mayfield's own *The Hit* and *The Long Night*.[3]

Members of the Guild had a sense of being outsiders in the house of literature. According to Rosa Guy, most of the Guild's participants in the early fifties had not yet published. Moreover, these aspiring authors saw themselves as working with subject matter — in particular the life experiences of young blacks — that was not fully accepted in American literary circles. In this connection, Richard Wright was an important literary model who, members felt, had written powerfully about the plight of black youth in *Native Son* and *Black Boy*. Deeply committed to their literary focus, they worried over the lack of opportunities for black novelists, fearing that an authentic vision of black life would not be achieved in print.[4]

Written at roughly the same time in the early fifties,

The Hit and *The Long Night* respond to experiences of marginality that Mayfield had not only observed but also undergone himself. Like the fathers in these novels, he found himself largely outside the mainstream to which he aspired. There was deep personal relevance in the question that he asked thematically in his fiction: how does one find fulfillment when one is obstructed from the American promise of success? The books' advocacy of self-knowledge based on one's own experience represented an affirmation of Mayfield's necessarily marginal vocation as a literary observer of Afro-American life.

Taking the ghetto world of Harlem as its setting, *The Hit* balances Hubert Cooley's failure at self-realization against his son's success. The novel is an optimistic affirmation of the possibilities Harlem holds for all its characters, and it dramatizes a universal theme: the need for all mature individuals to make the most of their circumstances.

The reader's contempt is immediately directed against Hubert Cooley, a janitor who desires to escape Harlem and his family for the life of a successful businessman on the West Coast. Hubert believes that God will provide for this plan by favoring him with a large "hit" in the numbers game. Mayfield condemns not only Hubert's desperate striving for his materialistic goal but also the world of fantasy that Hubert has built up to legitimize and promote his efforts. Hubert feels that he must leave Harlem because he is better than his fellow blacks, because he suffers with his present wife, and because his success will entitle him to the woman he desires. This network of delusions blinds Hubert to his true identity and propels him to a destructive end.

Indeed, Mayfield uses his opening pages to show that Hubert is no better than those blacks whom he despises. As he ambles uptown (where he will be arrested), we see Hubert castigating other blacks. However, the people he sees on the streets are no more flirtatious, shiftless, or reckless than he. Mayfield makes it clear from the start that Hubert's lack of self-knowledge is something more. Hating other blacks, Hubert clearly hates himself; his desire to escape Harlem is paradoxically an attempt to escape his own identity.

Hubert Cooley's belief that his wife, Gertrude, is not the woman for him is belied by what we quickly learn: she has stood by him through his various business failures, helped him raise a son, and assisted him in his job as a building superintendent. Although she is not a fully developed character, Gertrude is important for what she shows about her husband's stupidity and selfishness. Hubert's blindness to his relationships with women is appropriately punished in his relationship with his paramour, Clarisse, whom he does not understand until the end of the book. Despite her laughter and casual pats, Clarisse has none of Gertrude's devotion to Hubert. However, only after the hit and after abandoning his wife does Hubert see the folly of his choice of Clarisse as his companion on his projected cross-country escapade.

Hubert's ignorance of the system in which he places so much trust shows other delusions as well. To see the numbers game as part of God's providence is to misunderstand the highly fallible operation represented by John Lewis, a fledgling numbers banker who lacks the cash and the connections to pay off Hubert's extraordinarily large hit. The numbers operation is part of the fraudulence of ghetto life that Hubert detests. Ironically, in his frenzy to escape Harlem, he has put his hopes in one of the ghetto's dead ends.

Hubert Cooley's desire for success beyond Harlem is particularly significant in the light of his failures in the ghetto. He misunderstands the community, its people, and himself. In furthering his plans to leave, moreover, he ruins his relationship with nearly everyone he knows. Clearly, Hubert is unfit for life not only in Harlem but anywhere. And *The Hit* suggests that his chronic inability to adapt to society underlies his yearning for success.

In contrast to Hubert's tale, that of his son, James Lee, dramatizes the possibility of a satisfying existence in the Harlem his father wishes to flee. Unlike Hubert, James Lee Cooley can learn from experience and see himself from a detached perspective. In his rejection of his own follies, he is an exemplary character who dramatizes Mayfield's crucial principle that fulfillment is possible in marginal circumstances.

James Lee Cooley lives a life of degrading routines in Harlem. He exploits his girlfriend, Essie, who has aborted a baby for him. In his job as a taxi cab driver, he is exposed to racist taunts by his employers and passengers. He lives at home and there confronts the tenuous marriage of his parents. During the day depicted in *The Hit*, James Lee sees the collapse of the relationships that have shaped his life: Essie, asserting her dignity, leaves; his job is jeopardized when he beats up a dispatcher; and his father prepares to leave his family and begin a new life. In his selfishness, his exploitation of women, and his disgust with his present life, James Lee is much like his father. However, the breakup of his world forces him to confront the ideas that justified his behavior. Doing so, he recalls the wisdom of the eccentric McGowan, a fellow soldier during the Korean War:

> McGowan had said it! Life is a precious
> thing and you don't fill it up with dumb
> ideas just because there are plenty of them
> around. Now I see. There are all kinds of
> things trying to pull a man down, but mostly
> it's his own ideas. You've got to stay on your
> toes and you've got to keep thinking for
> yourself . . . always thinking for yourself . . .
> it's your only hope.

Here, in the novel's major reversal, James Lee rejects his (and his father's) exploitative ideas, creating the possibility of a new life for himself. Significantly, James Lee accomplishes this reversal and discovery within the world of Harlem, within the life that he had earlier compared to a dark subway tunnel. He emerges at the end of the book as a character who is freed to live significantly within that world because he has discovered a fundamental truth about human experience.

The Long Night presents a darker treatment of the earlier book's themes. Like *The Hit*, *The Long Night* contrasts a father's and a son's quests to realize themselves. However, unlike *The Hit*, *The Long Night* raises questions about the kind of self that can be realized in a place like Harlem. Paul Brown fails to mold himself in an image drawn from the larger American culture. Significantly, his son Steely insists upon his own values as he achieves his own heroic conception of himself. Steely's triumph reveals in the boy a self-knowledge that Paul lacks. This victory is accomplished by violating social norms; the issue at the heart of Mayfield's second book is the problematic nature of black heroism.

Paul Brown's deluded quest for fulfillment devastates himself as well as his family. A would-be lawyer, Brown struggles through college, fails law school, and abandons his family in despair over his inability to achieve his goals. Paul Brown's ambitions obviously are more heroic than Hubert's, but they are just as wrongheaded as his. Never a good student, he is unable to do the work in law school. More important, he pursues his goals in ways that are irrelevant to his best interests, spending increasing amounts of time discussing the race problem and drinking with a fellow law student.

To make matters worse, Paul misses his opportunities for heroism at home. Once he leaves law school, he loses much of his earlier energy, ambition, and zest for life. No longer pursuing a legal career, Paul abandons his role as parent and husband and finally leaves his family, ending up in the gutter. Through Paul's ongoing dissolution, Mayfield dramatizes the father's failure to grasp the opportunities for self-satisfaction that lie within reach at home. His son, Steely, has always been excited by Paul's vision of Negro progress and his enthusiasm for such figures as Jackie Robinson. In leaving home Paul fails to grapple with his real role as a father who must exemplify important virtues to his son, a role that would have provided an outlet for his vigor and imagination. Thus does he finally fail to discover a viable identity.

Juxtaposed with the father's failure is the son's triumph. Like James Lee, Frederick "Steely" Brown succeeds in achieving a stature and a maturity that his father lacks. By the end of the novel Steely has emerged as a heroic figure, who, unlike his dissolute father, has honored his commitments to his family. Consequently, the son can convincingly shame Paul into returning home and fulfilling his obligations. At the same time, Steely is a deeply problematic character, for he engages in outright crimes.

Steely Brown belongs to a Harlem gang, daydreams

about the intrepid figures he encounters in comic books, and idealizes Frederick Douglass, whom his father exalts. *The Long Night* begins with an incident that forces the woolgathering Steely to put his beliefs about heroism into practice. One day, as he returns home with money his mother has won by hitting the numbers, Steely is set upon by fellow gang members who rob him of his mother's winnings. Then and there he decides to recover the money, whatever the consequences. Steely's determined quest is a self-conscious act of identification with his heroes: he sees himself as "hard" (like his nickname), persistent, and scornful of his own safety.

In fulfilling this self-image, however, Steely becomes a threatening figure. He is willing to cheat and steal for his family. Although Paul tacitly forgives Steely for his crimes, Steely's character remains ethically ambiguous. And this ambiguity is deepened by his repudiation of his father's vision of the rising greatness of American blacks. However, Steely's criminality is not thoroughly repudiated by Mayfield. Indeed, it is seen as one of the givens of Steely's experience and a part of his relentless pursuit of his own vision of himself.

Harlem is always a marginal setting in Mayfield's fiction, and especially so in *The Long Night*. To sink from his dreams of heroism to the life of an ordinary laboring father in the ghetto means abject failure to Paul, for whom Harlem is a realm of social failure and ruined lives. Furthermore, the marginality of the ghetto seems to underscore the lawless and amoral character of Steely Brown's reckless pursuit to recover his losses. *The Long Night* dramatizes the way in which the conditions of Harlem shape the very tenor of life there. Self-realization on the periphery of society demands that, like Steely, one act without the sense of social legitimacy that accompanies life in the mainstream; one must accept the peculiar conditions that life imposes.

Mayfield's literary and political writing in the late fifties and early sixties uses the outlooks of his fictional characters to delineate the Afro-American cultural predicament. As early as 1959, he was arguing that the chief problems of American blacks were the lack of a well-defined identity, an inability to exploit their marginal position in society, and a willingness to neglect their immediate problems for participation in a largely inaccessible white world. As he saw it, the chief function of the writer and politician was to encourage blacks to establish a viable identity by meeting the demands of their personal, social, and political predicaments. As in *The Long Night*, this implies a confrontation with social and political realities that might be distasteful in comparison with an idealized white reality. Such an engagement meant an acceptance of the marginal but immediate black experience.

Mayfield developed the literary implications of this view in the article "Into the Mainstream and Oblivion," which appeared in *The American Writer and his Roots*, a collection of papers read at the AMSAC conference in 1959. Here Mayfield argues that blacks were faced with a crisis of identity, and he dramatizes a lack of self-knowledge in the American Negro that resembles the identity confusion of Hubert Cooley and Paul Brown: "He does not know who he is or where his loyalties belong. Moreover, he has every right to his confusion, for he exists on a moving plateau that is rapidly shifting away from the candid oppression of the past toward — what?"[5] This predicament is made worse because, like Cooley and Brown, the integrationist black leaders dream that "the future of the American Negro is . . .

an increasingly accelerated absorption into the mainstream of Amrican life where, presumably, he can find
happiness as a first-class citizen."[6] However, Mayfield
finds this dream a delusion. He argued that the Negro
will "occupy, to a diminishing degree, the position of
the unwanted child, who having been brought for a visit,
must remain for the rest of his life."[7]

As a result, Mayfield urges black writers to resist the
temptation of being drawn into the mainstream, which
they should instead explore from the perspective of
their marginal position. Indeed, Mayfield argues that
the stance of outsider might give the Negro artist an
advantage:

> He [the black artist] is indeed the man with-
> out a country. And yet this very detachment
> may give him the insight of the stranger in
> the house, placing him in a better position to
> illuminate contemporary American life as
> few writers of the mainstream can.[8]

The continuity between Mayfield's early fiction and
his later literary and political commentary suggests that
the first two novels were crucial to the development of
his thought. As we move from *The Hit* to *The Long Night*
to the early essays, Mayfield displays a deepening sense
that the very terms and conditions of Afro-American
life are different from those of what he calls the mainstream. As a result, he increasingly insists that blacks
should exercise a great deal more autonomy in their
lives.

To be sure, there was much that was poorly defined
in the key words "mainstream" and "marginality." However, these terms allowed Mayfield to structure his vision
of the Afro-American experience around the image of
a collectively maturing black America gradually coming

to grips with its marginal political and cultural predicament. As an essayist, Mayfield continued to think like the author of *The Hit* and *The Long Night*.

The fruit of this personal vision was the optimism that links the novels to his essay on the American mainstream. The lesson of the first two novels is that a realization of self opens up a world of potential, even in marginal circumstances. The sons in both *The Hit* and *The Long Night* have few prospects in purely economic and social terms; however, by the end of the two books we sense that their futures are open. So too in his celebrations of black writers and militant political leaders of the sixties was Mayfield optimistic. In the literary and cultural movements of that time, he detected a collective engagement with the marginal black experience on the part of black activists, writers, and intellectuals. For him, this engagement created a new world of political and literary possibilities. The sense of an open future that concluded his first two novels and "Into the Mainstream and Oblivion" is the link between the literary and political visions of Julian Mayfield.

PHILLIP M. RICHARDS

Notes

1. John Henrik Clarke, personal interview, 28 March 1989; William Branch, personal interview, 1 April 1989.
2. Branch, personal interview.
3. Rosa Guy, telephone interview, 6 April 1989.
4. Rosa Guy, telephone interview.
5. Julian Mayfield, "Into the Mainstream and Oblivion," in *Black Expression: Essays by and About Black Americans in the Creative*

Arts, ed. Addison Gayle (New York: Weybright and Talley, 1969), p. 271.
   6. Mayfield, p. 271.
   7. Mayfield, p. 275.
   8. Mayfield, p. 275.

Other Works by Julian Mayfield

NOVEL
The Grand Parade. New York: Vanguard, 1961

ESSAYS
"Into the Mainstream and Oblivion." In *Black Expression: Essays by and About Black Americans in the Creative Arts*, ed. Addison Gayle. New York. Weybright and Talley, 1969.
"You Touch My Black Aesthetic and I'll Touch Yours." In *The Black Aesthetic*, ed. Addison Gayle. New York: Weybright and Talley, 1970.

ARTICLES AND SHORT FICTION
"Numbers Writer: A Portrait." *Nation*, May 14, 1960, pp. 424–425.
"Challenge to Negro Leadership." *Commentary*, April 1961, pp. 297–305.
"Love Affair with the United States." *New Republic*, August 7, 1961, p. 25.
"And Then Came Baldwin." *Freedomways*, Spring 1963, pp. 143–155.
"Tale of Two Novelists." *Negro Digest*, June 1965, pp. 70–72.
"Legitimacy of Black Revolution." *Nation*, April 1968, pp. 541–542.
"New Mainstream." *Nation*, May 1968, pp. 638, 640.
"Crisis or Crusade: An Article-Review of Harold Cruse's *Crisis of the Negro Intellectual*." *Negro Digest*, June 1968, pp. 10–24.
"The Negro Writer and the Stickup." *Boston University Journal*, Winter 1969, pp. 11–16.
"Black on Black: A Political Love Story." *Black World*, February 1972, pp. 54–71.

THE HIT

This book is for

my father and mother,

Hudson and Annie Mayfield

Magically greased, out of the locks
and chains of definitions, slips the
personal I. In my Harlem, therefore,
find the Race, the Group, but, more,
find Me.

I, too, chase my dream, wrestle with it,
give it shape, but seldom taste it.

Not invisible then, nor yet outside,
but, like yourselves, searching in this
hell of earth, consumed with doing, .
enmeshed by my personal Me,
terribly afraid, painfully alone.

Chapter **1**

HUBERT COOLEY was the superintendent of
four tenement buildings on One hundred
and twenty-sixth Street in Harlem. In one
of these, on the ground floor, he and his family occupied a small apartment rent free. One Saturday night
during the summer, when it was very warm, he was
sitting with his wife Gertrude in their living room.
She had been reading the *Baptist News* for more than
an hour and was not aware that her husband was
staring at her. He was thinking: What a mess! How
I ever came to marry this woman I will never know.
Imagine living with her for twenty-five years! How
did I ever stand it?

"I think I'll walk a little," he announced suddenly.

"All right," said Gertrude.

Leaving the apartment, Hubert told himself that
Gertrude was not—and never had been—the woman for
him. She had not even looked up from her paper when
he spoke. She had not said Good night, God bless you,
or Good night, Dog. He certainly had no reason to
feel guilty about going to call on another woman.

Out on the street Hubert thought: Nothing short of
death can keep a Negro in his house on a Saturday
night. By this he did not mean himself, but his neighbors who were lounging on the front stoops and in

1

the open windows of their apartments. They were laughing and talking too loud, and some of them were drinking beer and wine. They greeted him, but he only nodded his head and walked on. They were not his friends, but Gertrude's. No, indeed! He minded his own business and he hoped they would mind theirs. He had no use for the trifling kind of Negro; they did not know how to act in public. Even now, as late as it was, their dirty little kids were playing in the streets, catching ball, pitching pennies, and playing three-card molly under the lamplight. As he crossed Lenox Avenue a very black boy driving an Oldsmobile tried to run him down. This was convincing proof that young Negroes went crazy as soon as they got behind the wheel of a car.

Sister Clarisse lived alone in a small two-room apartment near Seventh Avenue. Her husband had been a deacon at Little Calvary Baptist Church before he passed on to glory. Both Sister Clarisse and Hubert's wife Gertrude were very active in the affairs of Little Calvary. They were members of both The Willing Workers' Society and The Ladies' Auxiliary. Sometimes on Sundays they were referred to from the pulpit as "pillars" of the church, but to Hubert they were as different as night and day. Sister Clarisse was the kind of woman he should have married: sweet, gentle, and, most important, very feminine. She did not give a man a hard way to go, by contradicting him, arguing with him all the time. Gertrude was a thorn in a man's side, bothersome, constantly after him to do this or that. Hubert firmly believed that a man ought to have peace from his old lady and not a lot of lip.

Sister Clarisse's apartment was a first-floor front just above the sidewalk. This evening she was sitting in the window seat fanning herself. She laughed and said, "Why, Mister Hubert! What in the world are you doing over here?"

He answered that he just happened to be walking by, and she wanted to know why he did not come in and sit a while. He could see nothing wrong with this idea and soon he was seated beside her.

Sister Clarisse had lived alone for several years, and she enjoyed casual flirtations. It certainly was not her fault if some of the brothers happened to pass her apartment now and then. Keeping them at a respectable distance, she possessed a definite charm they could not and did not want to resist. A pleasant-looking, light-brown woman in her forties, she had a dark mole on one cheek that they never failed to notice. Hubert was fond of her high musical laugh. If he made a joke, she would spread her hands and laugh in a Southern way, saying, "You stop it now, Brother Hubert, coming over here and making a girl laugh herself almost to death over your foolishness." He would go to almost any lengths to make her laugh, because sometimes when she was really tickled she would slap him on his knee, and that would make him feel warm all over.

After saying good night to her, Hubert decided to walk down Lenox Avenue; he never wanted to go directly home after leaving Sister Clarisse. At the corner of One hundred and twenty-fifth Street he stopped to listen to a Black Nationalist who stood on a small platform making a speech to an audience of thirty or forty people. The Nationalist was a fine-looking man with glistening black skin. His mustache was thick like his eyebrows and trimmed neat and sharp. His tongue seemed crimson against the ebony of his skin. In a broad West Indian accent his screaming words slashed at his listeners: "Black mawn, wake up! Wake up! Drive this gowddawm white mawn out of Harlem where he comes and takes your mawney, mawn, out of your pockets. He molests your women while little children got no decent schools and go without food in their belly. Wake up! You hear me? I say, black mawn, black womawn! Wake up and recognize Africa as your true home. Do you hear me? Wake up!"

When the Nationalist finished, Hubert was so moved that he could not help joining in the loud applause, although he did not want to go to Africa or any other place where there were so many Negroes. He walked on.

At One hundred and twenty-fourth Street an old man with a clean-shaven head had somehow pushed taps into his bare feet and was dancing on the sidewalk. He must once have been a professional, for he moved effortlessly and gracefully in his small circle, setting up a machine-gun rhythm with heel and toe. Now he mumbled, "Pick up on this. Hey! . . . one . . . one . . . one two . . . one one one two two." Sometimes he would whirl six or seven times, tapping as he went. As he settled down he would shake his head sadly and say:

> "Old Bill Robinson is dead and gone
> But Lightfoot Charlie dances on."

Then he would compliment himself with a raspy laugh and a loud slap on his leg: "Goddog your time, boy. You know one thing? You're a dancing fool." He wore a white shirt with broad green stripes and pink trousers rolled up to his knees so everyone could see that the sounds were coming from his bare feet. But no one paid him any attention, and the old hat he had placed on the sidewalk remained empty. Hubert felt instant dislike for the passers-by who hardly glanced at the clownish dancer. Sure, he was foolish, but at least he was trying. Hubert felt a sudden kinship for the man. He dropped a dime in the hat.

Farther down Lenox Avenue a young woman brushed against him with her hips. "Hi, Pops." Hubert did not know her and resented the familiarity. And who was she calling Pops? He ignored her and walked on. At One hundred and twentieth Street he stopped to listen to singing that poured out of a little store-front church with white painted windows. As the congregation inside shouted the words, they stamped their feet and clapped their hands.

> *Lordy, Lordy, they keep crucifying You.*
> *Lordy, Lordy, they do it every day.*
> *Atom bombs and H-bombs,*
> *Crucifying You, Lord, in every way.*

A crayoned sign on the door said that this was the Happiness Holiness Church. Inside, the song went on and on. Women screamed and fainted. Everybody shouted and the song went on.

At One hundred and fourteenth Street in a tenement hallway a dark-brown boy was kissing a copper-colored girl. It was a long, sensuous kiss, and both of them moved their bodies in time with mambo music from a nearby jukebox. Hubert strongly disapproved of this kind of carrying on. No wonder, he thought, our people find it so hard to get along. They don't know how to act.

Farther on, Hubert saw a barroom where the Negroes seemed to be standing three deep. The jukebox, as usual, was turned up full volume, and they were laughing and shouting over its noise. Such scenes always disgusted Hubert. All these years of freedom had not taught them the most important thing about being free: to hold on to your money and make it work for you. Wasn't that the way the big white man stayed on top? Did you ever catch him spending a dime unless he expected to make two more? If the good Lord would let Hubert catch one of those lucky numbers he would show everybody that there was one Negro who knew how to put his money to work.

As Hubert neared the park he began to hear Spanish from groups of people clustered on the sidewalk. He wondered why foreign people would choose to settle in Harlem. Many of them seemed light-complexioned enough to live anywhere they wished. If Hubert had been blessed with fairer skin he would have crossed the color line and never returned.

It was a soft night, a gentle night on Central Park West. Girls and boys strolled arm in arm. Hubert sat down next to a man and a woman on one of the long benches. His thoughts turned to San Francisco, where he was going if he ever won at the numbers. Once someone had told him that Negroes had very good opportunities in the West. Some of them had their own businesses and all of them were industrious because that was the kind of city 'Frisco was—a place where willingness to work was rewarded. The very thought of himself on the West Coast made him feel

good. Impulsively he turned to the woman sitting beside him.

"You ever been to San Francisco?"

The woman was startled. She turned to her companion, a man of about thirty, who leaned forward
so he could get a better look at Hubert.

"What did you say, fella?"

Hubert didn't answer. He couldn't understand why
the man sounded so belligerent.

"Do you know this lady?"

"No, I don't," Hubert replied. Then he realized
that the man thought Hubert was flirting with the
young woman. That was silly. After all, a man his
age . . .

"Then what the hell are you talking to her for?"
The man stood up. He had a wide, tan face and a
lower lip that jutted out.

The woman said, "Aw, I don't think he meant
nothing, J.C."

"I think you'd better beat it, buddy."

"Aw, J.C. . . . ." She looked pityingly at Hubert.

"Gowan, Pop," said J.C. "Beat it."

What was there to do? Hubert got up and walked
away. It was just like a Negro of that low type to
show off in front of his girl. Hubert wished he were
younger and nearly the same size as that big yellow
bastard. He would have beaten J.C. until his socks
dropped off.

Behind him Hubert heard, "Aw, baby, the poor
little guy didn't mean nothing. Just a little off, that's
all."

"This park is full of nothing but freaks," said
J.C. "This whole city is full of all kinds of freaks.
They ought to exterminate 'em all."

Hubert walked down Central Park West. The farther he walked, the less he felt inclined to return to Harlem. And so it happened that he never went back home that Saturday night.

Chapter 2

HUBERT COOLEY had but one obsession, and that was to leave family, home, and Harlem as far behind as possible and create a new life for himself. He had lived with this idea for more than five years. He wanted to go to another city, San Francisco preferably, and set himself up in some small business. For this he had some qualifications. During the nineteen thirties, he had, at various times, owned two grocery stores, a dry-cleaning shop, and a poolroom. The fact that they had all failed did not disturb him. He believed that he only needed a few thousand dollars and some luck. So, whenever he could, he would bet as much as five or six dollars a day on the numbers. Since he hardly earned this much from his job, it is understandable that people thought him peculiar.

His luck was about to change. It was all in the hands of God, with whom Hubert had a rather odd relationship, one that would have shocked the members of Little Calvary had they known about it. Devoutly believing that God was responsible for everything that happened on earth, Hubert therefore concluded it was God who had done him wrong. This, although He knew that Hubert deserved better breaks, for surely industrious, honest Hubert was more worthy than those Negroes who had climbed up the financial ladder by devious means. Hubert's continuing faith depended on God's doing something it is not recorded He had ever done before: admit His errors and correct them. Once this was done, Hubert would surely have a change of luck.

So Hubert never fell on his knees to pray. His Sunday attendance at Little Calvary was more from habit than anything else. When Hubert heard the congregation sending up fervent prayers, he felt they were all strangers shouting at a personal friend of his. He himself talked with God any time it came to mind: standing in a crowd, working, walking down the street—anywhere. True, their long-standing relationship was undergoing considerable strain. Hubert had not received his due reward. Soon it would be too late; already he was more than fifty years old. But he was optimistic. Where was the meaning of life if God did not correct His errors? If Justice and Right did not triumph?

More than twenty-four hours after Hubert left home he found himself sitting on Central Park South. It was near midnight and he was tired. He sat on a bench and crossed his legs. He had been to Brooklyn, Queens, and the Bronx, and now he was thinking about returning home. He had never spent the night away from home before, and Gertrude was bound to be worried. But this did not bother him. It was simply that his money was gone and he would soon be hungry again.

On Central Park South the skyscraper hotels look northward over the park toward Harlem and the

Bronx. These hotels are like high glass fortresses that guard Manhattan's sparkling midtown district. What fascinated Hubert were the penthouses. Their tiny lights peeked out into the night like small, excited eyes. He wondered what it was like to live so far above the ground. This was an exceptionally hot night, but there were probably cooling, gentle breezes up there. Certainly it was quiet—not at all like One hundred and twenty-sixth Street, where the children whooped and yelled until all hours and the Lenox Avenue drunks raised holy hallelujah every night.

Hubert had never been inside such a fine hotel as the one across the street, and only in the movies and in magazines had he seen the interiors of penthouses. But as he stared up at their lights he could easily imagine the tall, casual men and the luxurious women with their soft, clear skin. He saw them lighting cigarettes and sipping chilled drinks from thin-stemmed glasses. He heard their pleasant, educated talk and quiet, refined laughter.

Across the street a taxicab drew up before the hotel and stopped under its white light. A smiling doorman in a blue-and-white uniform helped the passengers to the sidewalk, and the taxi moved away. The guests were in their fifties. The man was short, rotund, and a little lame, it seemed, for he walked with the aid of a cane. The woman appeared taller in her dark evening dress. There was something in her hair that sparkled; for a moment the hotel lights seemed to set it afire. There was a joke between them, and they were laughing. The doorman touched his finger to his cap as they passed, but they took no notice of him. The glass doors closed behind them and they vanished into the lobby.

Hubert was excited and breathless. It had seemed such a simple thing, and yet how grand, how magnificent the whole thing was! The way the guests had stepped from the taxi and had hardly looked at the uniform that saluted and held the door for them! And they seemed so at home in that wonderful setting.

Hubert thought: If I had been born white this would have been the kind of life I would have led. He knew, of course, that there were many white people who were almost as bad off as colored folk. But Hubert could not imagine himself being both white and poor. The two things simply did not go together. Even God, who had often disappointed Hubert, could not have been so cruel and thoughtless as to bless him with fair skin and leave out the silver spoon.

It was past one o'clock in the morning when a policeman stopped to chat with the doorman of the hotel. The doorman nodded toward Hubert, and the policeman started across the street. When Hubert saw the policeman coming toward him he told himself that he had no reason to be afraid. Central Park was for the public. He was not a bum, because he had an address and he worked for a living. Nor did he look like a bum. His necktie matched his blue suit, and, as always, his shoes shone brilliantly. No one, Hubert assured himself, could mistake him for anything but what he was: a respectable citizen. Still, he could not shake off a dark guilt feeling as the uniform of the law approached.

The policeman stopped a few feet away and took a good look at the little Negro man. He saw a small dark man with tense, nervous features. He did not know exactly what to think of Hubert. Manhattan was in the middle of a heat wave, and yet this man was wearing a heavy blue pin-stripe suit. It was just possible that Hubert was one of those foreign Negroes from Haiti or Africa or someplace like that. Perhaps one of those attached to the United Nations. They caused trouble when they were mistaken for local Negroes. The policeman, a man with fifteen years' experience, decided to proceed with caution.

"Hello," he said.

"Hello," Hubert responded brusquely.

"What are you doing there?"

"I'm sitting," Hubert's voice shot back. "What did you think I was doing?" The words sounded just the way he had wanted them to, bold and self-possessed. He was pleased with himself.

"I'm just asking you a question, Pop."

"Well, I just answered you," said Hubert. "And my name ain't Pop."

"What is your name?"

"Never you mind about that."

"You're up kind of late," said the policeman.

"So are you," Hubert replied. "So what?"

Thus far Hubert felt he had done well, but a deep-seated fear of and respect for white authority made him think he might have gone just a little too far. So he added, in a protesting tone, "I ain't done nothing. I'm just sitting here where I've got a right to be."

The cop moved two or three steps closer. He was a man with blunt features. He stood easily with his hands on his belt. He was not threatening Hubert, but the little man felt intimidated anyway.

"Come on, Pop," said the policeman, "let's move it along and call it a night, what d'ya say?"

If Hubert had stood up then and walked away, the matter would have ended there and most of his dignity would have been left intact. But again the policeman had called him out of his name, and this was something he especially disliked. Besides, he reflected angrily, this *was* a public park and he *did* have a right to sit there. He *was* a citizen.

So by way of replying Hubert used an old Southern expression: "You and Lets move it along if you want to. I'm gonna stay right here." He folded his arms on his chest and recrossed his legs. You couldn't let these people push you around all your life. Sometimes you had to stand up for your rights.

Before Hubert knew what was happening, the policeman had reached down, caught him by the shoulders of his jacket, and jerked him off the bench. In one deft movement Hubert was spun around so that he was facing away from the policeman. At the same time the policeman reached under the back of Hubert's jacket and caught a grip on the trousers' belt. With this grip the policeman jerked upward, forcing the breath from Hubert and causing him to stand on tiptoe to avoid being cut between his legs by the crotch of his trousers. All this happened very quickly.

The cop's patient voice now became a growl. "A nice quiet night and then *you* had to come along."

Keeping his grip on the belt and holding it so high that Hubert was forced to walk on the very tips of his toes, the policeman began taking long steps toward Columbus Circle. Naturally Hubert knew better than to struggle against a policeman. As he was being pushed and carried along, he tried to make it appear as if he were moving under his own power, but without much success. Hubert and the policeman passed a boy strolling arm-in-arm with a blond girl. Hubert could hardly see their faces in the dark but he was certain they smiled. He could easily imagine how ridiculous he must look with his trousers pulled high above the tops of his socks. It was very undignified.

At Columbus Circle they had to pause to let the cars go by. Both of them were breathing hard. "What's your name, boy?" the cop demanded.

Then Hubert had an idea which seemed exceptionally good. Here was his way to repay the cop. He would not reveal his name.

"Just call me Pop," said Hubert.

Instead, the policeman called him a so-and-so son-ofabitch and pushed the little Negro toward the precinct. But Hubert smiled fiercely. Now that he saw the cop was boiling mad, he somehow felt repaid for the indignity he was suffering. He was not afraid any more. They could pour hot oil over his naked body, set fire to his hair, and extract his teeth one by one. But he would never, never tell them his name. Never.

At the precinct station nobody seemed to care. After he refused to answer the first time, they shrugged their shoulders and continued their discussion of baseball. All of them agreed the Giants had a good team that year. One of them expressed the opinion that although the Dodgers had got off to a slow start, the team had now begun to catch fire and was steadily rolling toward the pennant. There was loud disagreement. They thoroughly reviewed the two previous seasons in defense of both points of view. This done, the desk sergeant took a look at Hubert and decided that the little man was a mental case, and all of his subordinates agreed.

"Hey, Al," the sergeant said to one of his men, "take this guy upstairs someplace."

"Okay. I'll put him with the Preacher. He's on his way to Bellevue tomorrow morning, too."

"My God, is Preacher back? What's the matter with those guys down on Psycho? Why do they keep letting him out?"

"They say he's just an average nut and they don't have any room for average nuts. The city's full of them."

The man took Hubert by the arm and walked him up two flights of stairs. He unlocked the door of a room that smelled of disinfectant and urine. He asked Hubert if he wanted to go to the toilet, and when Hubert said no, the policeman locked Hubert inside the little room and went away.

For several minutes Hubert stood just inside the doorway without moving. Out of the darkness came broken, unintelligible murmurings that might have been used in a prayer. Suddenly the words would halt and there would be the heavy breathing of a sleeping man. In a moment the murmurings would begin again.

"Lord, the cross is heavy . . . Lord . . . Thy will be done . . . down with the devil . . . pure and white for Thee I'll keep my soul, O Lord. . . . Though he tempt me I will never . . . Most High . . . never, never . . . Amen."

The man's voice was raspy and hoarse. Could he

be dangerous? Hubert turned and felt for a door knob but there was none, nor was there a place where one had been. Silently he pushed against the door, but it refused to move. He would have cried out but he was intimidated by the great stillness of the precinct building. When his eyes grew used to the darkness he saw the figure of a man on a cot with his knees drawn up in front of him. He lay facing the wall. He was praying and scratching himself. This was the Preacher.

Hubert walked quietly to the cot and let his weight down upon it slowly. He certainly had no intention of waking his roommate.

"Thy will, not mine . . . suffer . . . suffer . . . with clean hands . . . O Lord."

Hubert had never in his life been inside a prison and he had no idea what he should do next. He sat for a long time thinking about nothing in particular. He gradually became aware that he was very tired. Had he slept at all the night before? He couldn't remember. He wanted to lie back on the cot, but what if this Preacher fellow were to wake up and find Hubert off his guard? No, it would be better to stay awake. He would lie back and close his eyes for just a few seconds. He lay back, yawned, and, very much against his will, went to sleep.

This was the best dream Hubert had ever had. The others were usually so vague—confused images and sounds, like snatches from a hundred different motion pictures.

But in this dream everything was sharp and clear. Hubert and Sister Clarisse were having supper in the diner of a streamliner speeding toward San Francisco. The black waiters were smiling and bowing as they set the meal before the couple, both of whom were dressed fit to kill. She would say to him:

"Where did you get the money?"

And he would answer: "I turned the number around and played 417."

"Where did you get the money?"

"I turned the number around and played 417."

Over and over they said the same thing.

"Where did you get the money?"

"I turned the number around and played 417."

Sister Clarisse laughed and put her hand on his knee, which made him feel so good he wanted to scream. Then the train plunged into a tunnel, and Hubert and Sister Clarisse were enveloped in darkness.

He sat straight up when he remembered where he was. His fear rushed back. He had not intended to sleep. Why, anything could have happened to him as he lay there with his eyes closed. The Preacher seemed not to have moved. The man was probably not dangerous at all but some unfortunate fellow who also was being taken advantage of by the police. An automobile passed in the street below but barely disturbed the silence. The precinct building was a great sleeping thing, and Hubert lay awake in its bosom.

"Not my will . . . O Lord . . . but Thine," mumbled the Preacher.

It was true that now and then Hubert had imagined himself and Sister Clarisse together in San Francisco, but he had always put such thoughts down as wishful thinking. After all, she was a respected member of the church, a devout Christian woman. But now that the dream had again brought the idea to mind, there could certainly be no harm in thinking about it. The dream alone was evidence that he had reason to hope.

A man was a fool not to pay attention to his dreams, especially if they had numbers in them. Of course, with everybody dreaming different numbers, you could not expect them all to win. You had to be lucky and you had to have dreams so clear that there could be no doubt about what number was indicated.

Hubert lay back on the cot and cupped his head in his hands. It was true that he had played those three digits in every possible combination except in the order four, one, seven. The week before he had come close but had not hit it.

"Four-seventeen," said Hubert.

It had a good sound to it, and he felt good when he said it. If I get out of this jail in the morning, he thought, I'll start betting on 417. It probably won't pay off, but it's better to play and lose a few dollars than have it come out when you don't have a penny on it. The very day you turn chickenhearted and decide not to play, that's the day your number always comes.

He yawned deeply and felt drowsy again. He thought of Sister Clarisse and how different his life would have been if he had married her. Well, what was it they said? Life begins at forty. Or was it fifty? Who could say? Hubert Cooley might make his big splash yet.

Tomorrow I will play 417, Hubert said to himself. My luck is overdue.

"Amen," grunted the Preacher.

Chapter 3

LATER the same morning, at about six o'clock, a young Negro stood before the desk sergeant of the One-hundred-and-thirty-fifth-Street police precinct station. The Negro's extremely dark features were so calm and expressionless that they seemed almost sullen. His tongue played with his bottom lip and he frequently shifted his weight from one leg to the other. The desk sergeant was a white man in his forties, a hulk of a man with boyish red cheeks set on each side of a florid face. This sergeant was not just fat, he was gigantic. The younger man was preoccupied with his personal problems, but still he could not help wondering how much fat the policeman carried about with him. Two hundred and fifty pounds? No, it was surely closer to three hundred. But weren't there weight limitations on the New York police force? When the sergeant first joined he must have been much smaller. Jesus! thought the younger man, he must have a hell of a time trying to screw a woman. He tried to imagine how the whole act would look and sound but he couldn't.

The sergeant inhaled noisily and began a long, groaning yawn as he mumbled into the telephone. The skin of his face and neck crumbled into a thousand tiny particles. He was not tired, but he wanted his morning nap. Why, he wondered, was the grave-yard shift in a Harlem precinct always like the Fourth of July? They were always kicking up a fuss, these people, for the sole purpose of disturbing his five-o'clock snooze or preventing it altogether. He grumbled a bored thanks into the mouthpiece and hung up the phone. As he yawned again, more deeply this time, he let his eyes rest on the young man in front of him.

James Lee Cooley was blacker than the average American Negro. His was a liquid, whole blackness. He was a little over average height and gave the im-pression of being a dark reservoir of strength. His eyes were like those of a young boy: large, intelligent, uncompromising. But his manner was older, his ex-pression almost grave. He had a singular appearance that often caused people to stare—they never knew quite what to make of him. Just now the sergeant, finishing his yawn with a soft wheeze of relief and satisfaction, was thinking: Black as pitch . . . funny-looking face . . . like sculpture . . . never know what he's thinking. Now what was it I was just talking about on the telephone? Oh, yes.

"I was right. Precinct downtown called in a few hours ago that they had picked up a fellow who fitted the description of the missing Hubert Cooley." The sergeant explained that the fellow downtown was probably a psycho, at least they thought so be-cause he refused to give his name. What did the young man think? Could that be Hubert Cooley?

James Lee felt vaguely uncomfortable, a little dis-loyal. The man downtown was probably his father, and this fat sergeant was a stranger and a white man

to boot. But what did it matter? Fact was fact. "Yes,"
he said, "that could be him."

"You could save time by going down and having
a look," said the sergeant. "Of course, it's hard to
tell. The city's full of crackpots. But they say this
fellow fits the description. A skinny little dark-colored
fellow. Been missing since Saturday night, huh? That
ain't so long."

"My mother was worried about him," said James
Lee. "He never stayed away before."

"Do you know how to get to the precinct on West
Fifty-fourth Street right off Eighth Avenue?" asked
the sergeant.

James Lee knew how to find the precinct station.
Except for a very rude and unforgettable interruption
of twenty-three months spent in Uncle Sam's army,
he had lived in New York all of his twenty-six years.
Going back and forth to school, he and his gang had
raised hell on the subway trains, been chased by
furious conductors through the rumbling cars. And
there was that time when he had been unceremoni-
ously kicked—literally kicked—out of the Fourteenth-
Street station by two subway cops, a white one and
a black one who wasted no love on schoolboys. He
had hugged girls on the trains and pinched at their
nipples when he thought no one was looking, girls
with quick answers and chewing gum and bobby
socks. And later he had ridden the trains with girls
in high heels, nervous, long-legged girls, to basement
parties in Brooklyn and the Bronx, to the Palace
Theater and the Capitol Theater, and to the Roxy,
and to frenzied Saturday nights at the Palladium.
And some nights, cold, flat, gray nights, he had ridden from the Brooklyn end of the line to the Bronx

end. This was because he had been drunk and had slept past his stop. So now he said to the sergeant that he knew how to get to the precinct station downtown.

But the sergeant told him anyway, giving him detailed directions. James Lee mumbled a thank you and wondered if white people ever listened to anything Negroes said.

The sergeant punctuated his thought with: "And don't forget to get on the front of the train, d'ya hear, young fella?"

The young man reminded himself that the sergeant had been helpful, not nasty as a cop could be. So he called back a final thanks before leaving the station.

I'm all mixed up, James Lee Cooley was thinking. I don't know whether I'm coming or going. Running around, jumping into bed with everyone I can find. Hell, is that all I'm living for? I'm twenty-six years old and I don't know what it's all about yet. Damn!

As the train lurched out of the One-hundred-and-twenty-fifth-Street station he found himself a standing place in the front car near the engineer's booth. From here he could look ahead into the black tunnel. As the train was throttled forward, the tracks reflected the light of the onrushing cars and seemed to leap under their wheels. Staring straight ahead into the darkness, he imagined that the tunnel was like his future and that he was rumbling through it headlong. He had no control over where he was going.

There was not a single area of his life that was going as it should. First, there were his parents. Sure,

you had to give up something for them, to sacrifice
a little, but there were limits. Hubert and Gertrude
Cooley had already lived the better part of their
lives, while the best part of his was before him. It
was not fair of his father to go wandering away from
home, nor was it fair that James Lee should have to
spend his time looking for him. Oh, certainly, they
were getting along in years and had had some tough
breaks. But how could their quiet little lives compare
with his? Two years before, he had been in Korea
in the middle of a hot shooting war and he had damn
near got himself killed. But Hubert Cooley had never
been near a war, so what reason did he have for crack-
ing up? James Lee felt he had the remedy for what was
ailing his father: a good, swift kick aimed at a well-
chosen spot.

His biggest problem, he knew, had to do with his
girl Essie. He felt that if he could really make up his
mind what to do about her, everything else would
fall into place. She was waiting for him now over in
their room on One hundred and twenty-fourth Street.
She was probably still asleep, curled snugly in their
big iron bed with her knees drawn up in front of
her in that very special way she had. But no! She
was probably as mad as she could be because he had
left her alone all night. By now she had called him
everything but a child of God and was ready to throw
things as soon as he opened the door.

Now he turned his anger on himself. A sensible
guy with a girl in White Plains would keep himself
free on the nights she was able to get into town. You
did not have to be in love with her—he was never
certain how he felt about Essie—but if you saw she
was a good girl, in your corner, as the saying went,

you did not go out of your way to give her a hard time. Now Essie would be hell to get along with for two or three days. In the end, of course, she would thaw, come around as she always did. He would kiss and pet her, maybe buy her a present, and she would become her usual self again. But this time winning her over would be especially difficult, and he knew he had only himself to blame.

The express train flashed through the Eighty-sixth-Street local station. James Lee became aware of a deep-seated itching in his right buttock. He squeezed closer to the engineer's booth, where he put his hand under his jacket and into his back pocket so that he could scratch himself without attracting too much attention. On hot days when he perspired he itched around the scar tissue of his wound. When this happened he would think up special curses for the army surgeons who had assured him that they had removed all the metal pieces.

Why was it that whenever he found himself alone in a room with Essie he began to feel restless, hemmed in? Sometimes he told himself that he loved Essie and that he ought to marry her and treat her right. At other times he felt just as certain she was just another woman to please him in bed when he felt the need and that it would be the worst mistake to let himself think seriously about her. When he felt this way, he tried to get away from her as he had last night.

"Baby, I'm going out to the precinct to see if they've got any word on Pop. I'll be back soon."

"Okay, James Lee."

She had come around the bed and kissed him, keeping her lips against his so long that he felt he was being smothered. Then gently he had pulled away and gone down the stairs.

He really had meant to come back, he told himself, because it was the first night of her week's vacation. Essie had begged and pleaded with her employer in White Plains, Mrs. Ornstein, for the week off. Finally Essie had to threaten to quit before Mrs. Ornstein gave in. She had been excited about spending a whole week with James Lee, and he had felt good about it, too. But once they were in the room together he knew he would have to get away, at least for a little while. The strange thing about it was that of all the women he saw regularly, Essie was the only one who made him feel that way.

After leaving her he walked over to Bank's Bar & Grill, where he ran into Jacky and Harold. These were his two closest friends from high-school days. Now Harold was married and lived out in Long Island, and Jacky led the life of a Harlem sportsman. They only saw one another occasionally. Their meeting by accident certainly called for a celebration. At the beginning James Lee kept telling himself he should go back to Essie, but this seemed less and less important as the night went on. This morning he remembered only disconnected conversation, jumbled fragments of voices ordering gin, soda, ice, and—what was the crazy concoction that woman had been drinking?— oh, yes, Scotch, milk, and sugar.

"Send the ladies another round and ask them if we may join their party." This was Jacky speaking to the waiter at The Vet's Club. Jacky was always tailored in the best and seemed to have money to spend. He said he earned his money singing, but James Lee did not believe this because Jacky's few engagements in small Harlem night clubs never lasted for more than a week or two.

The women were picked up. They were not good-time girls and were so embarrassed Jacky had to work overtime getting them to relax.

"No kidding. You're really from Georgia?"

"Sure we are. What's wrong with that?"

"I told you guys, didn't I? I said, 'There's a Georgia gal if I've ever seen one.' "

"Aw, go on, man. Did he, sure enough?"

"He sure did." This was Harold, who was anxious to say something to prove that he was a regular fellow, which he was not. Harold was the most successful of the three. He had a job as a layout man with an advertising firm downtown. What was it *Ebony* magazine had said in their spread on him?

TALENT AND ABILITY
SMASH COLOR BAR

"That's right," Harold was saying now, " 'there's a Georgia gal, fellas,' he said."

"How'd you know?"

" 'Cause of that evil look on your face," said Jacky, "Everybody knows that Georgia women are evil as hell."

"I knew you were lying. I told these girls, I said, 'There's a man who was born lying. We better leave him alone.' "

"Let's have a drink."

"What're you having?"

"Tom Collins. I'm hot."

"Me too. Gimme the same thing."

"And you? What are you drinking, pretty?"

"Scotch, milk, and sugar, handsome."

"I told you those Georgia gals were crazy."

"Girl, why don't you stop showing off?"

"You drink what you want. I drink what I want."
She winked at James Lee, who so far had not said
much. He winked back and decided she was fairly
attractive.

"Waiter!"

"How do you girls happen to be out on a Sunday
night? Don't tell me you're playgirls."

"We all went to the ballgame today and decided
to make a night of it."

"Who do you pull for?"

"Dodgers, naturally. We all pull for the Dodgers."

"If you ask me, they've got too many spooks on
that team. It'll never work out. I used to pull for
Brooklyn before they got all those Negroes on the
team. Then I switched to the Yanks. You know Negroes never can work together."

The women protested. "Man, you talk crazy all
the time, don't you?"

"He looks colored but he talks cracker."

"I ain't kidding. I was out at Ebbets Field the other
day and so many boots came running out on the
diamond I went to the gate and got my money back."

The woman named Bernice pushed her chair back
and stood up. "I ain't gonna sit here and listen to all
this nonsense."

"Come on, girl. Have a drink. I'm just kidding.
I'm a Brooklyn fan myself. Jackie Robinson is my
first cousin."

Bernice sat down again. "Are you kidding? Is he
sure enough?"

"Sure he is. My name is Jacky and his name is Jackie."

Everybody laughed. Bernice asked, "Why do you fellows travel around with a crackpot?"

"That's because he's got all the money," said James Lee.

"Let's go someplace else," Harold suggested.

Jacky said, "Drink up, girls. I know a jumping joint on Hundred-twenty third Street. Drink up. Life is short, you know."

They paired off easily. James Lee found himself with the woman called Lottie. She was past thirty and seemed shapely, with high pointed breasts that pushed against him when they sat together in the taxi. The more he drank, the more he thought about them. Later, in her bedroom, her ample figure seemed almost liquid, dissolving and spreading when she loosened her girdle. By then he was drunk and, in a feeble sort of way, desperate to relieve himself sexually. Seeing her flabby breasts sagging on an overripe figure was only a momentary disappointment. Briefly he pictured Essie's animal young suppleness, but he pushed the thought away. Here was another woman to be had in another stuffy little bedroom.

"You're different, you know that?" She snapped off the light and lay beside him.

"What do you mean, different?" He was almost gruff. He wanted to get it over with. He did not want to talk.

"The way you look, for instance. Like you're thinking hard about something. And you don't talk much. That's what I mean, different. Like the Scotch, milk, and sugar I drink. I don't even like the stuff, but it makes me different, see?"

"Yeah."

"Everybody ought to have something that sets them apart. But not too much. I'm talking crazy, I bet. That's 'cause I'm scared. Here, feel my heart."

"Come on," he said.

She smelled of sweat and powder. In the dark her flabby ugliness made no difference. He gave himself to the situation, punished himself, going beyond the few feeble exertions he felt capable of, and, completely spent and disgusted with himself and relieved only by the knowledge that the stupid night was almost over, finally fell asleep.

Luckily he awoke early and was able to avoid the embarrassment that always followed these quick affairs—the strained familiarity, the halfhearted promises to see each other again, the saying good-by to a stranger.

Outside, daylight was just coming to Harlem. There was no need now to rush to Essie. He would need time to think of a good excuse. He had found himself walking near the One-hundred-and-thirty-fifth-Street precinct station when he decided to go in and inquire about Hubert.

Now, on his way downtown, he wished he could remain forever where he was, at the front of the subway train staring ahead into the tunnel. Its blackness was relieved only by the small red, green, and yellow signal lights that dotted the passageway. Perhaps if he stared into the darkness long enough he would find a way out of the dark confusion of his life. But the tunnel suddenly burst into the brilliant black-and-white-checkered Columbus Circle station. The Eighth Avenue "A" train roared to a halt. Its doors hissed open and the passengers pushed out.

James Lee turned his back to the engineer's booth, scratched himself energetically, then squeezed through the doorway and hurried toward the station exit.

"That's him," said James Lee.

Yes, of course he knew the little brown man with the sleep-red eyes and the wrinkled suit. This was his father, the queer duck of One hundred and twenty-sixth Street.

But, thought James Lee, I don't really know him, not really. When James Lee was very small, in the beginning, there were the three of them in what was called a family. But his father had never been a part of them. He was the man who came home to their little apartment, came home from stores, shops, and poolrooms, and talked dreams as they ate their dinner. "This is only for a little while," he was always saying. "Just steppingstones on our way to bigger and better things."

The most persistent memory James Lee had of his earliest years was his father's shrill, hope-charged voice insisting that nothing around them was real and per-manent. They were always on their way to a place where there were no railroad flats with greasy walls and piss-smelling hallways. This was a place where there was money, good food, and plenty of room to move around in. This was always coming next month, next year. Soon. These had all been lies. James Lee had understood that for a long time now. The rail-road flats with the greasy walls and stinking hallways were all very real. Only Hubert Cooley was unreal. James Lee could identify him as his father, but be-yond this Hubert did not exist for his son. They were strangers and had always been so.

"Don't he know," this new police sergeant was saying, "that he can get into trouble hanging around neighborhoods where he don't belong? Suppose something had happened there last night—a robbery, burglary, rape, or something? First thing we do is pick up all the loafers in the neighborhood."

James Lee told the sergeant that his father had never before been in any kind of trouble with the police and that he was certain Hubert would not loaf in the parks any more. The sergeant grumbled to himself, opened a large rectangular book, and began writing. After a few moments he paused and glared at Hubert.

"You wanna tell me your name now?"

Hubert mumbled his name. The sergeant's face was suddenly red with anger. His rock-hard voice roared at the little man. "Speak up, you! What's the matter? Can't you talk?"

Hubert took a deep breath, cleared his throat, and spoke again. "My name is Hubert Cooley."

Where did Hubert live? Where did he work, and what did he do there?

"I'm super of the building."

"What building? The one where you live?"

"Yes, and three more on the same block."

"Well, why didn't you tell me that in the first place? What am I supposed to do—read your mind?"

When the sergeant had received all the answers he wanted, he slammed the book shut, pushed it to the corner of his desk, and glared at Hubert.

"Don't you people have enough trouble without looking for it?" He pointed a thick, stubby finger. "Now hear me. If I ever catch you loafing around here again I'm gonna see that you get some time.

You can believe that." He was a heavy-set man, strongly built, not yet fifty. His steel-gray hair was clipped short and added to the impression of blunt strength. His voice boomed, his slate-gray Irish eyes threatened. It was as if he personally had been insulted and at the slightest provocation would leap across the five feet of desk and railing, catch the little Negro by his scrawny neck, and snap it.

"Now get the hell out of here," he growled. Hubert turned and walked from the building. James Lee followed.

"Pop, I hope you're going right home."

"Sure, I'm going home." Hubert was examining his reflection in a restaurant window. He set his tie right and then began buttoning his vest.

"Mama's been worried about you."

"She's always worried about one thing or the other."

Hubert finished buttoning his jacket and his vest. "A man ain't got the right to sit on a park bench any more, you know that?"

"I knew that before, Pop, and so did you."

Hubert changed the subject. "You got any money?"

"Why?"

"I need it for something," Hubert snapped. "Let me have five dollars until payday."

James Lee knew that Hubert disliked having to ask him for money and it made James Lee uncomfortable. His first urge was to give his father what he wanted so that the scene would be over as quickly as possible. But nothing annoyed him more than his father's expensive habit of playing the numbers. To James Lee the numbers game thrived on mass ignorance, and, though he might occasionally gamble at poker or dice, he had never chanced a nickel on the long odds of the numbers. Besides, his father's payday never came. His mother had begun to collect the small superintendent's salary. That was the only way she could be certain any of the bills would be paid.

James Lee took some silver from his pocket. "Here's fifty cents to get uptown with, Pop. This is the best I can do."

Hubert did not move. "I'll pay you the five dollars on payday."

James Lee fought down a desire to snatch one of the two bills from his pocket and give it to Hubert. But good money was good money and there was no sense in throwing it away. Besides, he would probably have to buy Essie a present to pacify her. This little man, the crazy fool! Why couldn't he be like everybody else?

"Nothing doing, Pop."

Without another word Hubert turned and walked toward the Eighth Avenue subway. For all his neatness, he was a shabby figure. James Lee returned the silver to his pocket. He had no urge to go after Hubert. He would call his mother and tell her his father was coming.

He felt as if his clothes were sticking to his body. He wanted a bath and a change of clothing, but first he would have to rush over to the garage. Suppose that dispatcher had given his taxi to someone else? He couldn't afford to lose a day's work. After picking up the cab he would rush home to Essie. He stopped at the corner and caught a crosstown bus.

Chapter 4

IN THE ROOM on One hundred and twenty-fourth Street Essie Dee Turner tried going back to sleep but her nerves were tense. A few minutes earlier Essie had been shocked out of her sleep by the shrill scream of a woman. She had sat straight up in her bed, wide awake, not daring to breathe. Then the woman had started crying, a low, throaty moan, and Essie had realized with relief that it was not a woman who had screamed but only that doggoned cat out there in the back yard. She was certain it was the same cat that raised so much sand every time she spent a night here. The good Lord knew, that old pussy would cause her to have heart failure one of these nights if she kept screaming like that.

She lay back on her pillow and tried to get to sleep. Where was James Lee? Could something have happened to him? As she thought about him it seemed that he was there, lying beside her, touching his lips to her ears and throat, murmuring all that foolish talk that always made her wonder if he was sincere. It was: Baby, you know I love you, don't you, honey? I'm crazy about you. You kill me with those crazy eyes. . . . New York nonsense talk, she called it, but she liked to hear it. Yes, James Lee, sweet black man

. . . he had her number, all right. The tension lifted. She yawned and fell asleep.

They were somewhere, the two of them, inside a house. She knew this house well and felt at home here. James Lee said something about being sleepy and she agreed that it was time to go to bed. She watched him take off his clothes, felt that same anxious sensation she always experienced when she saw the hardness of his body. And she saw that he was not really sleepy; nor, come to think of it, was she. They were together as one, she and James Lee, making love in that wild, clutching, fighting way that usually left her weak and trembling. But it was not definite to her, and she was vaguely dissatisfied.

And now they were in a living room. She could see this very clearly. The light-colored furniture was very modern, like Mrs. Ornstein's in White Plains. It was not cheap, either, not the kind they sell on One hundred and twenty-fifth Street, but solid stuff she would take good care of and polish each and every day.

And there were children. She could not really see them, but she knew they were there. Perhaps they were a boy and a girl or two boys or two girls. She was not certain of anything except that they belonged to her and James Lee. They were all over the place, those kids, running and giggling and making a racket, and James Lee was smiling all over himself because he really did like them, after all. Well, hadn't she been telling him all along that kids were the best things in the world? Essie had so much happiness that everything was soft and warm.

Then she saw the basin and she was living through the whole terrible episode again. That basin? She would never forget it, never! That was her blood, wasn't it, the pinkish splotches on the white enamel? At first she was not certain, but it had to be her blood because it was she who sat over the basin. It was strange to be looking at it like that. The pain was there, too, the one that was sharper than any other, deeper than any other; the one that made her go hot and cold and finally numb. It had been awful, terrible. God Jesus! there had been no words for it. She had felt the pain even in her teeth.

That damned woman! The wiry, mannish little woman that looked no more like a nurse than she looked like the Queen of Sheba. She was there, this woman, on her knees in front of Essie, probing with the long metal thing, scraping and murmuring: "It won't be long, honey, just a little more." But suddenly it wasn't the little ugly woman down there but James Lee, and Essie knew that it had been James Lee all the time. The hot pain was pulling at her spine and throbbing at the base of her neck. She heard the scream that was torn out of her body and she was thinking: Oh, Lord, Lord, please. I can't stand it, please, Lord! She pulled at James Lee's head and struck her fists against his shoulders. Please, honey, this ain't the way it's supposed to be. James Lee, baby, it was never meant to be this way. Can't you see? Please, please! She pulled at him, struck him, pleaded with him, but he kept right on. There, in her pain, she saw how terrible everything was, how wrong and awful to kill the baby that wasn't born, and if this was the way it was supposed to be, then they were better off dead. She had to stop it before it was too late. She had to stand up and fight a thing like that or there was no hope for anybody. She felt herself drowning, being sucked down into the heavy blackness, and her throat was clogged with a terror. She opened her mouth to scream but no sound came. She was lost.

Again Essie was sitting straight up in the bed. Her breath came in deep, noisy gasps. Her body was wet with perspiration and she trembled with cold. Her eyes were wide open and unseeing. She wanted to get out of the bed, but she could not will her arms and legs to move.

Above, on the next landing, she could hear heavy footsteps moving along the squeaky wooden floors of the hallway. This meant that it was seven-thirty and the plump, brown-skinned woman upstairs, the one that always reminded Essie of her mother down home, was getting her husband off to work before she left herself.

The woman's soprano voice seeped through the thin floors. "Lonzo, don't you forget to go by and see how Leo is."

Essie knew that Lonzo was about forty-five years old and baldheaded with a bulging pot of a belly. He said, "Woman, if you was to stop worrying about what *I* is supposed to do, and worried about what *you* is supposed to do, you'd be a damned sight better off."

"Lonzo!" Her high voice was full of shock. "Don't be cursing in the hallway like that so everybody in the world can hear how evil you are."

Now Lonzo was down to Essie's landing. He was mumbling to himself as he walked past her door. "With that woman, if it ain't one thing it's the other." Essie heard him sigh wearily as he started to let himself down the next flight of stairs.

The talk had served to pry her mind and body loose from the grip of the nightmare. She began to think. Quietly and slowly the thought formed itself: I've got to get out of here. Calmly and soberly it took body and grew. *I've got to get out of here.*

Still she did not move, and now her eyes darted from the dirty, streaked wall in front of her and swept around the room. They rested a moment on the black, greasy gas stove that she had scrubbed and scoured with steel wool and had never been able to clean; sped on to the single window that looked out onto the nothingness of other back windows with the same torn green shades and the gray grassless yards below; darted up to the dingy ceiling and stopped on the large heavy white patch of plaster that she had told James Lee would one day crash down and kill them. *I've got to get out of here.*

She had never liked the room, not from that very first moment when James Lee had swung open the door and announced that this was it. He had done this proudly, as if he had accomplished something in finding it. Yes, a young couple needed a place of their own. Each time they went to a hotel she was nervous and tense because she realized the clerk and all the hotel help knew that she and James Lee were not married. James Lee had said this was the way people did things in New York, but that did not make her feel any better. So she had agreed to the room. But this place was much too small, hardly large enough for the roaches, let alone her and James Lee. Why, the room she had in the Ornstein house in White Plains was fully twice as large. Of course, it was in the basement of somebody else's home, but even that was better than having to walk up four

flights of stairs through a dimly lit hallway to this
dirty little back room.

Essie's body trembled under the nightgown. It was
silly to be so cold when anybody could see that it was
going to be another hot day. *I've got to get out of
here.* But still she did not move.

Despite her dislike for the room, their first night
had gone well. They laughed about how much noise
the bed made and decided to get some lubricating oil
so that everybody in the house would not know their
business. James Lee declared that the last couple
must have been pretty old if they hadn't minded such
noisy bedsprings. Later in the night, after they had
given to and taken from each other, after they were
both drowsy and satisfied and ready for sleep, Essie
had gone to the bureau drawer and taken out her
nightgown. What the hell was that? James Lee wanted
to know. She answered that it did not seem right to
sleep naked, and he laughed so hard that Essie was
certain he would wake everybody in the building.
She had to kiss him on the mouth to shut him up, and
later they slept, her head on his chest, their bodies
warm against each other, and the nightgown on the
chair, where she had left it.

She forced herself to concentrate: I've got to get
out of here.

Now she moved for the first time, pushing back
the covers and throwing her legs over the side of
the bed. With her toes she found her bedroom slippers
and slid her feet into them. She jerked her robe from
the chair and wrapped it around her trembling body
as she stood up.

Who did James Lee think she was, anyway? He
certainly had his people confused. If he thought she

was going to sit there like a fool and wait for him
to make up his mind to come home, he had another
think coming. After pleading with old lady Ornstein
for these few days off just so she could spend some time
with this good-for-nothing, low-down snake of a Negro—did he think she was going to spend those days
sitting in their dirty room alone? Well, we would see
about that!

Her pink toothbrush lay on the bureau in the
glass container beside the tube of toothpaste. She
picked them up and gathered her washcloth, towel,
and soap from the bureau drawer. She pulled her
robe tightly about her and cracked the door to see if
there was anyone in the hallway. Finding it empty,
she pulled the door shut behind her and tiptoed along
the hallway toward the bathroom. But just then a man
came down the stairs from the floor above, a light-
skinned young man with a round porkpie hat. He
smiled—she thought it was more of a grin—and said
good morning to her. She only half nodded and hurried to the bathroom, where she locked herself inside.
When these New York men spoke to you they were
usually after something more than a good morning.
None of them had any respect for women. Why, even
married men had tried to get fresh with her! She
splashed cold water over her face and shivered.

New York men were no good anyway, Essie reflected. She had gone through the works with one by
name of James Lee Cooley and he was the last one
she ever would have. If anybody ever saw her going
with another New York man, trying to fall in love or
do something foolish like that, she wanted that somebody to give her a good swift kick.

Now she was hurrying frantically. She had to get

dressed and away before James Lee came. If he were to come in just now . . . well, she had let him change her mind before.

In her haste she dropped the toothbrush container and its thin glass tinkled over the floor. Impatiently scooping it up, she pricked her hand with a crystalline fragment. She said "Shoot!" and flung the debris into the trash basket.

Back in the room, she looked at the reflection of her slender brown legs in the mirror as she stepped into her skirt. Her thighs were lean and smooth, and she told herself for the thousandth time that she could use a few more pounds around the hips. But then, New York girls liked being skinny. New York . . . James Lee . . . maybe he could push these local girls around, but he was thinking like Grandpa dreamed if he had any idea he could do that to her. Men were crazy. All you had to do was let one of them know you liked him a little bit, and right off he . . . how did the song go?

> . . . *he'll start cutting a hog.*
> *Just be good to a man, Lord,*
> *And he'll treat you like a dog* . . .

She sat down before the mirror and began brushing her hair with quick, angry strokes. The ends were breaking off, and it was time to have it done again. Maybe when she got to her sister's house she would call Madam Johnson's for an appointment. But why not splurge a bit? Yes, it would not be Madam Johnson's this time but Rose Meta's. A good hairdo would pick up her spirits.

Suddenly the hand with the brush stopped in mid-air. She wasn't coming back! She had not really known it until that moment, but it was clear now. It was not just another of those times when he would melt her with a smile or a kiss. It was not just that he had left her alone on the first night of her vacation. Worst things had happened between them and she had walked out only to return at the first telephone call. But this was different.

So there was no hurry now. It no longer made any difference if he came in before she left. She knew he could not stop her leaving. He could get down on his knees, start cursing and threatening, even try to make love to her, but he would not be able to stop her.

She felt really happy, and it seemed to her that this happiness was a new feeling altogether. She looked into the mirror and said aloud, "Essie Dee Turner, you're a damned fool." And she thought, Excuse me, Jesus, for talking like that. When she finished her make-up she began throwing things into her suitcase. She would take only what was necessary. The rest she could get later.

She slammed the door behind her. Inside, something fell to the floor with a dull crash—probably the water glass that had been sitting on the basin. Even this made her feel good. For a moment she toyed with the idea of going back and smashing everything she could get her hands on. But now she wanted to be outside the house altogether. Walking down the steps, she hoped she would meet old lady Graham on the first floor. Mrs. Graham was the landlady from Barbados who always looked at Essie Dee as if she knew the girl was living in sin. One thing was certain: if she stuck her head into the hallway this morning, she would get a piece of Essie's mind. But old lady Graham, perhaps sensing danger, did not appear. Essie opened the door and stepped into the street.

The loudspeaker of the record shop at the corner was giving out with a hot record by a white woman who sounded almost colored:

> *Going to Chicago, sorry I can't take you,*
> *Going to Chicago, sorry I can't take you,*
> *Nothing up there a man like you can do.**

Essie decided that one day she would buy that record just to remind her of the day she broke free of James Lee.

She stopped at the corner of Lenox Avenue to change her bag from one hand to the other, and that was when the man bumped into her. He bowed slightly and tipped his hat and said, "Excuse me, Miss." He had a pencil mustache and he was grinning. Essie was sure he had bumped into her on purpose.

"Can I help you with your bag, Miss?" He still held his hat in his hand and showed a wide expanse of teeth.

"Look, joker," yelled Essie, "the way I feel about men this morning, you'd better get the hell out of my face!"

She had shouted at him so suddenly and so loudly she had frightened herself. The man's grin disappeared and he pushed his hat hastily onto his head. "Excuse me, Miss," he whispered and walked quickly toward One hundred and twenty-fifth Street.

Imagine cursing out loud like that! Why, she was

---

* From "Goin' to Chicago Blues" by James Rushing and Count Basie. Copyright © 1941 by Bregman, Vocco and Conn, Inc., 1619 Broadway, New York 19, New York. Used by permission.

beginning to sound just like one of those New York girls.

She raised her hand and hailed a taxi going south on the other side of Lenox. But a taxi going north was closer, and he gassed his car toward the curb where Essie stood. The driver making the U turn saw himself about to lose a fare and he put on a burst of speed. Their tires squealed as they slammed on brakes to avoid a collision. Essie walked around the intruding taxi and stepped into the one she had hailed.

That would really have been something, she thought, if the two cabs had run into each other trying to get to me. What in the world was the matter with her, thinking all these devilish thoughts and yelling at men in the street? She sat back on the seat and crossed her legs and smiled. You could say what you wanted about Essie Dee Turner, that she was not the smartest person in the world, that it sometimes took her a while to catch on; but one thing was sure: she never made the same mistake twice. Nobody could say that about Mrs. Turner's little girl.

Chapter **5**

THIS MORNING Gertrude Cooley told herself that she had too much to do to worry about Hubert. Monday was trash collection day, and all the cans would have to be out on the street before ten o'clock. In the house next door they were complaining about having no hot water, and she would have to get the furnace started. This was not an easy job once the fire died completely. A pane was broken in the front door of number 67 across the street and would have to be replaced. Sarah Anderson was complaining that her toilet would not flush, but this would have to wait until Hubert came back. She couldn't be expected to do everything.

She prepared bacon, eggs, hominy grits, and coffee for herself. She always ate a good breakfast before beginning her morning chores. When she had finished, she put the dirty dishes in the sink and covered them with water. A good meal for the roaches, she thought, but this morning she did not have time to skirmish with them. For seventeen years in this apartment she had been at war with the roaches, but they seemed as plentiful as ever. She sighed. Despite all the powders and sprays and the efforts to starve them out by keeping the kitchen clean and dry, it looked as if they would win in the end. "You'll bury me yet," she murmured, taking a halfhearted whack at a black peanut shape that scooted for refuge into a hole under the sink.

Gertrude put on her work clothes. These consisted of a green fatigue jacket and trousers James Lee had brought home from the army, which she had altered so they fitted her. She was a tall, heavy woman, bigbosomed, with strong arms and shoulders. Her movements seemed slow, but this was because they were so deliberate. The average task took less time in her hands. At almost fifty years of age she was in good health, though in the last few years she had begun to tire more quickly.

She went down to the basement and brought up two cans of trash. This was difficult, because the cans were large and heavy and she had to drag them up one step at a time. It was really a man's work, she told herself, and she ought not to be straining her back with heavy cans. But the job had to be done, and if Hubert was not there it was up to her to do it. James Lee helped occasionally, but he was not home much. Nowadays he often stayed away all night. She did not mind this. He had a right to his life without having to worry about the old folks. But she wished someone would see that she had some rights, too. Both her men, Hubert and James Lee, ought to understand that she could not keep up a house by herself.

She dragged the last of the cans to the front vestibule, where she paused to catch her breath. She would like to die, sudden-like, while they were both away from home. She could imagine their faces as they stood above her body. Maybe they would cry a little —not for her, but because they had treated her so badly and now they would not have anybody to wash, clean, and cook for them. It would serve them right.

She took a deep breath and began dragging the first can down to the street. It was not like Gertrude to indulge in morbid thoughts. She never worried about death and sickness. Besides, she knew that if she did pass on, they would not really care. James Lee might think he had loved his poor old mother, but neither he nor Hubert knew anything about love. Loving somebody was doing things for them and helping to make life easier for them. Clearly, nobody loved Gertrude.

"Good morning, Mrs. Cooley."

"Good morning, Mrs. Williams."

Mrs. Williams was a decrepit old widow who lived across the street. Her yellow, lifeless skin sagged on her bones and her trembling face always looked as if

she were about to cry. She lived alone in her little
third-floor front room with the idea that a mysterious
group of people was planning to kill her. This same
group had been responsible for her husband's death
fifteen years before. Like many people in the block,
she found Gertrude a sympathetic listener, and every
few days brought in new evidence she had uncovered.

"It won't be long now, Mrs. Cooley."

"It won't?"

"Oh, no, indeed," Mrs. Williams whispered. Gertrude detected the odor of the cheap wine Mrs. Williams drank. It was a sweet, heavy smell, oppressive
and sad.

"Any day now, Mrs. Cooley," she said. "In fact, you
might say any minute."

"What are you going to do about it?" Gertrude
asked. About this same time the previous year Mrs.
Williams had felt she was in immediate danger. At
other times she felt she had her enemies stymied. Gertrude had no idea what caused the old woman to feel
one way and then the other, but it was obvious that
all of Mrs. Williams' fantasies were very real to her.
This morning Gertrude was slightly annoyed. She had
troubles and complaints of her own. She wished she
could bring herself to be rude to Mrs. Williams, but
she could not.

"I ain't afraid of them, Mrs. Cooley. You know that,
don't you?" Gertrude nodded. Mrs. Williams' deep-
lined face seemed to grow duller even as Gertrude was
looking at it. "But this time I think they will win, just
the way they did with Mr. Williams." She rested her
hand on Gertrude's arm. "God bless you, dear Mrs.
Cooley. You're the only one that understands." And
with her odor of sweet wine and lace, with her petti-

coat showing beneath the hem of her dress, Mrs. Williams walked across the street to her little room with its quiet terror.

Gertrude went back to work. What was it like, she wondered, to be like Mrs. Williams, to think about unreal things as if they actually existed? Gertrude counted herself among the lucky ones of the world in that she was practical and down to earth. Everyone who knew her shared this opinion. She did not think of herself as especially bright. She had no idea what made the world tick, nor did she much care. But she looked upon herself as strong. She felt a measure of pride when friends said to her: "Gertrude, I declare, girl, don't nothing ever get you down, does it?"

No, nothing ever did. It was almost two years now since she had discovered that Hubert really intended to leave her. One day she had decided to clean his closet, and inside, pushed back into a corner, she had found the suitcase. Even now she could remember the smell of its new leather. She had never seen it before, had not known it was in the house. Under a transparent plastic covering were shirts, ties, socks, and underwear, all new. Certainly an ordinary thing, a suitcase with clothing, but when she thought of the hints and innuendoes, the veiled threats—"Woman, you just might wake up one of these mornings and find me long gone"—the suitcase and the clothing, hidden for she did not know how long, made sense to her as soon as she discovered them.

In the cellar of the house next door she began to gather kindling and paper for the furnace. Whenever Hubert wandered away and let the fire go out, she had to get it started again. The draft of the old furnace was not good. When she set fire to the paper and

kindling the cellar filled up with smoke. With stinging eyes, coughing and wheezing, she stooped over the
door of the furnace and tried to nurse the tiny flame
within. This was also a man's job, she decided, and
she was beginning to think she was the only man in
the house.

No, she never let anything get her down. She had
never mentioned finding the suitcase in the closet, nor
had he brought it up, though he knew she must have
seen it. It was a silent barrief between them. Well,
Gertrude, she told herself, you're pretty good. You
wake up one morning and find you don't have any
marriage, that the old man don't want you any more,
but you just keep on going like nothing ever happened.

Oh, she had known before that everything was not
all right. She had her ways of telling. It was before
the discovery of the suitcase, almost a year before,
that they had tried for love in bed. She had sought to
arouse in him a need, a desire for her, and he had
made an effort to respond; but nothing had come of
it, nothing but embarrassment and escape to opposite
sides of the bed and heavy, forced sleep.

The color of the fire changed from a dull yellow to
an intense blue and the smoke began to clear away.
She closed the door and set the thermostat. Then she
went to her apartment and washed her face. Her work
was not half done and she was tired already. She
looked at herself in the mirror and saw that she was
ugly. Not at first, of course, but gradually, as she was
able to imagine what *he* saw when *he* looked. Yes, she
was ugly. She swallowed hard and turned away from
the glass. "To tell you the truth," she said aloud, "he
ain't so hot-looking either."

Sometimes it was almost too much to bear, the dry, empty routine with its frustration: waking, eating and sleeping, working four apartment houses, going to church. "I'm forty-nine years old!" she said, thinking: Lord, only forty-nine, not old at all. She felt she was brimming over with life and she wanted to give everything of herself. She was hurt that nobody wanted her —not Hubert, not anybody. So she kept herself strong. When she felt a need to be needed, loved, made over, she teased herself and said, "You're not a hot girl any more, so keep your pants on." And sometimes she managed to laugh.

Where was she to blame? During the past three dull and empty years she had re-examined every particle of their lives together so that she would know where she had failed. But the most intense remembering, the going over in her mind of everything that had passed between them—all this had uncovered nothing to clear away her confusion.

She opened the supply closet and took out a pane of glass that would fit into the front door of Sixty-seven. With the glass, the tools, and the putty she crossed the street.

"Jesus, have mercy!" she muttered, and she meant have mercy on Hubert and James Lee and Gertrude Cooley. God knew she had done the best she could.

She had stuck with him through all the hard years. At the time they married, Hubert worked as a messenger in the garment district. He liked his job and his boss, Mr. Rosenblatt, who taught Hubert the value of cloth, how to measure and cut it. Hubert was a hard worker and thrifty. He began saving his money because he wanted to open a dress shop in Harlem. But

Mr. Rosenblatt was forced to shut down in 1932, and Hubert was out of work for a while. He used up his savings before he found another job. In 1934, Hubert rented a grocery store and managed to hold onto it for a year before it went under. In 1936, he rented another one, smaller and less ambitious, but this failed, too. Between these ventures he worked at anything he could find and saved until he could try again. Later there was a poolroom that was always crowded but never seemed to show a profit, and soon that had to be given up.

These were the lean thirties, bad thirties—the furious years of struggling just for food and a place to live. On gray, hopeless mornings Gertrude often sat on the "slave block." That was what colored women called the little park up in the Bronx where they were scrutinized by the white housewives who decided which ones looked honest and clean enough for a day's work in their homes. Gertrude was chosen often enough, but when she was away she had to leave James Lee alone. Each night she rushed home, cleaned, cooked, and laid out dinner for them. The boy, always dark and silent, would eat hungrily while Hubert talked away about how much money they had saved and how long it would be before they could lease the store or shop and go into business for themselves again. But somehow things never worked out the way he said they would.

The best thing of all happened in 1938. This was when she heard about the superintendent's job on One hundred and twenty-sixth Street. A job like that meant always having a roof over their heads and being able to draw a small salary besides. James Lee was ten years old that year, and it was time they were settling down in one place. At first Hubert had not understood how important it was. They quarreled about it, but gradually he came around. One day he walked down to Madison Avenue and talked with Reisling & Sons, Real Estate Agents. He came home with the job. For fifteen years now they had had an apartment rent free and always enough to eat.

It was a little past eight o'clock when Hubert came home.

"That you, Hubert?"

"It's me, Gertrude."

She made a vow. She would not argue with him. She would not start a fight and if one started she would not keep it up. What did it really matter that he had been away from home two days? What was wrong between them was deeper than that. She would do her best to keep everything calm. Nothing was going to get her down. She went out to the hallway where he was taking off his jacket and hanging it in the closet.

He said, "Gonna be hot today."

"Looks that way."

"How you feel?"

"Fine," she answered.

He did not look at her.

"James Lee call you?"

"Yes."

He said, "I spent the night in jail, y'know."

"I hear tell."

"Colored man can't even sit in the park no more."

He began unbuttoning his shirt. He was methodical and neat. She liked to watch his movements. Once the shirt was off he would find a hanger, put the shirt on it, and fasten all the buttons before hanging it in the closet. It did not matter that the shirt was dirty. Hubert did not believe in crumpling shirts into a ball and stuffing them into a hamper.

"You hungry?" asked Gertrude.

"Some."

"I'm fixing you some breakfast."

"Thanks."

After Hubert had taken a bath and shaved he came into the kitchen and sat down to the food she had prepared. He emptied his plate and asked for more.

"Did the trash get out all right?"

"Uh-huh. I put it out."

"Sorry I stayed away like that." Hubert spoke gruffly. This was an apology.

"That's all right." She sat down at the table and watched him eat.

"I like four-seventeen today. Dreamed it last night just as clear as anything."

She said, "Sounds all right." Gertrude sometimes played but never for more than a few pennies. Since Hubert had begun to bet so much on the numbers she did not like to think about them. They were silent for a while.

Suddenly Hubert said, "Do we have any money, Gertrude?"

"There's only seven dollars in the whole house. Just enough for the gas and light bill." Almost involuntarily she asked why.

"Oh, nothing," Hubert mumbled. "If we don't have it, we don't have it." He shrugged and went on with his breakfast.

When he had finished he asked Gertrude what work had to be done. She showed him the pad on which she scribbled the complaints of the tenants. They decided which ones should be taken care of first, and Hubert went out.

He worked diligently. He unclogged Sarah Anderson's toilet and stoked all the furnaces. He swept and mopped the hallways of 67 and then spackled over cracks that had developed in the plaster. He set traps, he painted, he hammered, he sawed. Hubert Cooley was absolutely the busiest house superintendent in Harlem that morning until eleven-thirty. That was when Gertrude left the apartment to go to the store. Hubert took this opportunity to slip into the bedroom and pry open her bureau drawer. He took out the seven dollars designated for the gas and electric bills. With the money tucked snugly in his pocket, he hurried away down the street.

Chapter 6

THE ONE PERSON in the whole world Iretha did not want to see this morning was her kid sister Essie. They got along together well enough, but Essie always chose Iretha's busiest days to come bursting in. On Mondays her schedule was always crowded, and today was no exception. At nine-thirty she had a beauty appointment at Rose Meta's that she simply could not break. Then she would have to rush back to the apartment, because at noon Lillian Sommerville, Dr. Sommerville's sister, was dropping by to discuss Iretha's candidacy for membership in the Wheatley Social Circle. This was the charity group that gave some of Harlem's most important social affairs and collected money for the poor little children in the West Indies. Also, sometime today Iretha would have to sit down and write a letter of resignation from The Fun Girls, that silly little club she had joined years before, when she had worked as a practical nurse at Harlem Hospital. Some of the members were bound to say she felt she had outgrown The Fun Girls, but that would not bother Iretha. She knew how they were—nasty, like crabs, pulling one another down. Goodness, she did have a lot to do! Tonight she and her husband Hugh were going to the theater. Trummy Carpenter, the well-known lawyer who was expecting a magistrate's appointment if the November elections worked out as expected, had given Iretha and Hugh tickets for the Broadway musical hit *Guys and Dolls*, which meant that Iretha would have to arrange for a baby sitter. It was really very thoughtless of Essie to come visiting at eight-thirty in the morning.

She knew it was Essie by the three short, insistent rings. Essie never came visiting except when she had had an argument with James Lee. She would moon around the house crying all morning, getting in Iretha's way and upsetting the children. Then James Lee would call, and Essie would go running back like a tamed puppy. Iretha resolved that today she would not listen to any of Essie's tearful stories. If the girl was silly enough to run around with low-class Negroes, she deserved all the trouble she was having.

Iretha had an impulse not to push the buzzer that would open the door five flights below. Maybe Essie would go away. Yes, that was it! She would not answer the bell. But she felt a tinge of guilt. After all,

Essie was her sister, unsophisticated and naïve, it was true, but her sister nevertheless.

Down below, Essie pushed the bell again, three short, compelling rings.

"Oh, darn," muttered Iretha. She pressed the buzzer and bit her lower lip as she waited. It was as if her kid sister had read her thoughts and said, "No, no, Iretha, that wouldn't be nice." Iretha decided to tell Essie that if she had to drop by unexpectedly she must try to avoid doing it on Mondays. But Essie would be crying when she came in. Well, Iretha would wait until she had calmed down and tell her then. Iretha would be firm.

No one could accuse her of having neglected Essie. When the girl had come up from their home in Cheraw, North Carolina, Iretha and Hugh had taken her in. This was when there had hardly been room for themselves, before they moved into this larger, more modern apartment overlooking Riverside Drive. They had introduced Essie to their friends and taken her to the Annual Christmas Ball given by the Upper Manhattan Lawyers' Guild in the Skyline Room of the Theresa Hotel. Iretha had insisted on buying Essie a gown for the affair, a white silk thing, not daring and only vaguely suggestive. The smart set had made a fuss over her. The young men had found one pretext after another to come over to their table and get themselves introduced to the new young face that seemed slightly out of place in the colored lights and restrained conviviality of the Skyline Room. Iretha had felt that the triumph belonged more to her than to Essie. She foresaw her sister making a nice marriage with one of the young doctors or lawyers—it did not matter who it was so long as the man was a profes-

sional who could take good care of Essie without her
having to work. Essie would not have the long hard
struggle for security that Iretha had had during those
first years in New York, before she married Hugh. He
was not yet forty and already was an inspector with a
gold badge at the post office. That night at the ball a
photographer from the *Amsterdam News* snapped
Essie and Ted Thayer, Jr., the son of the well-known
New Jersey real-estate man, as they danced. The picture had been displayed prominently in that Friday's
paper. But in the end the whole thing had come to
nothing because Essie was so stubborn.

Iretha sank onto her new chaise longue and lit a
cigarette. There was one thing you could say about
the Turner girls—meaning herself and Essie and two
other sisters who still lived in the South. There was
not one of them who was hard to look at. Iretha was
thirty-five, but she felt she looked ten years younger.
Perhaps none of them was light-complexioned, but
that was a handicap which was overcome by their tall,
slender figures and the teasing, chestnut brown of
their skin. Iretha had always felt that the baby of the
family, Essie Dee, would grow into the prettiest of
them all. She had been right.

"Tsk!" She made a noise with her tongue and
ground the cigarette into the ash tray. That was what
made it so damned tragic. A girl had to be sharp in
New York, on her toes every minute, ready to take advantage of the slightest opportunity. How she had
worked to get where she was! And she had not stopped
yet, not by a long shot. Any girl as pretty as Essie, with
a sister who had offered to pay the bills, as Iretha had,
had no business working for Jews up in Westchester.
Essie was stupid and ungrateful.

When she heard the elevator door in the hallway open, Iretha uncrossed her legs, got up from the chaise, and went to the door. On her face was the smile that was always there when admitting someone to the apartment. She was hoping that Essie would not cry very long and would leave soon so that she could get back on her schedule. She was surprised to find when she opened the door that Essie stood there smiling back at her.

"Hi, baby," said Iretha.

"Hi, yourself," responded Essie.

They touched cheeks. Essie seemed so happy that Iretha asked, "Girl, are you all right?"

"Well, look at me," said Essie, spreading her arms. "Am I standing on my own two feet or am I not?"

Iretha stared. There was a twinkle in Essie's eye that puzzled her. She did not like to be confused so early in the morning.

"I'm hungry," announced Essie. She went to the kitchen and swung open the door of the refrigerator. "What you got to eat, girl? I'm starved."

Essie began to take leftovers out of the refrigerator and soon was sitting at the table eating the remains of Sunday's dinner. What in the world had got into the kid? Iretha decided that what she had seen in Essie's eyes was not a twinkle at all but a glint. Essie looked as if she were at war. Iretha lit another cigarette and continued to stare.

Chapter 7

FRANK'S GARAGE was near the East River on First Avenue at One hundred and sixteenth Street, an old red-brick structure with green painted windows. There were sixty cabs and a hundred and twenty regular drivers backed up by a force of mechanics, garage helpers, and several extra drivers. Together they were supposed to keep each car on the street twenty-three hours a day.

Frank DaVini was a chunky Italian who smoked and chewed cheap cigars and had ulcers. He never nagged his men about averages. If a man's money on the clock began to fall consistently below the average, Frank would call him into the office and ask him what was wrong. Didn't he like working for Frank? Didn't he like having a new car to drive? Didn't he like having a whole army of mechanics waiting to take care of his car when it broke down? Didn't he like coming to work in the morning and knowing his car would be there waiting for him? Or maybe he would like to work for one of those companies where they made the men shape up every morning and sometimes a hackie didn't get a car at all. Or maybe he'd like to go to work for National and drive one of those Checkers, where a man couldn't make a living because the new DeSotos like Frank's were always stealing fares from him. Or maybe he didn't like being able to draw his money every day instead of having to wait until the end of the week. And having a paid vacation for a whole week every year. Frank never gave the hackie a chance to argue or apologize. He would get up from his green little desk, smile, slap the hackie on the back, and say, "All right, get on out there and put some money on that clock." Nobody's feelings were hurt. More often than not, the cabbie worked harder and produced more money. If he did not, he came in one morning and found that his car had been given to someone else.

"Jesus Christ!" screamed Frank DaVini this morning, as if he were in pain. It was a high, shrill exclamation, almost a squeal. "What the hell is this?" He stood in the middle of the garage pointing at car number three-six-eight, the only car parked in the entire garage. Frank's outraged voice shot into every corner and reverberated off the walls.

"Danny! Danny! Goddamnit! Come out here."

The mechanics at work on the second tier of the garage peeked over the railing to see what was ailing the boss. Danny O'Halloran came hurrying out of the dispatcher's office. He was a tall, blond young man, athletically built, good-looking. He did not think of himself as the best dispatcher in New York City, but he was certain that as a ladies' man he was unsurpassed. Among the drivers and the mechanics he was known as Young Genitals.

"Da-a-aneee!"

"What is it, Frank?"

Frank had not seen Danny come up. His deliberately soft, self-assured voice startled Frank. Danny always made Frank feel cold and off his stride. The syndicate that owned the greater bloc of stock in the garage had suggested Danny for the job and there had been little that Frank could do about it. On his own he would never have hired Danny. It was not just that he was too good-looking, a pretty boy, but he had never driven a hack. What kind of garage had a dispatcher who had never hacked? To Frank it was almost unethical.

"Danny, is this car in running condition?"

"Yeah, Frank, it is—"

"Then, Holy Jesus, what the hell is it doing here? It's almost nine o'clock."

"The driver isn't here yet."

"Is he the only one who can drive this friggin' car?"

"You know how things are in the summer," Danny said. "There aren't too many extra men around."

"Don't hand me that. There're plenty of guys around who'd be happy to drive a new car."

"What can I do, Frank?" said Danny with a spread of his hands. "If an extra man had come in, I would have given him the car—"

"Git on the phone; call some of the old drivers; do something and git that goddamned car out of here, Danny. You hear me!" Frank walked toward his own car parked in the driveway. He took quick, short puffs from the cigar. He was being loud and authoritative, but there was also a whining note of protest so that Danny would understand there was nothing personal in what he was saying. "Is that car making any dough for you or me or anybody else while it sits here in the garage? No. Take the car away from the damn driver if he don't want it."

He opened the door of his dark blue Chrysler and got in. "Jesus Christ," he exclaimed as he slammed the door shut and started the motor. "Nine o'clock and

the friggin' car sitting up here in the friggin' garage
and not a friggin' thing wrong with it!" He wiped the
sweat from his plump face with a handkerchief as he
backed through the garage exit. "Jesus Christ!" he exclaimed again as he drove toward Second Avenue.

Danny walked back into his office. He would give
Cooley hell when he came in. Who did that black
bastard think he was, not even calling the office to say
he would be late?

Evaline, the secretary and cashier, was seated at her
typewriter. She was a brunette, petite and attractive.
Danny stood behind her with his hands on her shoulders. As he talked he strained his eyes to see down the
top of her low-cut blouse.

"If I get any calls, switch 'em upstairs, huh?"

Evaline continued her typing. Her voice was cold
and contemptuous. "You've got to give me a rub-down
to tell me that?"

He took his hands away and walked out of the office. The little bitch! He would get her yet, just for
meanness, just to hear her cry. Yes, he would see that
she cried. Now he would tell the grease monkeys about
the virgin he had snared over the week end. He enjoyed seeing the looks of envy on the faces of those
married guys when they listened to his stories. He ran
a comb through his hair. Well, some guys had it and
some guys didn't. He had it. Was it his fault?

James Lee's fear of being late amounted almost to a
phobia. Somewhere he had heard that white folks believed Negroes always traveled behind time, and, although he told himself he did not care what white
folks thought, he always made an extra effort to be
punctual where they were concerned.

As he approached the garage he felt he especially did not want to see Frank DaVini. When Frank started yelling at you, he never gave you a chance to say anything and he always made you feel that you had done him a personal injury. Even if you did not like to be yelled at, especially by white people, you could never really answer Frank because there was something in his voice that made you suspect he was halfway right in what he was saying.

On the other hand, James Lee did not mind meeting the new Irish dispatcher they had brought in. He did not like the Irish anyway, and he would never take any guff off a young punk like O'Halloran. He took the dispatch card for his car and punched the time clock.

"Hey, Cooley, wait up!"

O'Halloran's voice sounded harsh and threatening in the empty garage.

"What is it?" James Lee asked.

Danny was descending the steps from the second tier. A cigarette was in his mouth and he was lighting it as he came down. He spoke with slight irritation in his voice. "Wait up a minute, will you? Another minute or two won't matter."

James Lee stopped and waited. His eyes measured the young Irishman. They were about the same height and size, slender heavyweights. Danny was fuller around the shoulders. Powerful wrists and hands projected from the sleeves of his shirt. A person would think twice before getting into a fight with O'Halloran. They faced each other in almost the same spot in which, fifteen minutes earlier, Frank DaVini had yelled, "Jesus Christ!", pointing at three-six-eight and demanding, "What the hell is this?"

"This is a fine time to be coming in, Cooley."

"I had something to do. Sorry."

Immediately James Lee wished he had not added the last word, for Danny pounced on it. "Sorry! My God! You drag in here at nine o'clock and all you can say is you're sorry."

James Lee shrugged. "That's what I said. What do you want me to do, crawl in here on my hands and knees? I told you I had something to do."

"This is a job, Cooley, you know."

"I know this is a job, O'Halloran. What did you think I thought it was?" He was thinking that O'Halloran reminded him of Captain Queens in Louisiana who had yelled at him, "This is the army, Cooley, y'know." He had had to swallow a lot in the army, but things were different now.

"This is a business to make money. Everybody loses when you keep a car laid up here this long. There were three extras around here but I saved the car for you."

James Lee knew this was not true. O'Halloran already had the reputation of not doing anybody any favors unless he was paid for it. He said nothing. He was aware of the mechanics peeping over the railing upstairs. He felt hot and uncomfortable around the neck.

"Some of you guys give us a hard time, dragging in here at all hours."

"Some of *what* guys?" James Lee demanded. Did he mean the Negro drivers, or hackies in general?

"Some of you friggin' drivers," said Danny, who had not meant that at all. He turned on his heels and walked toward the steps he had just come down. "If you want this job you had better start acting like it."

And, like Frank DaVini, he added: "Put some money on that clock."

James Lee got into the cab and drove it out of the garage. He thought back over the conversation to see if he had held his own. He always did badly in these examinations. Part of the price of being a Negro was that he was never satisfied with the fight he put up for his dignity and pride. He decided he had not said anything wrong but that he had not said enough. He should not have let Danny have the last word. He was a hackman with a good record. He could get a job anywhere.

Upstairs, Danny O'Halloran settled down onto his favorite stool near the grease pit. "One of these days," he said, "I'm going to kick that nigger where it will do him the most good."

The three mechanics agreed that they would like to see Danny try. It happened that all of them were small men and this fact spiced their resentment of Danny, who towered above them like a golden-haired Hollywood hero. They would like to see him in a scrap with somebody his own size, though they were not certain they would want James Lee, a Negro, to win.

One of them winked at the others and said to Danny: "So go ahead, kid. You had just got your hand on her brassiere and she had said, 'Please don't, Danny darling . . .'"

The young dispatcher ignored the sarcasm. "Oh, yes . . ." He closed his eyes and let his mind swim in the gruesome details.

There was a fan in the telephone booth where James Lee was, but he was hot. He had just come from the room in which he had expected to find Essie waiting for him.

"Hello, Iretha. This is James Lee."

"Hello, James Lee," said Iretha, as if they were old friends.

James Lee had met her only once and he had not liked her. It had been a dinner for three couples, a quiet, pretentious affair that nobody enjoyed. He had known what Iretha was thinking when she looked at him: that he was strictly no account and was taking advantage of her poor little sister.

"Is Essie Dee there?"

"Yes, uh-huh, she's here."

"Can I talk to her?"

"Just a minute." Iretha almost sang the words. James Lee hated her cooing voice. It was sweet and nasty, like syrup that clung to your fingers. It was typical of that phony crowd Iretha ran around with. Why did Essie have to run up there everytime she and James Lee had a fight? She had said she hated Iretha's way of life, yet as soon as something went wrong they became thick as peas in a pod.

"Hello, James Lee." It was Iretha's oozing voice again.

"Yes, Iretha?"

"I'm sorry, but Essie says she doesn't want to talk with you."

"But . . ."

"I'm sorry, James Lee."

Iretha had hung up the receiver. James Lee's lungs were empty. He wanted to hit somebody. He cursed into the dead phone and slammed the mouthpiece onto its cradle. He had passed three fares rushing back uptown to see Essie and now he did not have a penny on the clock. He cursed again and rushed outdoors to his cab.

Chapter 8

MORNING on Lenox Avenue was like a blue song, soft and soothing, with a steady bass beat, unhurried, going nowhere. The doors of the saloons, the shoe shops, and the fish-and-chip joints were thrown open, but it was too early for customers. One by one the corner bums took up their stations, the old folks brought their folding chairs out to the sidewalk or found seats near the open windows of stuffy apartments, and the blue song of Harlem wandered on.

"Hey, man," called Timmy, who was known as the Creep. "Whatcha know, John Lewis?"

"Man, I don't know nothing," said John Lewis as he shook hands with Timmy. When John Lewis took his hand away he had a dollar bill hidden in his palm that he put into his already bulging pocket.

"Let that roll on one-six-three," said Timmy, "and I'll be collecting from you at about five P.M."

"You've got it working, Pops."

John Lewis continued his morning stroll down Lenox Avenue. Beyond the door of Mabel's Beauty Salon was Mabel herself. She was plump, forty, and cheerful, with deep dimples and an extraordinary head of long, blue-black hair.

"Hey, John Lewis, you big black handsome thing, you."

"Hey, baby, you sweet little bundle of female, you."

Mabel left her customer and went to the cash register. She took out five one-dollar bills that she gave to John Lewis.

"I'm playing single action, John, honey. I want a four to lead."

"You got it coming, baby, you got it coming."

On down Lenox Avenue walked John Lewis.

"Hey, John Lewis, what you like today?"

"Everything, man. I like everything."

"Put my money on two-twelve."

"You got it coming."

Farther.

"Hey, John Lewis, sweet poppa."

"Hey, baby, you look good enough to eat."

"Take my money, you robber. I'm still playing six-nineteen, and it's beating me to death."

"It's coming, baby. Just hold on."

"John Lewis, you people must have those numbers fixed. You see how I missed those figures Saturday? I came so close I got a good mind never to play no more."

"Well, you know what Suzy Ann told Nappy Chin?"

"No. What?"

"She says, 'If you keep on gambling, you're bound to win.' "

"John Lewis, you're crazy. Here, put this on my regular figure."

"You got it coming," said John Lewis. "You got it coming."

The most popular gambling game in New York City, and especially in Harlem, is the numbers. The poorest, most miserable creature alive can play. To try his luck, all he needs is a penny, and if his guess is right the numbers bank will pay him six dollars in return. The odds against his winning are a thousand to one, and his payoff is only six hundred to one, but this disparity is somewhat compensated for by the comparative ease with which he can play this supposedly illegal game. The fat lady upstairs who sits at home all day with her cats and dogs, the grasping little man in the candy store across the street, the furtive, overdressed loafer with glistening shoes who is standing on the corner at sunrise—each will take a bet on the numbers. The penny bet is the stock in trade of a multimillion-dollar business with its headquarters downtown in the city's financial district. This business is incorporated, after a fashion; it has its stockholders, its officers, its workers, and its payroll. Its volume of business is steady, and it is seldom in crisis, for it is based on that most solid and persistent of all American phenomena—the dream.

John Lewis was a large brown man with a good-natured smile and a carefully cultivated mustache. He was extremely attentive to his long black hair, which was waved and set regularly in a local beauty salon patronized exclusively by men. His rich voice was warm and friendly and especially appealing to women. Men were uncomfortably aware of his masculinity, but they admired him. More important for his business, everybody trusted him. If your number hit, you never had to look for John Lewis. He would search you out and put every penny in your hand, no ifs, ands, or buts.

Before the war John Lewis had been a heavyweight boxer down in Washington, D. C. Promising, the wily managers had said, a real comer, a good strong boy who can take a punch. One night he was knocked out in the second round of a preliminary bout in Uline Arena. He blinked up at the lights and the counting referee and concluded that there was a lot more to boxing than being able to take a punch. He said to himself: John Lewis, stop making a fool of yourself. You better cut out this nonsense before you get your head knocked off. After that he quit the ring for good.

During the war he had distinguished himself not only as a truck driver in Patton's Transportation Corps, serving in Africa and Italy, but also as a black marketeer. He sold everything from sweaters and shoes to jeeps, and once, in Rome, he managed to dispose of a six-ton truck. Consequently he had a few thousand dollars saved at the end of the war. He decided to settle in Harlem, telling himself that a big man like him needed a big place to live. John Lewis liked handsome women and fast living, and so his savings disappeared quickly. But he had learned how to get along in New York City. Writing the numbers came natural to him. He walked the streets like a native. He was a good fellow to swap drinks with at the Theresa Bar or the Palm Café where the entertainers and the sporting crowd gathered.

Six days a week he took his morning stroll down Lenox Avenue, turning into the numbered streets along the way. He had trained himself to carry all the bets in his head, and a curious policeman could search John Lewis all he wished, he would never find a slip of paper with numbers written on it. Sometimes when John Lewis did more business than usual he would go home two or three times so that he could write the numbers down there.

By ten-thirty John Lewis had finished his pick-ups and was in his apartment where he and his wife Ada totaled the day's receipts. There, until early afternoon when the first race was run, people came in to place bets with him. At one-fifteen the pickup man came from the numbers bank and collected the money and the receipts. After the third race was run, if there had been any hits, the pickup man came again and paid John Lewis, who in turn paid the lucky player.

It was a good living for him. He carried a large book of regular players. He was certain of seventy dollars a week, and with his cut from winnings he often earned a hundred. There was really no risk involved. The big banker took care of any difficulty with the police, and John Lewis had no fear of losing any money because as the middleman he never risked any.

This morning as soon as John Lewis got home he sat down at a table and began writing down the numbers that had been bet with him on the street. Ada came out of the bedroom and spoke with her lips close to his ear.

"How's it coming?"

He shivered. This always happened when she petted him. It was silly. He could never understand how such a little woman could have so much power over a big man like him.

"Come on, baby," he said, "don't start your funny business. Let me write this down."

When he had first come to New York he had sported with the tall yellow glamour girls. It had seemed that a big man like him needed a shapely, statuesque woman to set him off well when he appeared in public. Ada had changed all that the day he walked into

Don's Bar-B-Que where she waited table. At first he had resisted the idea—"Why, she's only as big as a minute," he told himself—but six weeks later they were married.

Now she was wearing a black mandarin costume and Chinese bangs. The hair at her neck was caught with a bright red ribbon that matched the color of her lips. She sat on his knee and rested an elbow on his shoulder. She touched her lips to his forehead.

"Nora just called," Ada said in a voice that seldom went above a whisper. "She wants to know if we're going over to Atlantic City this week end."

John Lewis jotted down the last of the figures. "Baby, to tell you the truth, I don't know. Maybe I'd better stick close and see how everything works out before we start spending money."

She kissed his neck below the ear. "Is it going all right?"

"It'll work out, I think." John Lewis rubbed his chin with his hand. "I've got to play my cards close and I need a little luck."

This was absolutely true. Two weeks before, John Lewis had forsaken the relative security of the ordinary numbers writer. He had reasoned that a man could not stop growing. A big man had to step out and take a chance. Months ago he had sat down and taken stock of his progress. He and Ada had a few hundred dollars in the bank and he had just had a run of luck with the ponies at Saratoga. Why not make some real money for himself and step into the big league? Instead of just writing the figures and turning the profits over to someone else, why not *bank* them himself? He knew the numbers game and he had good contacts. If he nursed his little stake along he might build it into a real fortune. Others had done it.

He knew very well that you did not rush headlong into establishing a numbers bank. Harlem, like all of New York, was divided into carefully guarded sections, and each section had been allotted long ago to specific groups. The overall system was controlled by men with enough power to stay on top and dictate which groups operated and which did not. A new bank, even a small one of a few hundred dollars, could succeed only at the expense of another bank, so you had to have permission to operate. You had to pay off the right people and you had to have luck. If you opened a bank without permission, you very quickly ran out of luck. Many an upstart numbers entrepreneur had ended up dead.

But so far John Lewis had been smart. He had used his good contacts and had played them right so that the big boys had finally given him a nod. To be sure, it was not much of a nod. They had just made a little corner for him. They wouldn't help him, and he had to pay them to operate. But they wouldn't bother him. In a few months, with luck, he would be in the Cadillac class.

He had set up operations with two thousand dollars. Twelve playing days had now passed and his bank had grown to thirty-one hundred dollars.

Hubert could never relax until he had played his number. Whatever amount of money he had in his pocket urged him on toward his goal, the numbers writer. Until the bet was safely placed, he felt he was playing a foolish and dangerous game by carrying the money in his pocket. So he never tarried. As he rushed along the sidewalk, if anybody spoke to him he would give a hasty answer and continue on his way.

"Hey there, Mister Hubert," called Mrs. Jonas, the old woman who sold sweet-flavored crushed ice from her little cart on One hundred and twenty-sixth Street. "What you liking today?"

"I reckon a four," said Hubert and hurried on. Mrs. Jonas made a mental note of the four. All morning she would be asking passers-by what they liked. When she had decided which digit was the most impressive she would risk a quarter on it, hoping for a two-dollar return. This form of betting was called the single action, where instead of trying to catch three numbers you tried for one.

The fellows who stood in front of the Crystal Bar had Hubert marked down as a character who was always good for a laugh. They had learned from John Lewis that Hubert played large sums of money on the numbers and this convinced them that he was crazy. The numbers he played sounded weird to them, and, worse, he kept changing them all the time. This was something no good player was supposed to do. So each day when they saw him approach they would nudge each other and greet him with exaggerated respect.

"Good morning, Mister Hubert," they chorused, bowing at the waist.

"Good morning." Hubert's response was always brisk and unfriendly. Negroes who stood on the corners laughing loudly and drinking wine were the very ones who kept the race from advancing.

Flash was a kind of leader of the group because he was very resourceful in finding ways of obtaining sneaky pete, the local term for cheap sherry and muscatel. This morning he removed his hat and smiled broadly, showing several gold teeth that had been installed in better times. "May I ask what number you're playing today, Mister Hubert?"

"Four-seventeen," said Hubert. He always told them, although he knew they were laughing at him. It gave him pleasure to think that when his number came they would remember having heard it that morning.

They were sure that 417 was not a good number because fours and sevens had played the week before. So they had a good laugh wondering how much money Hubert was throwing away again. Flash remembered he had an aunt who lived at 417 St. Nicholas Avenue, but this disturbed him only a moment. He and his aunt were not on good terms—she had refused to have anything more to do with him until he found a job—and it was not likely that her address would indicate a lucky number.

Hubert spoke abruptly. "John Lewis, how much money do you get for a seven-dollar hit?"

"I don't know right off, Mister Hubert."

"Well, figure it up then," said Hubert impatiently.

After a minute John Lewis said, "That comes to four thousand two hundred dollars."

Hubert, thought about it. Forty-two hundred dollars was a very satisfactory figure. He held the seven dollars toward John Lewis.

"Put that on four-seventeen. Four, one, seven."

John Lewis took the money. "Boy, you're really playing them heavy."

"That's the only way I know how to play 'em."

"Well, good luck to you." John Lewis put the

money in his pocket. Hubert went out, and Ada closed the door after him.

"That poor little man," said Ada. "Just throwing away good money after bad. Don't you feel sorry for him?"

"If I started feeling sorry for people, I'd have to go into another business. The reason I will make it in this town is because I save all my sympathy for myself. And you, of course."

"But you know he doesn't have a chance, the way those fours and sevens were running last week."

John Lewis put his big hands on her waist and lifted her into the air. "Baby, remember that every number is a good number until it *don't* come out. Fellow was telling me just the other day about a time back in the depression when two led off every day for sixteen straight days. What do you think of that?"

He set her down and went back to the card table where he continued his figuring. Strictly speaking, it was true that yesterday's number might come back today, but it was highly unlikely. But why should he care if Hubert threw his money away? How could he make a living if there were no fools with money? He turned his mind away from the little man and the bad bet. The question was: How much money could he back with his own bank and how much would he have to pass on?

Chapter 9

Noon eased itself into the Manhattan
streets. The sun hung high over Harlem,
and its heat was heavy as a white cloak
over the flat roofs and the gray streets. Children
sought the coolness of dark basements and dank hallways. The old people sat near their windows and
looked with indifference out onto the shimmering
streets. Behind the lunch counters brown girls and yellow girls, irritated by the heat and their own perspiration, grouchily served up frankfurters with sauer-
kraut, hot sausages with mustard and relish and onion,
milk shakes, malteds, coffee, and orange juice; served
these to impatient clerks and laborers and helpers'
helpers, to shoppers, policemen, and hack drivers.
Preachers napped and dreamed of churches larger
than the Abyssinian. Lawyers and petty real-estate
brokers planned and schemed and gamblers figured. A
con man dropped a wallet with a hundred-dollar bill
in it to the sidewalk in front of the Corn Exchange
Bank and waited for a sucker to fall for the age-old
game. A hustler sat in her apartment on Sugar Hill
sipping cocktails with a white merchant from downtown who was taking a long week end, sized him up,
estimated his worth. Madam Lawson shuffled her
cards, Madam Fatima stared into her silver crystal

ball, and turbaned Abdul Ben Said of the ebony skin
mumbled an incantation to the black gods of old, and
lo! all of them saw glory in the morning if not sooner.
There, near the top of Manhattan Island, Harlem
sizzled and baked and groaned and rekindled its
dream under the midday sun.

As Hubert walked along One hundred and twenty-
fifth Street, he was, after his own fashion, praying to
God. These were hot, turbulent encounters accompanied by furious sounds and colors. The ordinary
hum of the city, the horns and the whistles, the murmur of voices, the hoarse breathing of car and truck
engines—all these city noises changed to shrill shrieks
and senseless tumult when Hubert had a go at God.
When he was a boy he had believed in the God of
the Southern Baptist Church, the know-it-all dispenser
of justice and glory at the end of a Christian life of
trial and tribulation, showing off miracles and casting
fallen sinners into the hellfire. Hubert had not really
lived with God then—had just taken His existence for
granted without really acknowledging it. But now he
knew that God really did exist and that He was
strictly responsible for everything, good or bad, and
whenever He did not straighten up and fly right,
Hubert gave Him down the country. Today as Hubert
walked along he sometimes gestured violently to em-
phasize a point he was making. He paid no attention
to the people who stared at him.

The tires of the car screeched to a halt. The driver
pushed his head through the window and said lazily,
"Hey, Pop, wassa matter? Got the blues? Tired of living, huh?" Hubert did not hear him. He stepped onto
the curb and continued on his way.

"God, You may be all-powerful, but as far as I am concerned You have been lax on the job. There's right to be done and You ain't doing it. I have worked and tried and been beaten only to get up again. I never asked You for too much, either. What's a grocery store, a shoe repair shop, a little luncheonette? Now, I don't understand You. You know I deserve it, but You ain't helping me to get it."

Hubert bumped into a girl who said, "Damn, Mister, what you trying to do? Knock me down?" She cut her eyes at him and passed on.

Hubert stopped in front of Blumstein's Department Store and startled people nearby when he suddenly threw up his arm and pointed toward the many stories of concrete and brick that imposed themselves over One hundred and twenty-fifth Street. Hubert's lips were moving, but no sound came from them.

"Did I ever ask You for a store like Blumstein's? No, 'cause I know that ain't reasonable. Blumstein's was here before I got to Harlem and will be here when I'm gone. I don't begrudge them the money I paid them for that refrigerator back at the beginning of the war, or the rug that Gertrude wanted, or the two lamps, or any of those things we bought from them in the last twenty years." He waved his hand toward Woolworth's five-and-dime store next door to Blumstein's. Nor did he begrudge Woolworth the nickels and dimes he had spent there during the same period. He had heard it said that buying and selling were the life's blood of the nation. He believed in law and order—he had taken no part in either one of the two Harlem riots where people broke windows and looted stores. He believed in the system and that Woolworth and Blumstein had a right to keep their places in it.

"But what about my place?" he cried aloud, and again people stared at him. He wanted passionately to buy and sell, to be a man of commerce, even in the smallest sense. "Damnit!" yelled Hubert, "I deserve something."

A mounted policeman in front of Loew's˙ movie house looked at Hubert uneasily but decided the little man was not worth the trouble it would take to dismount. Besides, he had quieted down now and was walking on.

Maybe You're punishing me for what happened between me and Gertrude, Hubert thought, but You know that ain't fair. If it wasn't for her I would've been out of Harlem long ago. In those days I wanted to take her with me. But she's the one that was responsible for me taking this job up here in Harlem and having to clean up after these no-account Negroes. I always could save money when I worked downtown, but once a man starts working up here he's lost. Another thing, God. I ain't never lost faith in You the way some folks have. You've got to exist or ain't nothing right."

Hubert walked on. "You owe me some luck, God. You owe me some luck."

Each time he saw Sister Clarisse he told himself: Lord, Lord, one of these days I'm gonna grab this little woman and I won't be able to let her go. That was the way he felt when he saw her face with its soft brown eyes and modest smile, the full yet young bosom panting under her lace blouse. Here was a woman! Half-forgotten urges welled up in him. He deserved a woman like this, he needed her, he would have her.

"I do declare now," said Sister Clarisse, "isn't this a nice surprise?"

Her twenty years in Harlem had in no way affected her soft Southern speech, and her voice created pictures in Hubert's mind. It was evening down home. Sister Clarisse, wearing a blue flowered dress, sat in a swing on the front porch. In her hand was a fan. Nearby, a pitcher of cold lemonade stood ready with two glasses. Hubert, a young man, had come courting.

"I hope you haven't had your lunch yet, because I've just been making some salmon salad I think you'll like." She indicated a chair for him and took a seat in the corner of the sofa. "Well, if you aren't the last person in the world I expected to see."

This was not exactly true, inasmuch as Hubert had of late become a regular caller, but it pleased Sister Clarisse to pretend she was surprised each time he came.

She walked around the screen into her neat little kitchenette. "Well, if we're going to have lunch, I'd better get it fixed. Did you ever see so much hot weather in your life? I declare, if it gets any warmer I'll just melt, that's all."

He did not answer. She was becoming used to his long silences and she went on talking. She had heard it said at Little Calvary that Hubert was "peculiar in the head," but this did not disturb her. After all, she was not married to him, and he always behaved himself while he was with her.

Later, after they had eaten and she had served Hubert a glass of cold beer, he spoke abruptly. "Sister Clarisse, what do you think of me?"

"Well, now—"

"Do you like me?"

"Why, yes, of course—"

"Then listen," he said, and he went on to tell her about his dream. As he talked he held her with his eyes. She felt uncomfortable. Why in the world was he being so serious?

" 'Where'd you get the money,' you kept saying over and over again," said Hubert. "And you and me, we were on our way to San Francisco . . . together."

She did not know what to say about such a dream. She shifted her weight on the couch and said nothing. Unaccountably, she crossed her legs.

"I want you to know I think an awful lot of you, Sister Clarisse," said Hubert.

She began to move her fan furiously. Leftright-leftrightleftrightleftright. "Well, I'm glad, Mister Hubert."

"I'm not happy at home, and I ain't been for a long time."

"Now, Mister Hubert, I don't think you should be telling me such personal things—"

"Hush now, Sister Clarisse. I want you to listen because I'm building up to something I want to say." Her fan took up a calmer rhythm as Hubert settled in his chair. He went on: "I been watching you and thinking about you and I've figured out that, like me, you must be awful lonely, too—"

"Mister Hubert, please—"

"It's the truth, ain't it?"

She hesitated. The fan slowed. Left . . . right . . . left . . . right. "Well," she said, "naturally, we all get lonely sometimes, especially somebody who is all by herself." Left . . . right . . . left . . . right . . .

"Well, now, I know you never gave me no call

to talk like this, but wouldn't you rather me speak what's on my mind than hide it?"

"Well, yes," she said, "I expect I would."

This was not true either. She was a woman who liked pleasant banter, but when the conversation took a serious turn she quickly lost interest, or, if it was pointed at her, she became warm and embarrassed, as she was now. She could not help noticing his eyes. They were definitely not ordinary. Remembering what they whispered about Hubert at Little Calvary, she began to wonder if she had been wise in encouraging his attention. She did not mind a casual flirtation but . . . left right left right left . . . What was he saying?

". . . out in California. They say a man with a little shop can live real comfortable there. Lots of people go out there when they're getting up in age because of the sunshine and all. Any day now, Sister Clarisse, I'm expecting to get the money and make this big move. When it comes—and it will come, it will come—I'll be asking you to come and go with me."

Her fan stopped abruptly. Only now did she understand fully what he was talking about. "Mister Hubert!" was all she could say, but the exclamation sounded ineffectual, without the outrage she wanted it to have. So she added, "Well, I never!"

"Well, now I said it," said Hubert, "and I'd be pleased if you'd think about it. I know it don't become a married man talking like this, but you know I ain't asking you to do no wrong. We're both lonely and we could make each other happy. If things work out right, would you—you know you ought to, but would you—come away with me?"

Sister Clarisse did not know what to say. She was

frightened and very warm. Left right left right left right. Somehow Hubert had moved over to the couch and had her hand in his. She wanted to take it away, to smile, to say something, anything to regain control of the situation. Could Hubert be dangerous? He was acting peculiar, talking fantastically about impossible things, and here she was, alone with him.

"Brother Hubert," she began, "I do think I may have given you the wrong impress—" She became aware of a man's unfamiliar breath. His lips touched hers and she inhaled sharply. He stood up.

"I'll be going now," he said, "and please think about what I've said." He left.

Now she was really angry. Who did this man think he was? She would have to get him told, really put him in his place. But he was gone. She raised her fingers to her lips.

Chapter **10**

JAMES LEE drew up to a corner where a red light was already holding a Checker cab. The driver was a Negro, and as a rule James Lee would have spoken to him. But halfway down the next block on the right-hand side of the street a lady was standing with a bag. She was almost certainly waiting for a taxi, and since both cars were empty they would have to race for her. So they pretended not to notice each other and waited for the light to change. The driver of the Checker was next to the curb and by an unwritten law the passenger belonged to him. James Lee could see that he was planning to jump the light as soon as it was safe to cross the intersection. James Lee had the same idea and a faster car. The light changed. James Lee jerked his foot off the clutch and simultaneously slammed the accelerator to the floor. The DeSoto leaped across the intersection. James Lee cut in front of the Checker, who gave a scream with his horn, and brought the DeSoto to a halt in front of the lady with the suitcase. She opened the door and got in.

"Boy, you sure must be hungry." The Checker had drawn up to the left of James Lee and the driver was yelling in an angry voice.

James Lee felt the blood rush to his head. "Aw, go get yourself a car and stop crying," he yelled.

The Checker driver was a middle-aged, stocky, brown-skinned man with rimless eyeglasses. "Some people will put their heads in a toilet for a buck," he said. He put the Checker in gear and drove away.

"Take me up to Seventy-third and Madison, driver. I'm in a hurry." She was a thin white woman with black hair and a voice that was cold and sharp. She was not the kind to take notice of two colored hackies who shouted at each other and almost wrecked their cars trying to get her as a fare.

James Lee eased the car into the traffic and headed uptown. He did not like having to beat another Negro out of a fare, and he wished he could explain to the driver that he really needed every nickel he could get that day to keep up his average. But why should he feel bad? It was dog eat dog out on the streets, and he had never noticed anybody holding back to let him get ahead.

"I do wish you would hurry, driver. I have a one-thirty appointment."

"I'm going as fast as the traffic will allow, Madam."

"Well, do the best you can."

He wanted to say something else, but the thought that he might knock himself out of a tip stopped him. Then he examined her face in his mirror. No, he decided, dried-up prigs like that would never tip more than a dime, not even if it were raining and you carried their suitcases for them. A dime was all they thought you deserved.

"I'm free as a bird," called Essie. Her voice sounded as if it belonged to someone else as it rang through the empty apartment.

"Do you hear what I say?" she demanded of the innocent walls and chairs and tables. "I'm free as a bird."

Yes, that black man had had her number, all right, but he could forget it now. She had danced to his tune long enough. From here on in, the men would jump when she said jump and no one would ever push her around again.

Essie snapped on the radio and found a colored station. A tenor sax man was carrying the melody on a jump tune. She danced around the living room, enjoying the music even more because she knew her sister disapproved of these stations. She said their music was too loud and only backward Negroes listened to them. But today Essie was playing a game. This was her apartment and she could listen to any station she wanted. She closed her eyes and she was dancing with Javan Washington down in Cheraw, North Carolina. Javan had been sweet on her. Once he had taken her to a dance contest and they had won second prize.

The tenor sax moaned as the tune ran out. The announcer spoke of how much nicer life was for girls with lighter, brighter complexions. A girl who used Black & White Bleaching Cream was certain to get the man of her dreams. Essie sat on the window seat and looked out over the Hudson River to the New Jersey coastline.

Free? What did she mean? It was easier to say than to know. Her mind grappled with the definition.

When she had first come to New York and lived with Iretha and Hugh she had been uncomfortable among them and their friends. Even though it had been exciting to meet the important people who came to the house, she knew nothing of the things they talked about and she spoke very little for fear of saying something wrong. Who was she but a poor little Southern girl whose mother still took in washing down home? Who was she to be sitting among these doctors and lawyers and these fancy women with their beautiful clothes? Essie wanted to get out on her own. "Stay with us," Iretha had said. "Go to school and take one of those business courses. With your looks you'll get a good job in no time. And don't worry about money. Hugh and I aren't rich but we're doing all right. Stay with us, girl. Besides, it won't look right, your being my sister and working in somebody else's kitchen."

It had been a real struggle getting away from Iretha and Hugh. They had done so much for her that she had felt guilty leaving them when they were obviously sincere about wanting her to stay. Still, she knew she could not live with Iretha and Hugh.

True, a sleep-in job was not much, but at least she had been on her own and free.

But not from loneliness. Then James Lee had made her days in the city complete and satisfying. During the hot months she especially liked to go to the beach with him. She loved his body, and when they played in the water she fancied she knew what was going on in the minds of the other women. And, if she said so herself, she was not bad looking. She belonged with him. On Thursday nights and the few week ends when she could come to the city they went to movies and parties and danced at the Savoy.

Sex with him had come about naturally. Their first night together had been good, complete and satisfying. Now sometimes she had thoughts that were frightening because of their strange and forbidden depths. In her sex experience she had unlocked a new and secret part of herself more wonderful than all her girlish dreams had ever imagined.

"I love you, James Lee."

"Do you, Essie?"

"I love you, I love you. There's a song that goes like that."

"Say it over again."

"I love you."

Their murmurings in the night had been strangely real. She had felt as if she had no skin, as if every nerve were tingling, every part of her alive and sensitive to his fingers and lips.

Essie trembled and closed her eyes. Despite all this happiness she could now feel that she was freeing herself. Where had it all started? She had to be able to put her finger on it and explain it to herself. She had to be certain.

The Sunday they went to Central Park was a fine, bright day, the first warm Sunday that spring. She had asked him to bring her because she had never been rowing before. She was wearing a brightly colored sailor's outfit, and James Lee teased her, saying he thought she was overdoing it for a mere rowboat. But she could tell he liked the way she looked.

He rowed well and easily, moving from one part of the lake to the other with little effort. His strokes were rhythmical, one oar biting the water at a time so that the boat moved along smoothly. She complimented him. She knew he was showing off a little, but that was nice, too. It was a peaceful day, and she was glad they had come. Then she thought that she would like to row.

"But why? Aren't you comfortable?"

"I just want to try. Please, James Lee."

"Aw, come on and relax," he said. "These oars are heavy."

She was vaguely disappointed. Why didn't he want her to try?

"Please, James Lee."

"Okay," he sighed. "Come on."

He frowned as he helped her into the stern seat and took hers in the bow. He would not smile when she winked at him. Like a boy, she thought, whose toys have been taken away. Well, she would not ask him anything. She would learn to row all by herself.

But he was right. The oars were heavy. She had hardly begun before one of them slipped through the oarlock into the water. She managed to retrieve it, but not before she had dropped the other, which he lifted from the water and passed to her without saying a word. In a few moments she was exhausted and frustrated with her inability to make the oars move with any sort of rhythm. She gave them up and went back to her seat, and did not say a word the rest of the time they were on the lake. For days she was angry with him—a quiet, frustrating anger because it puzzled her. They had bitter little quarrels over trifles. Then gradually she had stopped thinking about the lake, but she had never forgotten it.

Essie went to the radio, switched it off, and returned to the window seat. A tug with yellow lettering on it chugged down the Hudson, leaving a pencil of black smoke.

Only now, as she looked back, was Essie aware that she had attached so much significance to that little incident. Since that day there had been a new thing between her and James Lee. Figuratively she had tried many times to row the boat and he had prevented her.

The abortion. What had a rowboat to do with that? She shut her eyes tight. It hurt almost physically when she thought of it. They were connected, the rowboat and the abortion, both parts of a large pattern. She had given in to him on the most important of things, their baby.

"Don't you see, Essie," he had said, "that's the ugly way to get married? We'd always feel we'd been forced into it."

"But if we love each other . . ." She had paused, afraid of the thought that had come to her. "You do love me and want to marry me, don't you, James Lee?"

"You know I do, baby, but not this way. As soon as we're ready we'll get married and have a great big family. But let's not start out this way."

It had all been wrong. The reasoning had been twisted out of shape, but she had listened and been persuaded. Even now the memory of what they had done made her go cold all over, trembling because it was like yesterday, the abortion, and there was nothing anybody could do about it.

She opened her eyes. The tugboat with the yellow lettering disappeared around a bend of the river trailing its thin, black ribbon of smoke, and her thoughts rushed on.

Chapter 11

HE WAS CONFUSED. He did not want to lose Essie, but he did not want to marry her. That was what she had wanted all the time, that was the only thing that would really make her happy, and it was the one thing he was not willing to do. Why couldn't things ever stay as they were when they were going well? He was not in love with her. When you were "in love" with a woman you were carried away by her good looks, her way of doing things. Everything about her overpowered you and finally you gave in. That was being in love.

So he was not in love with Essie. He had been sleeping with her for more than a year and he felt he knew her like a book. She was that simple, and she was definitely not overpowering. She was just a pretty little girl from the South who was crazy about him.

But his life was stuck like a car in the mud. It was a lot of disconnected pieces and he could not make any sense out of them. He felt guilty about his treatment of Essie, and at the same time he knew he had nothing to feel guilty about. Women seemed born to hard luck. The trouble was that he was twenty-six years old and he did not feel he had hold of anything, that he was growing. Essie was about the only thing in his life that he was sure of, and he had the strange fear that if he lost her everything might fall apart.

The traffic was jammed for three blocks leading up to the pier. The *Queen Mary* gave a loud, anxious groan and waited. The traffic lurched forward a few feet and came to a sudden halt. The cab was a hot box, and James Lee's clothes were soaked with his sweat. His buttock itched, but he had two women passengers and could not give it the hard scratching it needed. He had to content himself with squirming in the seat, at the same time keeping an eye on his two passengers in the rear-view mirror to see if they were paying any attention to him.

He thought about his twenty-three months in the army. There were only three distinct things that ever came to mind: Leroy Butler, who stepped on a mine in Pyongyang and was blown to bits; the grenade that exploded behind him while he was crawling and the sensation of a thousand needles stabbing at him; and a man he had known named McGowan.

James Lee had been looking at Leroy Butler just before the mine heaved up the earth with a crushing jar, and when everything had settled there was no trace of the man who had been there a few seconds before. At first he had not believed that he could have been looking at Leroy. Then, when he knew that Leroy really had been there, he had become filled with a horrified wonder. Why, you could be walking along and suddenly lose everything, absolutely everything, even form and substance. He had not known Leroy Butler very well and he had seen other men go down. But the idea of suddenly disappearing from the earth, leaving hardly a trace of your former existence, filled him with cold fascination.

It was natural, too, that he should remember the grenade. When it exploded he was crawling along near the rear of his platoon, almost unafraid for a moment because they had just cleared the rear area and could move ahead without fear of snipers behind them. But the grenade had come from behind. The explosion made everything seem ludicrous. When he remembered that winter in Korea and the big push toward the Yalu, it was neither the bitter cold nor even the frozen corpses that came to mind. It was a question: How could an enemy have been behind them when they had just cleared the area? It was crazy, absurd, like everything else that bizarre year.

He could not say why he thought of McGowan, who was only one of the many characters he had met. Besides, he had never liked the man. By all rights he should have forgotten McGowan long ago. . . .

He was a Negro on the same ward with James Lee in the hospital near Yokohama. His bed was in a corner and James Lee had the bed next to him. He was squat and ugly and only shaved for inspection. The few other Negroes in the ward were ashamed of him and tended to avoid him because of his blunt manner. James Lee probably would have done the same, but during those first few weeks he was unable to get out of bed. The first time McGowan spoke to James Lee was on the second morning during breakfast. He was sitting up in bed with the tray across his legs. He had a habit of chewing and talking at the same time.

"Boy, what are you doing over here?" There was not even a hint of friendliness in his gruff greeting. "You're a long way from home."

"I guess you are, too," said James Lee.

"Damn if I ain't," he agreed, and he laughed as if he had not considered that before. "They tell me you got your backside blasted. That right?"

"Yeah, that's right."

McGowan chuckled and went on with his breakfast. It had been only a few days since James Lee was wounded and he was in constant pain. He was sullen and angry. "I'm glad you can see something to laugh at, fella."

"Boy, if you can't see something funny in that you ain't got no sense of humor. Here you come all the way over here carrying that rifle and that other silly stuff they give you—all the way over here, just to get your butt busted open." He gave up the struggle to keep from laughing. His stunted little body shook so hard that he had to push his tray away to keep from knocking it over. "Man," he said, controlling himself for a moment, "you could've done that at home with less trouble."

James Lee watched in silence. The man was obviously crazy. He wished he could lift himself out of bed and get near enough to smash his fist into that open mouth with its uneven teeth.

McGowan finally stopped laughing, pulled his tray back into position, and began piling his mouth full of food. "Where're you from, boy?"

"New York. Why?"

"New York," he grunted. "I thought they made some smart Negroes up there. Me, I'm just a Southern boy myself. Born and bred in Kentucky. Don't pay no attention to me 'cause I ain't got no sense."

"That," said James Lee dryly, "is one thing I can believe."

"What the hell were you doing over there in those hills, boy?" McGowan pointed in the general direction of Korea.

"They sent me over there," James Lee retorted. "What did you think?"

"The question is what did *you* think?" said Mc-Gowan. "You look halfway intelligent. Didn't you know you could get killed over there? Or did you think those Koreans and China boys were fooling?"

"Well, what were you doing over there?" James Lee assumed that everybody in the ward was a war casualty.

"Over where?" McGowan looked shocked, but his eyes twinkled. Again he pointed. "You mean over *there?* Boy, I wouldn't be caught dead or alive over there, not as long as they're shootin' and fightin' 'and fussin' and carryin' on." He winked at James Lee. "I got stomach troubles, man. They started just as soon as I heard where we were going and they ain't give me no rest since. My stomach bothers me all the time." He took a large bite of his food and chewed at it viciously. "You see, doctors don't know too much about the stomach."

"You mean there's nothing wrong with you?" James Lee said coldly. He had spent a lot of freezing nights in the mud of Korea and he had a few buddies who were still there. And then there had been Leroy Butler.

McGowan frowned. "Shhh, man. What you trying to do? Spoil my play?"

Later that same day he asked James Lee, "Say, man, do you know what these people are fighting about?"

James Lee said, "That's a silly question. How the hell would I know? Do you know?"

"No, I don't," McGowan laughed, "but I sure thought you did, coming in here with your butt full of lead and steel. And I'll tell you something else, Mister. If I ever go somewhere where they're shooting and killing, I'm gonna have a better reason than 'They sent me.' You can believe that."

James Lee grew to hate the man in the bed next to him. But he also became fascinated by him. Each morning he woke up with the thought: What is this fool going to say next? He learned that McGowan was from Louisville, Kentucky, and had spent a year in a Southern college before he was drafted. He was one of the few men on the ward who used the Red Cross library, but to James Lee he did not talk or act like an educated person. Nobody liked him, and for good reason. He was ill-mannered and aggressive. If the other men on the ward had a general joke, McGowan could see nothing funny about it. But when they showed movies in the ward McGowan always burst out laughing during the emotional scenes that were underlined with sentimental music, thereby embarrassing those who were involved in the picture's plot. The wonder was that nobody ever jumped him and gave him a good beating. Fights were not unknown on the ward, but everybody avoided McGowan and paid him a grudging respect with their unsuccessful attempts to ignore him.

One day he said to James Lee, "Man, you know what's wrong with you? You're in danger and you don't know it."

"What kind of danger, Professor?" James Lee had begun calling McGowan by the name the ward had given him.

"When that Chinese boy busted your backside with that grenade, didn't it make you stop and think? I'm not talking about being scared, but something else. Didn't you say to yourself, 'Why, I can get killed and won't have a damned thing to say about it'?"

James Lee had thought along those lines—or, more accurately, he had felt along them—but he said nothing.

"Most people just go through life dancing to somebody else's tune," McGowan went on. "They get caught up early and they keep going along with the act just like sheep. And when they die it doesn't mean a damn thing because they never lived in the first place." McGowan put his head back on the pillow and stared up at the ceiling. "The first right is the right to live, boy. You got so many years and days and minutes to do something with your life. The only way you know what to do with your life is to think. Life is precious, man, and it makes me feel bad when I think of all those people who never had a life of their own because they let somebody else or some other thing have first call on it. It's like you're a house and you rent out all the rooms to other people and you end up sleeping outside because you didn't save any room for yourself. That's what it's like."

Lots of what McGowan said was too vague for James Lee to understand, but it almost always made him uncomfortable. He could seldom think of anything to say in reply.

One day McGowan suddenly asked, "Boy, you got a girl back home?"

"I got lots of 'em. Why?"

McGowan snorted, but James Lee felt he was on sure ground. It was true that he always had been popular with the girls and this was certainly something that little, ugly McGowan could not claim.

"I guess you trim 'em up a lot, don't you?"

"I guess I do 'trim 'em up' a lot, Professor," said James Lee with a sneer at the country expression.

"Boy, you sure are stupid," said McGowan.

James Lee's temper flared. "Have *you* got a girl?"

"Nope, but I got a wife," said McGowan, and already there was a snapshot in his hand that he passed to James Lee. The smiling woman was on the plump side but not unattractive. She held a baby in her arms. James Lee was surprised that she was not ugly. How in the world had she got stuck with a runt like McGowan?

"To really appreciate a woman, boy," McGowan was saying, "you've got to do more than trim her. You've got to get inside her soul and take a look at yourself. Then—and only then—you are cooking with gas." He took the snapshot and put it under his pillow. Then he lay back and closed his eyes and went to sleep.

The doctors were extremely attentive to McGowan. They were of the opinion that he had the only interesting case on the ward. He was constantly being fluoroscoped and X-rayed. Visiting specialists in internal medicine were always taken to McGowan's bed first. Regularly his stomach became upset and he was unable to hold anything on it.

"The secret," he said, "is concentration. I don't know why, but all I have to do is think I'm sick, and the next thing I know my stomach is acting up."

But one day McGowan's luck ran out. This was about five weeks after James Lee arrived. The chief of the medical service, Colonel Weylan, came in to see Private McGowan. He was to be congratulated, said the colonel. After exhaustive studies the medical staff had decided there was nothing wrong with Private McGowan that the rigors of infantry life could not cure. After a few more days of routine tests McGowan could rejoin his old outfit. The colonel and the private shook hands. McGowan thanked the officer for the kind treatment he had received. The colonel left.

James Lee had his first good laugh in weeks. He himself had several more operations to undergo and no expectation of returning to the battle zone. It pleased him when he thought of McGowan being shot at in the continuous blizzard of a North Korean winter, and he suggested to the professor that he might even be killed—adding that no one deserved it more.

For his part, McGowan seemed to accept the tragic news with equanimity. He was happy, he said so that everybody could hear, to be leaving the hospital at last. He was an active man and did not like sitting around in a robe and pajamas with nothing to do. He promised to send them a post card when he got to China.

It happened at three o'clock one morning. The hospital was quiet and peaceful when McGowan suddenly began to scream. They were blood-curdling shrieks that shocked James Lee out of a deep sleep. The lights began to go on. McGowan was sitting up in his bed staring straight ahead as if something on the other wall had pushed him beyond the border of sanity. His shrill, horrified cries made every man tremble. Sleepy-eyed nurses, orderlies, and doctors came running. They approached the frenzied, stunted little man cautiously. McGowan swung suddenly and viciously and knocked one of the orderlies cold. The others jumped him, but with surprising strength he threw them off and jumped out of bed. With agonizing screams he ran through the ward breaking windows and overturning tables. Suddenly he stopped screaming and began to sing and dance.

> " 'Cause my hair is curly,
> 'Cause my teeth are pearly . . .
> That's why they call me Shine."*

His pajama bottoms had fallen off now, and his immobile face with its frenzied eyes made him look like a crazy, wound-up doll. They rushed him again. He fought them off, striking out savagely at anyone who came near. James Lee sat in his bed transfixed, certain this was a bad dream that had suddenly erupted in his sleep.

The scene became as bizarre as a Halloween party, as more orderlies arrived, equipped with a strait jacket and sheets. They fell upon McGowan as a mass, and he went down, still struggling and singing and kicking his feet as if to dance. A doctor was standing

* From "S-h-i-n-e." Words by Cecil Mack and Lew Brown. Music by Ford Dabney. Copyright MCMXXIV and copyright MCMXLVIII by Shapiro, Bernstein & Co., Inc., 1270 Sixth Avenue, New York, N. Y.

near with a hypodermic ready. When McGowan was safely fastened inside the jacket the doctor approached and injected the sedative. The muscles of McGowan's face seemed to relax immediately, and he was taken out of the ward. But as he was being dragged through the door—and about this James Lee was absolutely certain—McGowan turned his head toward James Lee and winked.

"Driver!" The woman's sharp voice jerked him out of his thoughts. "Driver!"

"Yes, Madam."

"Is this the quickest way we can go?"

"It's the quickest way I know," James Lee said. "Midtown is always slow at—"

"Well, go over to Park Avenue. It seems to me that Park Avenue ought to be quicker than Fifth."

Of course she was right. Park Avenue was always quicker than Fifth, but his mind had not been on his work. When they reached the beautiful six-laned avenue the traffic was moving slowly but steadily. James Lee glanced at his passengers in his mirror. The woman's husband was embarrassed because his wife had created a scene, but her look was one of sharp-faced triumph.

The one good thing about driving a cab, thought James Lee, is that when passengers get out of your car you will probably never see them again. He gassed his car into the Park Avenue overpass above Grand Central Station and thought of Essie again.

No, he did not want to marry Essie. But what did he want? What did he want of any woman? Damn! In four years he would be thirty. Time, they said, went faster after that. In almost no time he would be forty. His life was slipping away from him. He had to get himself in hand. The trouble was that a man's life ought to make some sense and it didn't, not his anyway. You spent all your time doing one thing or the other, and all you were really doing was trying to make life make sense. You never succeeded, he suspected, but you kept trying because there was nothing else to do. At twenty-six you ought to know something of what it was all about.

When his cab was empty again he drove to the West Side and pointed the car uptown. Perhaps he would go to Iretha's apartment and see Essie. It was better to settle these things before they became too involved.

Chapter **12**

IT WAS ONE O'CLOCK and John Lewis had a problem. He had sorted and checked all the bets he had received that morning. There was a lot of little money on some of the "hot" numbers and most of this he was passing on to the regular bank. All of the single-action money, the bets placed on a single digit, he was passing along because the odds against the player were cut down from a thousand to one to eight to one. He himself banked all the money that had been bet on odd numbers, those combinations of three numbers on which only one or two people were betting.

The problem concerned the money that had been played on the six possible combinations of seven, one, and four. Aside from Hubert's bet of seven dollars on 417, there were at least fifteen additional dollars bet on one of the other combinations of those three digits.

What puzzled John Lewis was that not one of the possible combinations was considered "hot." Most of the so-called hot numbers or lucky numbers changed from week to week. But some held on for months, and a few, like 711 and 510, have been considered hot for more than twenty years.

These lucky numbers were passed from block to block, and they reflected themselves in John Lewis's books. Two weeks before, 941 had played, and on the previous week either the four or the one had shown up in the numbers every day. So it was odd that anyone would consider a combination of the four, one, and seven lucky. Yet here were more than twenty dollars on those figures.

John Lewis separated this money from the rest on the table. He was no numbers player himself, for he knew there was no profit in it for anybody but the men behind the game. But without risking his money he sometimes tried to guess how the number would run, and he was beginning to pride himself on having pretty good luck. This morning he told himself that if he were a player he would not bet a penny on any combination of four, one, seven. This was sure money for the big banks. John Lewis made a sudden decision. He would keep this money himself and add it to his bank. There was not one chance in fifty thousand that a four or a one would show up that day, and certainly not the whole number. It was almost a certainty. He folded the bills, among them Hubert's seven dollars, and pushed them into his pocket. Now that he had made the decision, he felt relieved. Why should he send good money to the white man's bank? He went to the kitchen and returned with a cold bottle of beer. He imagined he could see the horses at the starting gate in Saratoga. "Let 'em loose," said John Lewis. "Let 'em run."

And so the great dream machine was wound tight. The nickels were in the slots and the players waited. Only a turn of the handle was needed to set the whole thing in motion.

Oh, Lord, please let that number be 316 today. You know my life ain't been easy, me with three mouths to feed and that man of mine done snuck away like a dirty little coward. I done forgive him, Lord, the way I know You wanted me to—I never think no evil of him no more. But it's hard trying to feed these three kids on thirty dollars a week. Now, with a twenty-five-cent hit I could get shoes for little Johnny and Mary and Sarah Lou, and clothes to keep them in school. . . . So if You please, Lord, let that number come 316 . . .

A girl needs nice things or men just look the other way . . . dresses, slips, a handbag . . . Honest to goodness, I'm out of just about everything. Just can't seem to make enough to keep up. But if I can hit 212 today . . .

How a man can work so hard and never have any money I just don't know. If that 530 don't come today, I just don't know what I'm going to do. There's the television set to be paid, the refrigerator, the furniture and the car, all of which comes due the first of the month. Not to mention the rent that never stops and the gas and electricity and the telephone. I could take care of these things if 530 was to jump out just the way I played it. . . .

Let 728 come, and Harlem's gonna wake up and find out that I am here. I'll rent myself a suite up on the top floor of the Theresa and throw a party that will last a week. Then I'll buy myself the prettiest Cadillac Harlem ever saw. It'll even have a television set in it. I might even send some money to Mama down home, too. She ain't been doing so good lately. . . .

Lord, I'm needing a new church so as I can help set these people back on the path of righteousness. I saw a nice big store at One hundred and thirty-sixth and Lenox, and I have made inquiries, and I know that store can be acquired for a hundred and twenty-five a month. Now, they want two months in advance, and You know I don't have that kind of money. It's the perfect site for the Blessed Lamb Holiness Church. From there, Lord, the truth of Your loving word will flow all over Harlem and bring these wayward sheep back to the fold. The number is 471, Lord, and I have played it in a six-way combination. Now, if in Your loving kindness You could see fit to make things go that way, O Lord, we would be eternally in Your debt as we are already. All these things we ask in Jesus' name.

Amen.

Chapter **13**

AT TWO O'CLOCK Mabel's Beauty Salon was working at full capacity. The three booths were occupied, and there were two women under the drying machines. The two operators who worked with Mabel paid her rent for the use of the facilities. There was a competition among the three as to who could do the fastest and the best work. Mabel was the oldest and, in a sense, the boss. She often complimented her two operators on their work, but the praise was always bestowed in a condescending manner, as if from the master to the student. Each one took great pains to point up the merit of her individual work. Each had her regular clients and each took great pride in sending them away fully satisfied. All things considered, they got on well together, for the shop was small and they had to make one another company for long hours six days a week.

Mabel was running a hot comb through a young woman's hair. "Girl, I swear it's getting longer and prettier every day."

"Oh, you think so, Miss Mabel?" The girl was pleased. Her mother was one of Mabel's customers and, no doubt, if she ever had a daughter she would be sent to Mabel's, too.

"I guess it's time you were thinking about getting married and making a family," said Mabel. She was intensely interested in the personal life of every one of her customers. This amounted almost to a passion, and a customer was hardly in the chair before Mabel, in her friendliest manner, began probing. Through the women who came to the shop Mabel managed to know what was going on in a large part of Harlem.

"Planning anything soon?" Mabel asked sweetly.

The girl smiled and blushed. Mabel laughed good-naturedly and dropped the subject. The girl's mother had an appointment for the next day, at which time Mabel would get the whole story.

Lucille was washing a client's hair. "What in the world did she do that for?" asked Lucille.

The running water muffled the woman's voice. "She said she was tired of living with him."

"At her age she won't get nobody else."

"I told her, but she said she don't want nobody else."

"Hmmm," said Lucille incredulously. "She ain't that old."

The third operator, Alice, called over. "What did he do, hit her or something?"

"No. She said he was running around with other women."

"Is that all?" Lucille clicked her tongue in disgust. "Well, what if he was? He's just a man. Everybody knows that a man is lower than a dog. He's just as good as the rest of them. She better hold on to him."

All the women in the shop voiced their agreement with Lucille. The voice of the announcer interrupted the swing music on the radio. "We have the first race in from Saratoga. Here are the results of the first race from Saratoga." Alice sat down beside the radio, where a pencil and a sheet of paper were waiting. She scribbled down the win, place, and show money as the announcer read them off. The music resumed. Alice frowned when she had finished adding up the total.

She looked at Mabel and asked, "What did you play today, girl?"

"I just put five dollars on a four to lead," Mabel replied in her sweetest voice.

"Well, wouldn't you know it." Alice pushed the paper and pencil aside and went back to her customer. "As bad as I need money, and Mabel's hit that number again. There ain't no justice."

"Well, I play to win, girls," said Mabel. "Ain't no need in y'all getting mad at me."

Lucille said, "Don't tell me that number's a four when I have all my money on sixes."

"It's a four the way I figure it," Alice said.

Lucille left her customer and sat down in the same chair. "Here, girl, let me figure this thing out for myself." She began to count aloud. After a minute she said, "It's a four, all right." She crumpled the paper and threw it into the wastebasket. "Mabel, where in the world do you get such luck?"

Alice said, "That baldheaded old man of hers sure must be giving her some good treatment."

All the women laughed except Mabel, who smiled serenely.

"That I wouldn't deny," she said.

A pimp walking down Seventh Avenue looked down at the man who was shining shoes and said,

"What's happening today, Pops?" And Pops looked up from the shoes and said, "Four times."

When the pimp got to One hundred and twenty-eighth Street a policeman was standing on the corner twirling his nightstick. "What's happening?" he asked the pimp, and the pimp replied, "A four's running."

The cop walked over to Lenox Avenue, where some young men were sitting in a car drinking beer. One of them said to the cop, "What's up, Doc?" The cop held up four fingers and walked on.

An old woman sitting in the shade of her newsstand called across the street, "What did he say?" The young men told her what the first number was.

The word went out from thousands of apartments and shops and stores. It crackled through the streets like electricity. People held up four fingers, whispered it out of windows, and tapped four times.

In a few apartments Negro girls examined long lists of three-number combinations from which they separated all those that had four in them. From these they separated all those that began with four. When they had the results, they presented them to their bosses, who got on the phone and began placing bets on the next two numbers with larger banks. This scene was duplicated thousands of times on the east and west sides of Manhattan, in the Bronx and Brooklyn by white girls sitting at adding and calculating machines, and by their bosses who got on the phones and began placing what they called insurance money bets.

In a tall building downtown suave executives, the kind who first grow gray at the temples, and nervous executives, the chubby ones who sweat and chew cigars, checked with their accountants on the state of business, now that a four had played. The girls at the switchboards channeled the sudden flood that poured in at the same time six days a week. Here, at the summit of the business, men and women accepted these calls from district banks, then immediately sent the figures off to the accountants.

And in John Lewis's apartment he looked up from his pad and slapped his head with his hand. "A four! Well, what the hell do you know about that!" he said. "A four! Where did that come from?" He took his list and checked off his four money. There was no rush, no emergency. It was a routine matter. He smiled. Well, the suckers guessed *one* number right, anyway. He phoned in his insurance money but did not disturb the twenty dollars in his pocket.

Chapter **14**

"A BLACK WOMAN shall see hard times," Gertrude Cooley quoted to herself as she walked toward Lenox Avenue. A few minutes before, she had discovered her bureau drawer pried open and the seven dollars missing. It was possible that someone might have sneaked into the apartment and stolen the money, but, as Hubert was missing, too, it was more than likely he had taken it. The gas and electric bills were long overdue and Consolidated Edison had already threatened to shut off the power. Gertrude did not know how she could get the money back even if she caught up with Hubert before he bet it, but she had to try. She walked in the general direction of John Lewis's house, hoping she would see him.

Mr. Curtis's candy store was empty except for the old man himself. He was sitting behind the counter reading a newspaper with the help of his steel-rimmed glasses. The store was old and dusty, chock-full of penny candy, comic books, vending machines, notebooks, pencils, and a variety of useless gadgets for children. The few people who patronized the store came from force of habit. Mr. Curtis did not seem to care any more, so long as he kept a roof over his head and was his own boss.

"Mrs. Cooley, ain't seen you in I don't know when. Come on in here. How are you?" He was a short little man, a brown West Indian with a completely bald head. His lively eyes smiled and frowned as their owner's moods changed. "Mister Hubert? No, he ain't been in here since last week sometime." Then he swung to his favorite subject, politics and The Black Man. "Say, did you read this week's *Amsterdam?*" He held the paper up in the air and slapped it with the back of his hand. "The white man's up to the same old tricks. They appointed this fellow Clarkson to the Interior department. You know him—his father owns all those funeral homes. Sent that boy to Harvard. He's supposed to be one of us but he wouldn't give a black man the time of day. He made an Uncle Tom statement about that boy they're trying to frame down there in Florida. But he's supposed to be in Washington representing us. Can you beat that!" He looked over his glasses at Gertrude and saw that she was not listening. "Are you all right, Mrs. Cooley? Something the matter with Mister Hubert?"

"No, nothing's the matter, Mr. Curtis." She walked to the door. "I'll be seeing you."

"If I can do anything to help, Mrs. Cooley," he said, "you just give a yell."

"Nothing's the matter," said Gertrude, "but thanks anyway."

Gertrude walked to Lenox Avenue. The afternoon was hot, but there were quite a few people on the street. Lord, Lord, thought Gertrude, where in the world am I supposed to start looking for that crazy man? Where did I sin to deserve all this misery? I must be about the unhappiest woman alive.

She had known Lenox Avenue for more than thirty years, but now she seemed to see it with new eyes, with deeper, more terrible understanding. Many of the faces were familiar: the young men on the corner laughing and boasting of empty accomplishments; old Slim Thomas who had drunk enough wine for the day and now lay asleep on the sidewalk near the Paradise Bar; the old men and women who sat on their folding chairs outside the stores and shops; the boy with the suit on the hanger stealing into Sol's pawnshop; the girl chewing gum behind the hot-dog stand on the corner; the insurance collectors and the furniture collectors and the salesmen with their bags full of sparkling junk and Bibles and cheap tapestries—all these familiar parts became a whole, complete picture as Gertrude looked at them, and the street with all its superficial color and sound became one flat, bluish gray, a dull, monotonous drone. Among these parts Gertrude saw herself, ungainly and ugly and tired in her work clothes. Most of us are just strivers, Gertrude thought, but strivers who never get anywhere. We just follow one day after another until the end comes, and, thank God, it comes soon. Gertrude knew, as she always had known, that you had to make the best of a bad situation. But today remembering the thirty years of her life spent near Lenox Avenue, years that seemed completely wasted, it was almost too much for her.

Suddenly she wanted to scream. She wanted to put her clenched fists to her head and yell bloody murder at the top of her voice. She wanted to break out of herself and make her voice heard everywhere. You couldn't just sit and take it forever. You had to cry for help. If you were being sucked under, if you were drowning, you screamed for somebody to throw you a lifeline.

She clenched her fists and opened her mouth to give way to that desperate need, but that was all. She was Gertrude Cooley who lived in One hundred and twenty-sixth Street, and everybody in her block knew her. When she walked down the street they said, "Good morning, Mrs. Cooley," and "How are you today, Mrs. Cooley?" They respected her, and women often came to her for advice because they knew she was one of the strong ones. She could not let herself go, not ever. She let her arms hang loose at her sides, and as she relaxed she began to tremble. She felt she had just had a narrow escape from something terrible and unknown.

She motioned to Flash, who was standing on the corner with his friends. He immediately detached himself and came over, removing his hat as he approached.

"Flash, is the first one out yet?"

"Yes, ma'am. It's a four."

"Thank you, Flash."

"Any time, Mrs. Cooley, any time."

She walked toward home. There was no use trying

to find Hubert now. She would have to find another way to pay the gas and electric bill. Perhaps James Lee would have the money.

On One hundred and twenty-sixth Street Mrs. Jonas was scraping ice for two little girls who held their hands high so Mrs. Jonas could see their pennies. She put the ice in paper cups and flavored it with chocolate syrup. The girls squealed eagerly as they exchanged their money for the cups.

"I declare, Mrs. Cooley," Mrs. Jonas said, "you ain't looking so good today. What's the matter?"

Gertrude sighed. "A black woman born into this world shall see hard times."

"I know it's the truth," Mrs. Jonas said. She believed in all the old sayings. She sat on her folding chair and drew up the other one that she kept for company. "Come on, Mrs. Cooley, let's sit and chat a while."

But Gertrude did not feel like chatting. She excused herself and went into her apartment.

Chapter 15

ACTUALLY, he had no business worrying about Essie, he told himself. She was only one woman, and he had plenty of opportunities to make time with other girls, especially the ones who had gone to school with him. When he happened to meet them on the street they usually made it plain that they would welcome a call from him. Very often when Essie was working in White Plains he took advantage of these opportunities. Then there were the women he met when he worked the night line. He wondered what Essie would think if she knew that there were many women who would rather sleep with him than pay their fares. They were not usually whores, either, but ordinary women, colored and white, often very well-to-do. They liked his looks. He wondered what Essie would say if she knew that the city was full of opportunities for a man like him. But why worry about Essie at all? She was just—

"Where're you going, driver? Isn't this the address I gave you?"

The passenger was a man who usually ordered people about. He and his companion wore cool summer business suits and an air of self-importance.

James Lee mumbled, "Sorry," stopped the car, and backed up to the entrance of the apartment building where a tall, gray-haired doorman touched the visor of his cap as he helped the passengers to the street. The fare was eighty cents and the man told James Lee to keep the change.

"Thanks."

"That's all right, George," said the man pleasantly. He walked into the apartment building with his companion and the doorman slammed the taxi door shut.

Late one Saturday night not many months before a white passenger had called James Lee "George." James Lee had brought his car to a sudden halt, dragged the man out of the back seat, and knocked him to the sidewalk, where the man had apologized, explaining that he called everybody George, not just colored people. James Lee had driven away and left the man sitting there. He was often confused about what to do when he was called "son" or "boy," because an older white man might call anybody that.

But he was never in doubt about George. This time, however, he had been caught completely unaware. The man had gone into the building and there was nothing he could do without feeling silly. He could not even show the minimum protest—to curse the passenger and throw the change in his face. A taxi drew up behind, forcing James Lee to drive away. Petty frustration gripped at him.

Then he knew what he had to do. He would go see Essie and have it out with her. This day everything had gone wrong for him, and it was all her fault because she was on his mind, bothering him. Nothing would be right until he settled with her. He pointed the car toward Harlem.

He had been to Iretha's apartment only once, and he had not liked it then. Now he disliked it even more, and he knew why. It was in one of those modern buildings at the foot of West One hundred and fifty-third Street. Negroes had only recently moved in, and there were still a few white families in the building. Most of the new occupants were big-shot professional people—doctors, lawyers, real-estate brokers, well-paid civil servants, and racketeers—that group of colored folks who always seemed to have everything going their way. When James Lee was around them he felt almost insignificant, just the way he did when rich white people got into his cab. That time Iretha had invited him and Essie to dinner—just to examine him, he was sure—he had felt clumsy and uncomfortable all evening.

"Oh, it's you," Essie said. She held the door open for him and told him to come in. She was calm and pretty. He was irritated that she had obviously not

been crying. He remembered now that he had not had
a bath or changed his. clothes, and he needed a shave.
The fancy apartment intimidated him, made him
feel dirty. Who the hell did Essie think she was?

As they faced each other in the living room he began aggressively, "Look, baby, what is this business? I
call you up on the telephone and you don't want to
talk to me."

She shrugged. "I didn't want to talk to you, period.
I don't want to talk to you now. I don't have anything
to talk to you about. You and me, we've had it." She
gave a little wave of her hand.

"Look, about last night . . ." He had almost forgotten about last night, the drinking and the woman
called Lottie. He would have to think of something
good to tell her.

"Frankly, I'm not interested." Essie sat down on the
couch and crossed her legs, smoothing her skirt down
over her knees. This made James Lee even more uncomfortable. Now he was the only one standing in the
center of the living room. As large as the room was, he
felt too big for it in his wrinkled clothes. He did not
know this Essie. She was too calm. He wanted an argument or anything that would make her someone he
recognized.

He said, "I only wanted to explain."

She returned, "You don't have to. You can go home
now—or wherever it is you spend your nights."

He was being dismissed like a small boy who had
come asking for something and had been refused. For
a moment he felt it would be better to walk out of the
apartment and try to forget the whole thing, but that
would mean he had been defeated. He forced himself
to laugh. Then he started shouting at her.

"Why, just look at little Essie. Where do you get off? You're nobody to me, you understand, and I mean *nobody!* I picked you up and I can drop you just like that. Where do you get off sitting up in this apartment putting on airs like a two-bit whore—"

She was stung. The viciousness hurt and shocked her out of her calm. She jumped to her feet.

"Nobody asked you to come up here," she yelled. "Why don't you just go away somewhere and leave me alone? I don't want nothing to do with you, and I mean *nothing!*"

Now that she had lost her temper, he felt he was on even ground. His voice mocked her. "If you're mad about last night why don't you say so? I come up here to explain something and you start acting like a fool—"

"You're the fool but you just don't know it," Essie said. "That's right. You don't know it and you never will know it, but you're the fool."

His words slipped out easily. "Here I've been thinking it was time we were getting married—"

"I wouldn't have you on a bet."

Their words clashed against each other. She was standing close to him, flinging her words into his face. He put his arm around her waist and snatched her to him. It seemed the natural thing to do.

Then everything went wrong. Something, perhaps a thousand such scenes in the movies, had made him expect that she would, after a moment's resistance, give herself to his embrace. But she twisted and she struggled, she kicked and she screamed, and he had to let her loose. Struggling for breath, she fell against the wall.

Then he knew he had to hit her. He had to punish

her for what he was feeling. He had made a fool of himself, and she was the cause of it. But if he beat her, hurt her, she would know whether he was a man or not.

She must have known what he was thinking, for she stood quite still, almost in a crouch against the wall. But even as he raised his hand he knew that he was not going to strike her. This was not the way he had wanted it to be. It was all messed up. James Lee Cooley, he thought, what the hell are you up to now? You don't have the slightest idea. Just plain mixed up, that's what you are, Cooley. He lowered his hand and cursed—not Essie this time, not himself, but everything. He opened the door and walked out of the apartment.

Essie did not move for several moments. She continued to stare ahead of her as if he were still there. Then, suddenly, Essie thought she knew something that she had not known before, something that helped to explain everything that had happened. It surprised her because it was not about James Lee but about herself.

Chapter **16**

JAMES LEE fought off all thinking as he wrenched the wheel of the car, jerking it out of its parking area and merging it into the southbound traffic of Riverside Drive. He had no destination, yet he drove with a fury, switching incautiously from one lane to the other, jumping traffic lights before they turned green. He rigorously avoided thinking about Essie. He felt as if he were being chased.

At One hundred and twenty-fifth Street he swung eastward under the elevated subway at Broadway. At Amsterdam Avenue a white man and woman with luggage gave him a frantic hail. Damnit, he thought, there's a three-dollar job to La Guardia or International Airport. But he passed them by because he did not want to stop the car. He sped on, catching the lights at St. Nicholas and Eighth Avenues.

He came to a sudden halt when he swung his car south on Seventh Avenue and plowed into the rear of a brand-new Cadillac that was double-parked in front of the Theresa Hotel. The noise from the crash barely made itself heard over the traffic sounds of the intersection, but those people standing nearby turned to look. Some of them pushed their way toward the scene of the accident. James Lee was unhurt, for he had braced himself when he saw he would not be able to stop his car in time. Sitting behind the wheel of the car with the people coming toward him, he took a deep breath, closed his eyes, and tried to relax.

There are a thousand stories about Negroes and Cadillac automobiles, of which probably nine hundred and ninety-five are not true. But the very prevalence of these stories testifies to the high regard that Negroes, like other underprivileged groups, hold for a Cadillac car. It is not just a better-than-average piece of machinery that takes you from one place to the other; it is a symbol of accomplishment, of triumph. When you drive a fishtail Cadillac you're serving notice that the world is no longer kicking you. The situation has been reversed, and you are kicking hell out of *it,* riding it like a bronco buster, breaking it in to fit your style. They say, "A Caddie is due respect," meaning not the car but the man who is driving it. They say, "Man, that woman ought to be riding in a Cadillac," meaning that she is good to look at, and, if they had their way, they would see that she had the best of everything. A woman who is not so favored has no business in a Cadillac. Many a young man whose fortune has taken a sudden turn for the better has traded in not only his Ford or his Chevrolet but also his woman.

This particular Cadillac was a powder-blue affair with immaculate white sidewall tires and bumpers trimmed in sparkling chromium. On the previous Saturday night the young owner had managed an extraordinary run of luck by throwing seventeen passes in a floating crap game. Each time he had left his winnings on the table and they had multiplied. On the seventeenth pass he broke the game. Sunday had been a day of acute frustration for him because all the car dealers were closed. But this very morning, he had gone to the showroom and bought his Cadillac for cash. When the collision came he was standing under the Theresa Hotel marquee talking with his cronies, some of whom had made generous contributions to the game on Saturday.

He turned and saw that it was his car, but he could not believe what he saw. He drew in his breath sharply and closed his eyes, then opened them again. It was true: there was really a yellow taxicab sitting up on the rear end of his powder-blue Cadillac. He turned pale with rage, and from his head he snatched his hat, an expensive Panama straw (also new), slammed it to the sidewalk, and stamped on it with both feet. Clenching his fists, he looked up at the sky and swore a long and terrible oath that would have shocked and offended many of the bystanders had they all not felt as he did, that a man with a Cadillac had certain sacred and divine rights and that among these was immunity from collision.

Flanked by his companions, he walked weakly toward the scene of the accident. He attempted to regain some of the calm he had felt that morning. "Well, I'll be a monkey's uncle!" he said. "Boy, the good Lord just don't like colored folks." His friends tried to cheer him up. "Don't worry, man, you got to get paid. All those taxis are insured." He shook his head. "But, man, it'll never be like it was. Never."

Glumly James Lee and the unhappy Cadillac owner went through the formalities of exchanging credentials. While each was copying down information about the other, bystanders helped to untangle the automobiles. When the ceremony was over, James Lee drove away toward the garage.

"Jesus Christ Bloody Mary! Look at that!"

They were all watching as James Lee parked the car. The mechanics stared over the upstairs railing and Evaline came to the door to see what Danny was yelling about. Well, let them watch, thought James Lee as he prepared himself for what he knew would be an uncomfortable scene. Just so they don't start anything with me.

Danny tramped loudly down the metal steps and took a quick look at the car. "I'll be damned, a front end!" At all garages the driver was considered at fault if the front end of his car was damaged. Front ends ran up the insurance rates because they indicated the garage employed careless drivers.

"How did this happen, Cooley?"

"I ran into a guy."

"You mean it was your fault?" Even with a front end a New York hackie never admitted he was at fault. It was against tradition.

"Yeah, I guess that's what I mean," said James Lee. "I was at fault."

I don't have to stand here and be grilled by this punk, thought James Lee. He turned to Evaline and said, "Give me one of those accident forms, will you, Evaline?"

"Well, hell's bells!" Danny called. "Wait a minute, will you, and tell me what happened."

"I'll put it all down on the accident form and you can read it."

"I don't want to read it, I want to hear it—from you!"

"You gonna have to read it."

"Well, get a load of him, will you, fellas?" Danny spoke to his audience of mechanics, who were following every word from the second floor. "He brings in one of our cars half wrecked and he can't even take time to tell me about it."

He walked toward James Lee, who thought: He's just like that Marine poster in front of the Apollo Theater on One hundred and twenty-fifth Street, with his blond hair and blue eyes. He's the clean-cut American boy like the movie heroes, and I guess I'm scared because he's just as big as I am, but this is one day he can get a fight if he wants one.

Danny lowered his voice. "Look, sonny, I'm just the dispatcher around here, you know?"

"I don't care who you are"—James Lee was conscious of Evaline standing in the doorway—"and who the hell do you think you're calling sonny?"

"Look, Jackson, all I ask—"

"—and what's this Jackson business? My name's not Jackson. You know my—"

"—to hell with what your name is. I don't give a—"

James Lee swung first, a hard-aimed right that he did not know he was going to throw. But it was the next logical thing to do. Then all the accumulated fury and frustration exploded, and there were not just James Lee, Negro-American, and Danny O'Halloran, Irish-American, squaring off at each other in a taxi garage. James Lee was facing all the people who had irritated him all day, all the confusion that had kept him from understanding. There was Essie who was trying to show him up and make him feel small and inferior, and his father who was making a fool of himself, and McGowan with his crazy ideas, and the white man who had called him George and left a twenty-cent tip for the privilege. O'Halloran had none of this to drive him on, and he had been caught by surprise. He fought well because he had been in street fights and barroom tussles before, but there was nothing outside the natural desire to win and keep from getting hurt that impelled him.

James Lee thought, I will kill him if I can or I'll make him wish he was dead. When Danny caught him by the shoulders and slammed him to the floor he got up thinking, He's a good wrestler and I'll have to stay out of his reach. Swing now and keep him off, swing now and move right and move left and swing and keep on moving because if he catches hold of me I'm done for. But Danny did catch hold of James Lee's

-head with his left hand, pushing it down and slapping it with several cutting rights that left James Lee struggling for consciousness. In desperation he thought, I'll break his guts, and he brought his knee up into Danny's stomach and he heard the wind break from the Irishman's mouth. James Lee stepped back and with one vicious blow to the head he staggered Danny, who was dazed and fighting to catch his breath. With short, chopping blows James Lee beat against the dispatcher's head, thinking, Goddamnit! get down, down, down. Finally O'Halloran was on one knee and then the other. A grunt of final effort tore from James Lee's lips as he slammed the heel of his right hand down on the back of Danny's neck. The dispatcher sprawled face downward with a deep groan, unconscious.

Neither Evaline nor the mechanics had moved, had hardly breathed, during the few savage moments of the brawl. Now for another full minute they stood as if impaled by what they had seen. Then the mechanics began running down the metal stairs, setting up a jarring racket. Evaline stared at the unconscious figure of Danny, stifling a scream with her hand over her mouth.

James Lee, breathing heavily, turned and stumbled toward the garage entrance. Come and get your blond god, he thought. He felt good. He had been afraid of this fight, but now he had won it, and he knew that this was the way life ought to be, full of gigantic struggles that were won in the end. He had no thought now of Danny or the police or of finding another job. He was full of himself and the problems that were closest to him. The edge was on him and he knew he could hack his way through those problems like a steel ax. On the street people noticed the bruises and the blood and made a path for him. He wanted to smile, but his lips were swollen. That's right, he thought, get out of my way. He plunged on through the crowded streets toward Harlem.

Chapter **17**

HUBERT STOOD on the One-hundred-and-twenty-fifth-Street bridge that looks southward over Harlem toward downtown Manhattan. The bridge is of steel and concrete. On a hot day no one ever walks across because it intensifies the heat like an oven. There was the constant blare of automobile horns and occasionally the groan of an old boat as it chugged down the narrow Harlem river. There were many other sounds: the drone of an airplane dropping toward La Guardia Field, the beat and grunt of a jukebox going full volume in a bar down on Eighth Avenue, the sudden roar of baseball fans in the Polo Grounds. Beneath all these separate noises, pushing more persistently, was the great hum of the city. It was like an orchestra with a thousand bass viols constantly repeating a single, groaning note. If you concentrated by deliberately shutting out the other sounds, you could hear it, the drone of millions of lives spending themselves in stifling intimacy.

Hubert grasped this humming with his attention, wrapped himself in it, and there he existed for a while. He was absolutely alone now, and his isolation was complete and different from any he had ever ex-

perienced before. This was a complete involvement
with thought: He considered each of his problems, re-
acted to a thousand irritations, and wished for pleas-
ures. It was passionate, it was sensuous, and every inch
of him was alive, hot, and tingling. No one really mattered when he was like this, neither Gertrude nor the
boy nor what they thought of him. It was almost pain-
ful, as if his skin had been stripped away and the least
speck of dust caused a sensation. A thought could
make him cry or yell out in anger.

Already two of his numbers, the four and the one,
had played. It would soon be time for the third race.
There was nothing unusual about his being only one
digit away from a winner. He had come as close before without winning. Whenever this had happened,
new enthusiasm had been born on the spot for the
next day's number. Six days a week he had a chance
to win, and this was what kept him going. When he
had tentatively selected his number for the next day,
he would turn it over in his mind, switching the digits
to different positions. He would speak it aloud, ac-
centing different syllables. He would rub his tongue
over his lips, tasting the number as surely as if it were
a tangible thing. Once a number had passed this inspection, nothing could shake him in his determina-
tion to play it.

But today Hubert knew that all of that was over,
that he would never play another number again. He
knew his time had come and that the last digit would
be a seven. Hubert was talking to God about it. It was
long overdue, his hitting the numbers, but God was,
after all, a just God who made things come right in
the end. God would have to help him a little further.
There was the matter of Sister Clarisse. Nor did Hu-

bert underestimate the difficulties of setting himself up in business in a new city. Once all of this had been taken care of, God could forget about him. Hubert would take care of himself.

The noises from the traffic jam on the bridge pushed their way into Hubert's thoughts. He had been standing in the sun and he was drenched with perspiration. He walked toward the barbershop at the crest of the hill where One hundred and fifty-fifth Street joins St. Nicholas Avenue.

The fans in the shop droned. The barber was called Smitty. He was in his thirties, already fat, with the beautifully contoured lips of a man who enjoys talking whenever the opportunity presents itself. He and his customer were discussing a murder that had recently occupied the front pages of the Negro newspapers.

"The guy was crazy for playing around with a chick like that. Him with a wife and five kids." Smitty's scissors moved with a rhythmic chatter around the man's head. He had finished the haircut sometime before, but he would never let the customer know it until the conversation was finished or another customer entered. "She was bound to kill him if his wife didn't get him first. The cat never had a chance."

"She swore it was his gun and she took it away from him." Both men laughed.

Smitty nodded toward Hubert who entered just then. "Hiya, Mister Hubert, you're next."

"No, Smitty, I don't think I need one today." Hubert cleared his throat. "What was the last one?"

"A seven," said Smitty. "Can you beat that? I've

been playing five-twenty-nine for a month now and can't come near it. A poor man ain't got no win."

"You said it," said the customer.

"Thanks, Smitty," said Hubert. He walked out of the shop.

"As I was saying," continued the customer, "some of the smart boys are laying odds that that little girl will never serve a day. Somebody told me—and this boy ought to know because he's got good connections himself—that that little girl has some of the right folks behind her from downtown."

"Well," said Smitty, summing it up, "it's a woman's world any way you look at it." A new customer had just walked in. "You're next," said Smitty, and with a flourish he finished the haircut.

Hubert was choked full with feeling, and the hot tears flowed easily. The hum of the city enveloped him in a new way, becoming for him a song of triumph.

As he walked toward John Lewis's apartment he saw again familiar objects of Harlem, the occasionally familiar face without a name. These people . . . his people . . . these Negroes . . . he was not angry with them any more, not resentful, not concerned with them. They could not hurt him any more. He was surprised to find that he really felt sorry for them, for all the Harlem black and brown and yellow folk, all the colored people all over the world who had never made it. Good-by, you poor fools, Hubert said to Harlem. God bless you. Soon Hubert would push them into the past like a bad dream.

John Lewis wore a large grin when he opened the door and looked down at Hubert.

"Man," he exclaimed, "am I sorry I ever laughed at you!" John Lewis gave a low whistle and slapped Hubert on the back. "You sure must've got up on the right side of the bed this morning, Mister Hubert. That's a lot of money you've got coming."

Hubert was uncomfortable. He did not like to be slapped on the back. He shifted his weight from one foot to the other.

"What are you going to do with all that money, Mister Hubert?" asked John Lewis.

"Oh, I've got a few ways to spend it," answered Hubert.

John Lewis said, "Well, I know this ain't no social call. You want to get your hands on that loot and I don't blame you."

"Well, I want it as soon as I can get it."

"I tell you what I'm going to do," John Lewis said. "Just because it's you, I'm going to pick it up myself. Suppose I bring it by your house at, say, seven o'clock, huh? How's that for speed?"

"That'll be fine," said Hubert.

On the way to the door John Lewis slapped Hubert on the back again. "Man, this is your lucky day, huh?"

"I'll see you at seven," said Hubert. It was not his lucky day. He was receiving his due. Life was settling its account with him. No luck about it.

As soon as the door closed behind Hubert, the smile vanished from John Lewis's face. He pushed his hand into his trousers' pocket and jerked out the money he had there. He crushed the bills in his big fist and hurled the green ball against the wall. It landed silently and bounced back to the couch. John Lewis sat down heavily and squeezed the ball again. "Well, kiss me one time!" he exclaimed. He gave himself a solid slap across the forehead. "Ada! Ada!" he called to his wife, who was napping in the bedroom. When he heard her mumble in her sleep he yelled, "Get up and come on out here!" He bit his lips, he cursed, he scratched his head and drove his fist into the couch. "Goddamn!" he growled as he lit a cigarette with unsteady hands. He unraveled the ball of money and walked over to the window, where he tore it into little green bits. He held a hand out the window, where a suggestion of a breeze caught up the green flakes and scattered them over the Harlem streets.

"John Lewis, boy," he said glumly, "you're a fool." For once in his life he was sure he knew what he was talking about.

Chapter 18

HUBERT LOOKED at women again—not a particular one, but all of them—in a great sensuous conglomerate. He was the young male animal appraising each female he passed on the street. The young woman with the green outfit was easy to look at, and those earrings set her chestnut-brown complexion off just right. Hubert reflected that in all the world there was nobody who could beat a colored woman wearing earrings.

And it seemed to him that the women were taller than they used to be. At One hundred and twenty-fifth Street he paused to look at the young girl who stepped down from the bus. She was tapioca-colored, with red lips. Around her waist was a wide belt that matched the deep black leather bag she was carrying. Hubert wondered what in the world she would want with a bag so large. She had fine legs, slender yet strong. As she walked away, Hubert concentrated on the swing of her hips and the way her tight skirt emphasized the swing of her thighs.

She was taller than Hubert by two or three inches. He could not remember women being so tall when he was young and really after them. They had been good-looking, all right. Yes, indeed, women had always been pretty when a man was on top and had life where he wanted it, but Hubert did not think they had been so tall.

He walked on. Now he had more to do than watch young girls. There was a woman, a real flesh-and-blood woman waiting for him, although she did not know he was coming.

Surprise and disapproval were on Sister Clarisse's face when she opened the door. She had not forgotten their conversation earlier that afternoon. "Mister Hubert!" she frowned. "Twice in one day? What will people think?"

Without waiting for an invitation he walked past her into the room. "It hit," he said.

"What did?" she asked.

"My number. It came just like I played it."

"Good for you," said Sister Clarisse, who was still wondering why he had returned to her apartment. "How much did you hit for?"

"Seven dollars," he announced.

"Aw, gowan," Sister Clarisse laughed. She knew that no one ever hit the numbers for seven dollars except big gamblers and people like that. With poor colored folks a hit for seven cents was more likely.

Hubert said, "That's more than four thousand dollars I got coming."

His seriousness frightened her. "Mister Hubert, you're joking, aren't you?"

"Not a bit," he answered, then added with a bold flourish, "not a damned bit."

The language was unusual for her apartment, but she took no notice of it. "Well, my goodness," she said weakly and sat down on the couch.

"This is what I was talking about when I was here a few hours ago, Sister Clarisse, only I just didn't know how soon it was coming. Here's our chance, yours and mine."

Sister Clarisse was only happy in a routine she understood. Problems bothered her because she did not know how to begin to handle them. She had never solved a major problem in her life. There had always been someone else to take care of them for her or she had left them to take care of themselves. Now she felt trapped. This man standing in front of her actually had ideas about the two of them going away together. It occurred to her that a woman with good intentions could get into a lot of trouble by just being nice to a man.

"I've been unhappy and dissatisfied for a long time, and you probably have, too. For more than ten years I've been waiting to kiss Harlem and New York good-by and go somewhere and start all over. All I needed was a little money to buy myself in because I found out a long time ago that a man has to own something to be on the inside. He needs money in the bank and a check book in his pocket. That's the only thing that makes him somebody."

Now, somehow, he was on the couch beside her and

she had not even noticed that he was so near until he spoke again.

"I'm a man you could live with because I'm a man who could love you and be a partner with you in everything. We're not children any more—I'll be fifty-one my next birthday. I figure that we've got a little good living coming to us, Clarisse. Now, if you say yes, by eight o'clock tonight we'll be on our way to a new life together."

It was a wild idea. From time to time she had thought of doing wild and irresponsible things, but she had never been what she would call "bad." She raised her eyes and looked at Hubert. Yes, she liked his face. It was a man's face, smooth and strong. She liked the heavy black hair of his mustache, the firm lips. But the eyes bothered her. They seemed brown at first and yet darker, almost black. And intense, like the eyes of a troublesome boy. He had the eyes of a wild boy with wild dreams. Such dreams had to be beaten out with the practicality of adulthood. A man of fifty-one had no business with such eyes.

"Are you coming, Clarisse?"

Once, when she was seventeen and still a girl in Alabama, she had spent several months with relatives in another county. There had been a boy with such eyes, a restless boy, intense and passionate, who spoke to her of the wildest things. They had said that he drank and gambled and would never amount to anything, but none of that had mattered to her. She had given more of herself to him than to any man since. She had loved him. But nothing ever came of it. What happened? . . . a quarrel? She could not remember. And later, when she heard that he had been killed in an ugly gin-mill brawl, she cried for days. Later she came to realize that everybody had been right about him all along. Loving that boy was the last irresponsible act she had ever committed.

Hubert was waiting. She had to say something.

Then she saw them as they really were. She was forty-eight and a widow. No matter what some jealous folk said, she led a good, Christian life. Her husband had been a deacon of Little Calvary. Hubert was a man with a family, and everybody said he was peculiar in the head. Suppose she were to do the crazy thing he proposed? That would really give the sisters something to talk about. She could see them now, buzzing around Sister Gertrude with their sympathy and advice. No, Sister Clarisse would never give them any real ammunition to use against her. Besides, she was a good Christian woman and would never dream of doing such a thing.

She smiled and her laugh fluttered. "Well, Mister Hubert, my goodness! What would everybody say?" She knew it sounded childish and silly, but how else could she put it? You could not come right out and talk about a thing like that.

Hubert stood up. He looked at her for only a moment. Then he turned and walked out of the apartment. The vacant smile lingered on Sister Clarisse's face for several minutes. Her feeling of relief was tinged with sharp regret as she stared at the closed door, and she only remembered to remove the smile when she turned her eyes away.

Chapter **19**

At FIRST the coming of the seven did not ring a bell with the corner bums at all.

They lounged dispiritedly outside the Crystal Bar and went through a variation of their daily routine.

"Boy, money and me, we hate each other."

"You and me both, Pops."

"And here I am, dry as a nun's tit."

"Boys, I would put my last suit in hock and get us all a drink, but I did that yesterday."

"If my old lady would straighten up and act right, I could get a drink for us. But since she got this job of hers, she's acting kind of cool toward me."

"It wouldn't be so bad if I had come close to the damned number, but God knows that figure wasn't supposed to be no four-seventeen."

"I'm gonna quit playing myself. That's a promise."

"Yeah, no use making those number boys rich when the number is running wrong all the time."

Suddenly Flash gave himself a hard slap on the head and stamped his foot on the sidewalk. "Well, I'll be!" he yelled.

"What's ailing you, Flash?"

"Boys, don't none of us ever deserve another taste of sneaky pete." Flash snatched his hat from his head

and slammed it against the wall. He gave the trash
can a hard kick and sent it spinning into the street.
"Man, ain't none of us got no sense at all."

"Well, get hold of yourself, man, and tell us what's
happening."

"That's the number old man Hubert gave us this
morning. Don't you remember? Four-seventeen.
That's just what he said. I remember it because my
aunt lives at Four-seventeen St. Nicholas Avenue, and
at the time I said to myself, I ought to play that number just in case. Ooooooh!"

He moaned and groaned and slapped himself on
the cheeks with the palm of his hands. He finally lay
down on the sidewalk with arms outstretched, pleading, "Somebody please kill me dead right this minute. Anybody as stupid as me don't deserve to live."

This behavior was not unusual for a numbers player who thinks his own foolishness has caused him not
to hit. But there was no one to comply with Flash's
request because all his companions now recalled the
number Hubert had given them and each of them
went through the same kind of antic. It now developed that each had thought the number was good but
for one reason or another had not played it. Each con-
fessed that his own stupidity had lost him a fortune.

After a while they began to speculate on how much
money Hubert had won.

"Well, you know what John Lewis said: that Hubert don't never bet less than five dollars."

"Great day in the morning! Count that up, Flash.
You're good at figures."

Flash calculated and told them the total. They all
agreed that it was a magnificent sum, and then the
discussion naturally turned to what they would do if

they had that much money. The consensus was that a down payment on a Cadillac would be worth while and the rest would go toward parties, women, and good wine and whisky.

When James Lee approached, one of them yelled, "Jesus, look at the kid."

"He looks like a truck backed over him."

"Two trucks."

The blood from James Lee's nose had dried into a black stain on his shirt. His jaw was puffed and one of his eyes was swollen.

"Boy, look at your hair standing at attention."

"And your eyes going in every which direction."

"And your jaw trying to take off like the mumps."

"Your old man's done hit the jackpot, boy."

"What are you guys talking about?"

"Don't you know about four-seventeen?"

He did not know. They told him. He hurried on.

Earlier, when Gertrude had returned home, she had sat in the big overstuffed chair and begun to cry for the first time in many years. No, life had not been good to her, but she had taken everything without a whimper. She had known that life was something you did something about, you *acted,* so there had never been any need for tears. But now there was nothing to do. She felt herself a raw, tender thing who had been roughly handled and hurt. At first she had cried softly. But these tears seemed to open up a well within her, and her large body shook with great sobs. She choked and coughed and cried until she was exhausted. After this she felt relieved. She closed her eyes and went to sleep. She did not hear James Lee when he came in. He went to the bathroom where he washed and changed his clothes.

"Mama."

She opened her eyes. James Lee was kneeling beside her. Although he had washed, she could see the bruises.

"Honey, what in the world happened to you?"

"What happened to you? You've been crying."

"No. I was just sleeping," she said.

"Where's Pop?"

"Lord, I don't know. He took our last seven dollars out of here this morning and I ain't seen him since."

"Did he say what number he was going to play?"

She said, "No, I don't think so."

James Lee asked, "Did he say anything about four-seventeen?"

Gertrude sat up now, fully awake. "I remember he said he had a dream last night and he was going to play four something or other."

"It was four-seventeen," James Lee said. "He told the guys on the corner. If he played it he hit it."

"Call John Lewis and be sure."

James Lee went to the phone and found an old booklet with the pages curled at the edges. He thumbed through it, found a number, and dialed it.

"Hello, Ada. This is James Lee. Do me a favor and ask John Lewis if Pop was right today." He listened a moment, then said, "Thanks." He hung up the receiver.

"Pop hit for seven dollars," said James Lee. "John Lewis is supposed to bring the money by here in a little while."

Gertrude said nothing. He asked, "What're you going to do, Mama?"

She sighed. "I don't see nothing I can do. I guess if a man hits for that much money we ought to be happy."

The front door opened and Hubert came in.

Without speaking, he went to the hall closet and took out his bag, the one he had never used before, the one that for three years had been sitting in the closet with new clothes in it. He went into the kitchen and came back with a cloth that he used to wipe away the dust. After unfastening the two straps, he unsnapped the lock and laid the bag open on the couch. James Lee watched, somehow fascinated by his father's slow, deliberate movements. Each activity was logical, growing out of one thing and leading to another. But all together they made no sense.

Hubert came out of the bathroom with his toilet articles. He carefully wrapped them in newspaper and placed them in a compartment of the bag. James Lee's voice sounded weary as he spoke.

"Pop, what do you think you're doing?"

"I'm packing a bag, boy," said Hubert, "as any fool can plainly see." He went to the closet and took out a suit.

"You going someplace?"

"That's right," said Hubert. "You get the idea."

"You mean you're leaving home—Mama and everything?"

"That's right."

James Lee was suddenly exasperated. "You're crazy, you know that! Just plain crazy. Why, you little jerk! You couldn't make it on your own with fifty thousand dollars if you didn't have somebody to play nursemaid to you." He yelled, "You're a number one first-class jerk!"

The words had no effect on Hubert, who went into the bedroom. James Lee turned to Gertrude. "Mama, aren't you going to say something? Try to stop him?"

"Not a word. Let him go. I can't take it any more." Her voice was low and tense and she was trying to keep from yelling.

When Hubert came back to the room James Lee said, "If you're trying to hurt Mama, you can forget it. You've already done that."

"Not trying to hurt nobody," he said. "I'm just leaving. Never did like it around here. I've been wanting to get away for many a long year." He went on with his packing.

James Lee looked at Gertrude, really looked at her, and saw a large, ungainly woman, tired and beaten. He remembered old snapshots he had seen in an album that used to be around the house. They were photographs of Gertrude and Hubert when they were young. James Lee used always to wonder why his mother had married his father. She was very handsome. James Lee always remembered his mother's dark, beautiful eyes in the photographs. They had been large and eager, and he had wondered that his mother was ever so young. Now—he forced himself to think it—she was almost ugly, so large, so worn.

"Goddamn you!" He spat the words at his father. James Lee had never cursed Hubert before nor had his mother ever heard him use such language. He rushed out of the apartment.

Hubert and Gertrude heard him walk quickly through the hallway and down the steps outside. Then, for a while, in this room where man and wife were, there was silence. Finally Hubert brought more clothes from the closet and went on with his packing.

Again James Lee walked the streets without seeing. The sun seemed beyond the Hudson now, and the heat was lifting. As the coming-home rush hour approached, activity increased on Lenox Avenue. At One hundred and twenty-fifth Street the subway seemed to cough up people who pushed their way through the exits and dispersed. James Lee felt the rumble of the heavy old Seventh Avenue trains below the street as they dragged themselves farther uptown. A girl in a blue bonnet, somehow pretty without rouge or lipstick, stood near one exit selling religious magazines. Shoeshine boys in tight-legged motorcycle dungarees stood near the corner and yelled at prospective customers. People paused in front of the newsstand to snatch a *News* or *Mirror* or a *Jet* magazine that they began to read while waiting for the traffic light to change. A bus already packed with passengers roared past its stop and halted in the middle of the block to discharge some of its occupants. Some of the people who had been waiting at the stop set up a yell of protest and pushed down the street toward the bus. A mounted policeman, a black man with dark glasses, galloped down the block and drove the people back onto the curb. The smell of grilled frankfurters came from a nearby stand where a dark-brown girl was irritably reminding the crowd that she only had two hands. The soft, steady daytime beat of Lenox Avenue shifted. Picking up its darktime rhythm, it became feverish, mad, syncopated.

James Lee turned west on One hundred and twenty-fifth Street. He was biting his lip and talking to himself. He wished he could have said to his father and mother what was on his mind and in his heart. Once they had loved each other. . . . But people did not

think like that, did they . . . about love? Not really.
But they had loved each other. What else could you
call it? And something had caused that love to break
down over the years. You had to have something else
besides love to keep from turning out like his parents.
You had to become better or you became worse. It
was as simple as that. His father had been an okay
person, but look at him now . . . a mean, ugly little
man who was hurting the only one who cared anything about him. His mother . . . those eyes in the old
snapshots . . . Why, my God! They reminded him of
Essie!

He stopped abruptly in the middle of the sidewalk.
The people pushed past him.

Twenty-five years ago his mother had been about
the same age as Essie. She had met this fellow named
Hubert and decided that this was the man with whom
she would spend her whole life. Look what a mess
they had made of it. Could the same thing have happened to him and Essie? James Lee Cooley had given
her a rough time just like Hubert Cooley's son might
be expected to.

He began walking again. His steps quickened. He
turned at St. Nicholas and headed uptown.

Where did I get these silly ideas that I've been
carrying around with me, he was thinking. Treat the
girls rough, they like it . . . variety, man, the spice of
life . . . screw 'em all while you can . . . do her wrong
before she does you wrong. How many times have I
wanted to really talk to Essie?

McGowan had said it! Life is a precious thing and
you don't fill it up with dumb ideas just because there
are plenty of them around. Now I see. There are all
kinds of things trying to pull a man down, but mostly

it's his own ideas. You've got to stay on your toes and you've got to keep thinking for yourself . . . always thinking for yourself . . . it's your only hope.

Suddenly James Lee was conscious of his direction. He broke into a run toward Iretha's apartment, where Essie was.

Chapter **20**

THE AFTERNOON RUSH hour in Grand Central Station is a long one that begins at about half-past three and only subsides toward seven o'clock. In the vacant white lights that spill down from the high chandeliers thousands of people rush toward New York Central commuter trains that carry them out of the city's heat to small green residential towns farther north. During these hours the station is like a well-organized but overcrowded beehive. From the world's busiest center, Manhattan's midtown, the car horns, the millions of voices, the thousand other distinct sounds, combine into a single persistent din that envelops the station and seeps through its walls. The hollow voices of the public address system and the clatter of racing footsteps echo off the high hard ceiling.

The young Negro woman who walked down into the station from the west-side entrance carried her head high. She had been shopping, and, besides her overnight bag, she carried a large hat box filled with her purchases. She moved with a jaunty step that was not without youthful grace. There were pride and sophistication in her walk, and anyone watching her would have said definitely that she knew where she was going and what she was going to do when she got there.

When you go through life being afraid, she was thinking, you're really asking for trouble. And you don't have to wait long before you get it. Poor little Essie. I just had to have a big strong man to lean on. I couldn't stand the thought of being alone in this big old city. He never took anything away from me. The things that counted, I gave. But I'm somebody too.

She stopped in front of the ticket window and bought a round-trip fare.

No wonder he wanted to hit me. If your pet dog starts acting up, you give it a beating. Well, Essie, you live and learn. After I tell old lady Ornstein I quit, I'm coming back down here and live in this old town. That was all a lot of nonsense anyway, going up there. Just a case of being scared again. I'll get a job, go to night school . . . heck, I can even live with Iretha. Nobody scares me, not any more.

A frantic-looking young Negro man rushed into the west-side entrance and moved his eyes searchingly over the bustling crowd below. When he had found the person he was looking for he called out, but his voice was drowned in the great murmur of the station. He bounded down the marble staircase three at a time, jostling commuters and excusing himself as he rushed by them.

"Essie. Hey, Essie!"

He was so happy he had found her that he had forgotten how angry with him she must be. "Hey, Essie, it's me. Iretha told me what train you'd catch."

"Hi," she said as she returned his smile, but she

kept on walking. For a moment he stood watching after her. Then he caught up and fell in step beside her.

"Hey, where're you going?"

"I'm going to White Plains." She did not slacken her pace nor did she look at him. He caught her by the elbow and gently pulled her to a halt.

"Hey, this is me. Remember James Lee? You know me."

"Yes, I remember you." She smiled. "I'll always remember you. Now I don't want to miss my train. Good-by, James Lee."

She walked through the gates that led to the tracks. He followed her onto the platform. He had to talk to her. He had to explain what he had been thinking and feeling. He caught up to her again.

"Look, Essie, about last night and that crazy stuff today in Iretha's apartment—" That wasn't the way he wanted to begin. "—Well, look, all that is dead and I know it now for what it was. I wish I could make you understand how different I feel. I've been looking at Mom and Pop and I know how a person can get mixed up the way I was. But listen to me, I don't want to be that way. I don't, Essie. Believe me."

She felt his sincerity. "James Lee, you and me, we've had all we can get from each other. I don't love you, not any more, and I don't think you ever gave a rap for me. Understand, I'm not blaming you. I thank you for what I got, the good times, the hard times, all of that . . ."

She paused. For the first time since she had known him he was listening to everything she was saying. Even this made her angry, and she knew she did not have to be, so long as she knew what she was going to do. But as she looked at him she could not keep her anger down.

"You pushed me around—" She stopped. She had not meant to shout. She spoke in a fierce whisper. "Well, nobody's pushing me around any more. That's all I'm trying to say."

She started to walk again, and he was beside her. She was crying now because she was thinking how wonderful everything could have been and how nasty and stupid it had turned out. She thought about the baby. She knew there were tears in her eyes, but she would not wipe them away. She said, "I'm crying because it didn't work out."

James Lee had been listening in silence. Glancing around, he saw something that made him stop so suddenly that she stopped too.

"What is it?" Essie asked.

"Baby, please don't get on the train yet," he said. "We've got to talk."

James Lee walked a few feet away into the path of a man who had just bought a ticket and, with overnight bag, was rushing to catch an express train that was taking on passengers on the other side of the platform.

He who fights and runs away
Will live to fight another day

was the crazy rhyme that repeated itself in John Lewis's mind. Some people had the luck and some people didn't. He had been going along just fine, with a great future, and then a crazy, stupid number like this 417 had to show up. Why hadn't he bet the money with the big bank in the first place instead of

taking a silly chance? Four . . . one . . . seven . . .
those three numbers could ruin a man's whole life.
Together, the hits against him came to seven thousand dollars, and he did not have nearly that much.
And his reputation! This was what really mattered.
Well, no one could say he hadn't tried. He really
wanted to pay off the winners. He and Ada had been
on the phone two hours trying to round up some cash.
They had called every big wheel they knew without
any luck at all. Guys he had drunk with and gambled
with, guys who could have raised the money with a
telephone call—they had turned him down. When a
new bank got busted, everybody swore it off. If his
had been an old, established bank that suddenly
came up two hundred thousand short—well, that
would have been different. But those low-down rats
would not back him for four thousand. They were
willing to let him go under. But John Lewis was a big
man and he would show them. This was what they
called a temporary setback. A couple of months and
he would be back. Numbers players are funny people.
Right after they hit and don't get their money, they're
liable to kill you. But give them a little time to think
it over and they will chalk it up to experience. If that
little guy, Mister Hubert, had been the only winner,
there would be no need to leave town. But two of the
others were the kind of low-class Negroes who were
mean enough to start cutting and shooting. So the best
thing for John Lewis was to absent himself until the
storm blew over. Anyway, it might be a nice vacation
for him and Ada up there in Syracuse in her mother's
house. Ada would take care of the apartment and
drive the car up later. Oh, yes, it was just a vacation

because he would be back. New York was a big city
and God knew that John Lewis was a big—

"Say, John Lewis. Where're you going?"

John Lewis stopped. James Lee was the last person
in the world he expected to see. "Hey, man," laughed
John Lewis. He put his big hand in James Lee's and
tried to sound pleasant. "What are you doing down
here?"

"Are you making a trip?" James Lee asked.

"Well, kind of . . ." John's mind was working frantically. "Say, did you know your old man just finished
cleaning me out? Got to go dig up some more loot."

James Lee was puzzled. "You mean you already paid
Pop?"

"Yeah," said John Lewis. "I got it a little quicker
than I thought, so I took it on over. He's a rich man
now." John Lewis's eyes shifted uneasily. He was trying to keep them looking directly at James Lee, but
they moved away involuntarily.

"Say, what do you mean, he cleaned *you* out? I
didn't know you had a bank of your own now. I
thought you were still just writing them."

"Did I say *me*? What I meant was *us*. He cleaned
us out." He was trying too hard to explain. He realized
this as soon as James Lee did. "Well, man, there goes
my train."

James Lee said, "Say, wait a minute. You're not
trying to run out with my old man's money, are you?"

"All aboard," called the platform conductor.

John Lewis said, "Man, you must be crazy. I told
you I've got to catch a train."

James Lee did not know what he was trying to do,
but he felt he had to hold on to John Lewis. He
reached out and caught him by the sleeve.

"What's the matter with you, boy?" yelled John Lewis. "You know better than to be pulling on my clothes. Have you lost your mind?"

"I think you're taking a powder. Look, John Lewis, my old man is counting on that money. It's like a sickness. He's got to have it so he can find out—"

"I don't know what you're talking about," John Lewis said. "I told you I already paid your old man." He pushed James Lee's arm away. Some of the passengers, seeing two heavyweight Negroes arguing, stepped off the train onto the platform hoping to see a fight.

"All aboard!" called the platform conductor with finality. The train creaked to a slow start.

"Look," said James Lee as he caught John Lewis's arm again, "stay and catch the next train—"

"Boy, I told you."

In one movement John Lewis jerked his arm free and dropped his bag near his feet. He was an ex-boxer with a quick job to do. Already James Lee was swinging a hard right that he blocked easily at the same time he hooked his own right into James Lee's stomach. John Lewis followed this up with a quick left to the jaw and a jarring right to the head. James Lee gasped. He fell face downward and lay there. John Lewis scooped up his bag and dashed for the moving train. He had only a few feet of platform left when he jumped onto the observation car. The train jerked into the tunnel and disappeared.

An elderly white man, one of those who had missed his train to see the fight, cautiously approached James Lee. "Are you all right?"

James Lee tried to clear his head and pushed himself to his knees. The jaw that Danny had bruised first now felt as if it no longer belonged to him.

"Are you all right?" The white man had sandy hair and was carrying a battered briefcase. James Lee thought the man was grinning, but he could not be sure because his eyes were not focusing well. He felt hot and embarrassed. He tried to picture what all these white people were thinking of two Negroes fighting in Grand Central Station. It would give them something to talk about when they got home that night.

"I'm okay," he said. He wanted to yell at all the staring faces, but all the fight was out of him now. He felt Essie's hands helping him to his feet.

"You all right?" she asked.

"I guess so."

"What in the world was all that about?"

He told her briefly about John Lewis and his father. Then he asked, "Are we really through, Essie? I came down to ask you to try again."

"I'd like to try again," said Essie, "but you see, there's nothing left to try. No use trying to breathe life into what's dead. And it is dead . . . like our baby."

They were silent.

"All aboard." The platform conductor had walked across to the second train now.

"Good-by," she said.

"Good-by, Essie."

She touched his hand. Then she walked into the train. He watched her go, feeling strangely happy for her, although he felt cold and empty already. After a moment the train began to move. One by one its cars were pulled into the tunnel. Essie was gone.

Evening approached Harlem. Hubert had taken his suitcase and set it on the small landing outside the vestibule. From there he would be able to see when John Lewis turned into One hundred and twenty-sixth Street from Lenox Avenue. He sat down on the suitcase to wait.

The news of the big hit had spread up and down the block. Many of the Cooley neighbors rushed through their dinners so they could see John Lewis when he brought the money. Coming home from work some of them had stopped to inquire, "You taking a trip, Mister Hubert?"

"Yep."

And when they had asked him where he was going he had smiled and said, "Any place that comes to mind."

When there was no one asking him questions, Hubert talked to himself. "A man hopes and prays all his life for something like this to happen, and when it comes he can't back down. It's a deal he makes with himself and that kind he can't break."

In their homes from time to time the children of the block had overheard their parents say that Hubert was crazy. Some of them now gathered under a street lamp a few yards away from the Cooley apartment. They played halfheartedly at their games. They were really watching Hubert and waiting for John Lewis. Hubert looked at them for a long time. Then he spoke aloud, softly, insistently.

"It's no good around here," he said. "You never get a chance to do any living. Babies are born here and old folks die here, but in between there ain't no living."

And later he said, "I don't blame Gertrude and I

don't blame the boy. I tried to give both of them ambition and I found out that you can't do that. They never understood me. I don't believe I was born to spend my whole life on this street or any other street in Harlem. I've wanted to be too many grand and wonderful things to find out in the end that this was all I was ever meant to be."

It was almost completely dark when James Lee came down the street. Hubert did not seem to know him. The young man spoke gently, in a tired voice.

"No use waiting, Pop. John Lewis won't be here." James Lee explained what had happened at Grand Central, but when he finished he knew that Hubert had not listened to him. His father sat with his eyes fixed on Lenox Avenue.

James Lee said, "It's past eight o'clock, Pop. Believe me, he's not coming." He put his hand on Hubert's shoulder. "He never comes, Pop. Don't you see that? John Lewis never really comes."

Hubert did not answer. James Lee became conscious of people watching from nearby houses. He looked at the kids who had stopped their game under the streetlamp and were staring. James Lee went into the house. He would bring the old man in later. Now he wanted to tell his mother.

After a while Hubert gave a low chuckle of satisfaction. "They laughed at me and said I would never make it, but I did. Maybe it ain't true that every dog will have his day, but I'm going to have mine." He laughed and wiped the sweat from his forehead with the back of his hand.

Now he was tired. He felt as if he had no strength in any part of his body. He took a deep breath. "Come on, John Lewis, come on. I gave this street too much precious time. Gave it my youth, gave it my strength. Ain't gonna give it no more. Come on, John Lewis, come on."

A fire engine, clanging and hooting, roared down Lenox Avenue. Night settled over Harlem but brought no rest. The murmur of living, like the river, flowed on into the evening toward the dawn.

THE LONG NIGHT

TO ANA LIVIA

Agwé Arroyo, protect your children,

Sea-shell in hand, care for your little ones . . .

A Voudoun prayer to the Haitian sea god **Agwé**.

one

The hallway was dark because the light bulb had burned out a long time ago. Probably one or another of the tenants had thought of replacing the bulb from time to time, but no one had ever got around to doing it. Neither had the old, alcoholic superintendent, who, as much as possible, avoided climbing stairs. So once you reached the fifth floor of this Harlem tenement, you found yourself in almost complete blackness. But the enveloping sounds and smells told you that you were still among the living. Radios and television sets squawked, and people hollered at one another behind invisible doors. A heavy staleness hung in the hallway, relieved only by the occasional piquancy of hotly seasoned frying pork. You saw, after your eyes became adjusted, that there was a vague light after all. Along the dank hallway you could now discern several heavy wooden doors, some with ancient, grease-filled cracks in them. The doors stood in a line like weary old soldiers in the night, protecting the living quarters beyond.

At the rear of this hallway was an apartment of two small rooms. Here on a warm Saturday afternoon Lieutenant Frederick Brown, ten years old, lay on his cot reading a Superman comic. He was waiting for his mother to come home from the laundry where she worked. She would relieve him of the guard duty he was standing over his little brother and baby sister.

He was a member-in-good-standing of The Comanche Raiders, the dominant neighborhood club. All the boys now called him Steely because he had gone through the initiation exercises without a whimper. Just before he had run the gantlet, made up of the biggest boys in the club, he had told himself that he wouldn't cry, that he mustn't cry. Some of the blows had been sharp, but he had gritted his teeth and run on. One of the boys had suddenly stuck out his leg and tripped him, spilling him to the ground with tremendous impact, scratching his arms and face and causing his nose to bleed. But he had not cried out or even opened his mouth. He had crawled until he could struggle to his feet. Then he had run on, ignoring the grinning faces and the yelled threats and the strange cruel looks in the faces of the boys about to strike him. He had run on, knowing that he had already been through the worst and that he would pass the test all right. At the end of the ceremony the Supreme Commander, Shotgun (the one who had tripped him), nicknamed him Steely and commissioned him a Second Lieutenant in The Junior Comanche Raiders, which was the section of the club that a boy served in until he was thirteen. Steely was very proud of his rank because the other boys who had undergone the same initiation were only sergeants. None of the boys his own age ever challenged him any more. Even those guys two years older knew that Steely was nobody's pushover.

He was a very black boy, tall for ten years old, but skinny. He knew better than to wrestle when he got into a fight because the average boy had the advantage of weight and could slam him to the ground. But Steely was fast and slippery. He could hit and move away and hit again before his opponent knew what was happening.

And he could run. Nobody could run like Steely. When the cops came on the scene Steely took off like a bat out of hell, and even the older boys had a hard time catching up. Running was his passion. When he felt confused and angry and did not know what to do about it, he would take off, his black knees pumping up and down, his sneakers hardly seeming to touch the sidewalk. Sometimes Steely would run for no reason at all, just because he had nothing else to do. Off he would go with no particular place in mind, running until he was exhausted. Then he would slow down to a walk. All his strength would be gone, but he would feel better somehow, freer.

Suddenly he sat up on the cot and yelled, "Get out of that window!"

His five-year-old brother, Robby, a bumptious, obstinate boy, liked to play in the window leading to the fire escape. Steely knew that a lieutenant's principal duty was to maintain discipline; his voice was sharp and hard when he spoke to Robby. Seeing that Robby was slow about obeying the order, Steely lunged at his brother, caught him by the waist of his short pants, and jerked him back into the room. Such arbitrary treatment infuriated the younger boy. He swung wildly but missed. Contemptuously Steely pushed him to the floor, where he sat with his legs outstretched. He opened his mouth and let out a howl. This woke Carol Ann, who was only a little over a year old. She sat up in her crib and gave a long frightened wail. The children's crying sounded like a duet of sick air-raid sirens.

"Shut up!" Steely screamed at them, but they only yelled louder. He decided to ignore Robby. He went to the crib, which they had bought second-hand at the Salvation Army and painted a bright yellow. He took his sister in his arms and hugged her. She was only a baby, Steely reminded himself, and he could understand why she might not show proper respect for his authority. He loved Carol Ann and told her so now as he rocked her back and forth, kissing her cheeks and her little arms and hands. She stopped crying and laughed and started to play with his ears. Robby's interest was attracted by two fuzzy blue-black flies that flew through the open window and hovered over the pots on the stove. He stopped crying and rolled up an old magazine. There was nothing he hated more than flies. He took vicious but ineffectual whacks at them, exhaling anguished grunts as he saw how little damage he was doing. After setting Carol Ann back into her crib, Steely went to his cot and opened his comic book again.

Being a leader was very important to Steely. His father had told him about Toussaint L'Ouverture, a black Haitian who had revolted against Napoleon and liberated his people from slavery. Steely's father had also told him about the great Douglas, after whom he had been named Frederick—a man who had been born a slave in the United States but had overcome many obstacles and become a great leader of his people. That was the kind of goal Steely was determined to reach. To attain it he would be hard and unafraid and would risk death a thousand times.

But neither Toussaint nor Frederick Douglas were as real to him as his other heroes, Superman and Davy Crockett. True, it made a great difference that Toussaint and Frederick Douglas had been colored men, but not everyone had heard of them. Superman and Davy Crockett were famous. If a game was being organized on the street and you said you were either of these two, the other guys did not ask, "Who's that?"

So now as he stretched on his cot he was not Steely any more but Superman, the strongest person in the whole world. He could lift anything, run faster than a bullet, and his eyes were so powerful that he could see through a steel wall. Best of all, he could fly like a jet plane, even faster. When there was a war he could knock them out of the sky with one hand. Now he glided lazily over Harlem, swooping down occasionally and scattering his enemies. At One Hundred and Twenty-third Street, with one great blow he completely demolished The Black Ravens, who were traditionally the bitterest enemies of The Comanche Raiders. Picking up speed, he soared eastward over One Hundred and Eighth Street and Madison Avenue, where the Puerto Rican boys lived. When he found the clubroom of The Conquistadores he brought his fist down hard and The Conquistadores were destroyed forever. Then he sped southward over Yorkville where the white boys were gathered. There he swept all The Avengers and The Hawks into the East River and watched happily as each of them drowned.

Steely sighed. The first thing he would do if he were really Superman would be to circle low over Harlem until he saw his father below. He would swoop down, catch his father in his arms, and soar with him through the clouds high above New York. Steely would tell his father how mad his mother was but that she would probably let him come back home. Then Steely would ask the question that was bothering him, the one that only his father could answer—

Smack!

The blow was a hard, thumping one across the back of his head. It knocked him off the cot onto the floor.

Smack!

This time it exploded on the side of his face, stinging and hurting him, jarring his whole body, making him see bright red and yellow dabs. He huddled against the wall and tried to cover his face with his hands, expecting that another blow was impending. He made a point of never crying, but right now he hurt very much.

"Damn you, Frederick! I thought I told you to watch these kids. I can't trust you to do nothing, can I? Look at that boy up there in that window!"

It was his mother. He parted his fingers and peeped into her face. The familiar deep brown eyes were fastened on him accusingly. Her dark lips were thin and tight. Quickly he shifted his gaze to the window. Again Robby was playing happily on the fire escape. He played like a lamb, with no idea of the shock in store for him; the commotion indoors had been drowned out by the street noises. Mae Brown reached out and caught him by the pants. He struggled until he saw that it was his mother who held him. She jerked him into the room and stood him on the floor in front of her.

"How many times have I told you to stay off that there fire escape?" she demanded. "Tell me, huh? How many times, Robby?"

Robby's lips moved but no sound escaped.

Smack!

Robby tried to twist away, but Mae Brown held him fast.

"Are you gonna mind what I tell you and stay out of that window?"

He nodded his head up and down and tried to speak, but fear choked off the sound.

Smack!

She loosened her grip and Robby sat down

where he had been standing. From deep within him, softly at first, then growing ever louder, camc wailing, pitiable sobs. Steely's ears still hummed, but his head had stopped hurting. He wished he could cry like Robby—then surely he would not feel so bruised inside. His mother's voice was so even that it was almost a monotone as she spoke angrily to her sons. The threatening words fell quickly and sharply. They were the harshest of Southern sounds, which are seldom very harsh.

"Neither of you is any good for a damn thing. As hard as I work trying to keep this family together! I've told you over and over again that you're gonna have to learn to take care of yourself, but you won't do it. Both of you act just like babies. You, sitting there with your head in that picture book, the house coulda burnt down and you wouldn'a knowed a damn thing about it. And you, if I *ever* catch you out there on that there fire escape again, I'm gonna whip your behind until it smokes. Hush now, Carol Ann"—here softening her tone and hugging the girl to her— "you know your mama loves her little baby, yes she do." Now she shifted her eyes back to the boy on the floor, whose wailing continued on a maddening and exasperating note. "Robby, you better shut up that yelling 'cause you ain't got half of what you will get if I ever, and I mean if I *ever*, catch you out there again. You're both growing up to be no damn good, just like your daddy. You better learn to mind me like I tell you or I'm gonna beat the living daylights out of both of you. Robby, you got just two seconds to shut up that noise. *Two seconds!*"

Obediently the boy stifled his crying. Mae devoted herself to Carol Ann. Steely remembered how different everything had been when his father was home. Mae and Paul Brown had argued sometimes, but they had also laughed a lot. His mother had been nicer then; she was not always yelling at them and slapping them for the least little thing. There had been lots more to eat, too. Both his mother and his father used to bring home good food when they came in from work. After dinner his father would stretch out on one of the cots or sit at the table and tell stories about great colored men. His father was a wonderful storyteller, and Steely liked to listen to the fascinating tales.

"Make some milk for this baby, Frederick," said his mother without looking at him. She called him "Frederick" only when she was angry with him,

"Fred" at other times. He had told her that everybody now called him Steely, but she insisted on
using his old name. He went to the cabinet, con-
sisting of three shelves in a wooden frame. It was
hooked to the wall beside the sink. Covered with
a flowered yellow cloth, it contained nearly everything they used for eating. He took out one of the
brown packages and measured the orange powder
carefully into a bottle. He filled the bottle from
the running faucet, pushed a nipple onto its neck,
and shook it.

"Does it have to be heated, Mama?"

"No, boy. Just give it here."

He went back to his cot and sat staring across
the room through the open window. Far away and
high up, fluffy gray clouds hung over the city.
Through the haze of smoke it seemed he could see
a thousand tenement roof tops. He lay back on the
cot and stared at the ceiling. Nowadays he was
always thinking about how life used to be, and it
seemed that he could remember every little thing
that had ever happened to him. He could remember back a long time, even before Carol Ann was
born. He could close his eyes and see his father's
face just as if he had seen it only yesterday. Paul
Brown was wine-colored, lighter than Mae. He

was a slender, active man who always used his hands when he talked, as if he were drawing pictures in the air. He was never without a joke, a riddle, or a story. Usually it was about Negroes and how they were getting ahead. Sometimes he would get so excited he would stand in the middle of the floor and make frantic gestures like one of those street-corner speakers. He was certainly the most wonderful person Steely had ever known.

"Look here, boy," he would say to Steely. "Do you know how lucky you are?"

Steely would know there was a joke working, but he would not know what to say. Before he could put up his dukes Paul would give him a punch and say, "Don't you know you're about the luckiest kid in the whole world because . . ." And then Steely would know it had all been just an excuse to sing.

"Don't you know, boy,
You got a pretty ma?
Say, don't you know, boy,
You gotta a rich, rich pa?

Mae Brown would say, "I ain't denying I'm good-looking, Paul, but where is your riches?"

Paul would answer, "Don't you know that money

makes you unhappy? It's only because I love my family that I don't bring home more money. Right, Fred?" The boy would nod his head, not really understanding, and Paul would laugh and say, "Oh, boy," in that special way of his. When he said that, Steely didn't know why his heart jumped so. Perhaps it was because his father almost sang the two words, stretching out the "oh" on a real low note, then snapping in the "boy" real short.

A moment later Paul would speak seriously. "It's only a little while longer and then I'll have that diploma. I'll be able to get a decent job and we'll live better. You'll see."

That diploma! Nobody showed any real excitement about it, yet Steely had known they were all waiting for it. His father worked in the shipping room of a dress factory downtown. As far back as Steely could remember, Paul Brown would rush home in the afternoon, eat a hurried dinner, then rush out to catch a train for Brooklyn, where he was going to college. Very early Steely had come to believe—to know—that life would be better for them when Paul finished college and got that diploma.

They had made Steely stay at home with Robby that night of the graduation exercises. When Mae and Paul returned, Steely had asked to see the diploma and was disappointed when they told him it would come in the mail. They had been waiting all this time for something that the postman would bring. It didn't seem right.

Their lives had not changed as they had expected. They had gone on living in the same two rooms and eating much the same kind of food. Steely had expected that they would move to a nicer apartment or maybe even buy a house of their own. But Paul had suddenly decided to become a lawyer, and for that he would have to go to school longer. There had been a big argument about it, with Mae saying that Paul had to remember he didn't live in the world by himself, and after all the years of waiting, it was time he put his education to work and got his family out of the dump they were living in. It was a luxury, she had said, his trying to become a lawyer, with a wife and three children to take care of. Besides—she had thrown this in as the argument became more heated—he had not shown himself to be so smart as he evidently thought he was, having had to make up several credits in the last two years. There were good jobs around for college graduates. Why did he have to subject the family to further hardship by indulging some whim of his? This was the gist of Mae's argument, which she had concluded with a flat question: "Anyhow, what in the world ever put this idea into your head?"

Paul Brown had argued that the race needed lawyers. ("What for?" Mae had retorted. "Far as I can see, they're just looking out for Number One like the whites.") Paul said that only by becoming a lawyer could he realize himself. He assured her that he was smarter than she thought he was and that he would make out all right. The thing wrong with Mae was that she had no vision—she couldn't see beyond her nose. He wanted to become something that his children could be proud of, and she had to understand how important that was. He would not be held back, he shouted. Mae Brown threatened that she would leave him, take the children, and force him to support them. Then Paul revealed that he had already registered and paid his tuition, so that was that. Mae was beaten; their lives went on as before. Steely admired his father. He could see that Paul Brown was a man of his word. He never gave in.

Mae put Carol Ann in her crib and set about making dinner. She said to Steely, "Go down the hall to Miz Anderson and see what the number was."

He put on his Comanche Raider jacket. It was luminous green with black arms. The name of the club, in fancy lettering, was on the back above the emblem. The jackets had cost each boy seven dollars and ninety-eight cents, an amount that had taken Steely ten Saturdays to earn. Now he never left the apartment without the jacket, no matter if the distance was long or short, or the weather hot or cold. It called for stern measures on his mother's part to persuade him to leave it off long enough to have it washed. He had earned every cent of the money it had cost, and had the right to wear his jacket proudly.

The hallway was dank and cool. Somebody was frying chicken; Steely could hear the hot grease popping in the frying pan. At another door he sniffed pungent neck bones and boiling turnip greens touched with a piece of fatback. Corn bread was browning in an oven. The smells filled his nostrils and made him hungry. At the end of the hallway he stopped in front of a door and rapped. There was no response, but when he rapped again the peephole snapped open, shooting a beam of white light across the corridor.

"Who that?"

The woman's voice was aggressive and demanding. At the movies Steely had seen people open their doors without knowing who was on the other side, but he had never seen such a thing in real life. Women were especially cautious in always demanding complete identification.

"It's me, Mrs. Anderson," he said. "Steely from down the hall."

"Who?"

"Steely—Frederick Brown from down the hall."

"Oh."

The door swung open and the pale white light from the naked bulb washed into the hallway. The woman was large and yellow with a fluffy, baglike bosom. Her features were shadowed because the light was behind her.

"What you want, Fred?"

"Mama told me to ask you what the number was."

"Tell her it's three-twenty-one," said Mrs. Anderson and closed the door.

"Three-twenty-one," his mother repeated when he had told her. "Are you joking, boy?"

He shook his head and assured her that those were the figures Mrs. Anderson had told him.

"Three-twenty-one," his mother whispered again. Then she laughed and threw her arms around him. He ducked, thinking at first she was going to strike him, but a moment later he knew he was being embraced.

"Dummy, don't you see? That's my number!" She kissed him, making him feel hot and uncomfortable. "I hit!" Immediately she started figuring. "Now we can get you some shoes for school. And we'll get some for Robby, too, because he'll be starting next month. And there're a couple of things we can get for Carol Ann."

Steely's love for his mother always lay just beneath the surface. Now it stirred and was awakened by her happiness. He knew they did not have much money now that his father was gone, and he sensed that she would be nicer to the children if she did not have so many worries. He felt ashamed of all the spiteful thoughts that recently had begun to pass through his mind about her, especially when she slapped him. Shyly, fumblingly, he returned her embrace.

He asked, "What about you, Mama? Ain't you gonna get nothing new for yourself?"

"Heck, what do I need when I got you and Robby and Carol Ann?" But she winked at him.

"Who knows? Maybe I will get me a pair of stockings or something like that."

She wrote out a note and gave it to him. He knew where Mrs. Morgan lived. He was to go there and give her the note. She would give him twenty-seven dollars and some change. "You put your hand in your pocket," said Mae Brown, "and you hold that money tight, and you better not let go of it until you get back here. You hear me?"

He worked his head up and down with enthusiasm. Now he was Lieutenant Steely Brown being sent on a dangerous mission.

"You be careful now, Fred, and you remember what I told you. Come straight back here and don't you stop for *nothing* or *nobody*." When he got to the door she added, "And if you lose that money, boy, don't you come back at all."

"I won't lose it, Mama," Steely promised. He had just been knighted by the queen. The government was sending him on a top-secret assignment. His life was at stake, but what did that matter when the fate of a nation depended on him? He ran the length of the hallway and down the wooden steps three at a time.

t w o

Steely plunged into the brownish gray of One
Hundred and Sixteenth Street. It was that time of
late afternoon when the crisp white light of day
suddenly colors and the night shades come. Steely
half ran, half walked through the little knots of
men and women who still haggled over prices and
weights in the Park Avenue market place. Overhead a twilight train pierced the gathering darkness as it hummed toward One Hundred and

Twenty-fifth Street, the Bronx, and points north. As Steely ran, the smells changed swiftly from crated cabbage and collard greens and damp kale to frying fish and pork chops and *cuchifritos*. Here on One Hundred and Sixteenth Street factory girls and shopgirls and office girls hurried homeward in wedged heels and bargain basement dresses; here hurried also the factory boys, the stock boys, the shopboys, the garage boys, the kitchen boys, and the messenger boys; the handlers, the day laborers, the unskilled helpers; rushing toward pocket-sized apartments with their mustard-colored pay envelopes containing their rewards for services rendered to downtown commerce. It was still early for the petty pimps and the two-fifty whores, but a few of these already loitered on the corners near the saloons like hungry, impatient birds of prey. For all these people—the producers and the parasites, the black, brown, yellow, and white, and all the shades thereof—Saturday night exploded with unrepressed fury, releasing stocked-up passions and recharging dwindling hope and wavering confidence. Saturday night was a Roman candle shot aloft once a week, glowing red-hot momentarily, then, toward morning, disintegrating from acute, sensual exhaustion.

But of course nothing of this sort occurred to Steely, the ten-year-old black boy who at times was Superman or Frederick Douglas, Toussaint L'Ouverture or Davy Crockett, and now again was Lieutenant Brown of the Junior Comanche Raiders, an officer charged with high responsibility. The people who walked One Hundred and Sixteenth Street seemed only quick dark shadows to the running boy. At one corner a cluster of fellow Junior Raiders signaled him. Steely returned the signal but did not stop.

"Who that?"

The woman's voice crackled in the hallway like an old phonograph record. It was thin and fragile, as if the knock on the door had awakened old fears. She was looking through the peephole but could not see anyone. Steely stepped away from the door into her line of vision.

"It's me, Mrs. Morgan. Fred Brown." He wondered how many years it would be before everyone called him by his new name. "Miss Mae's boy," he added.

"Oh," she said.

The peephole snapped shut with a metallic click, and from within the unlocking of the door began.

The heavy steel pole of the police lock was lifted from its place and set to one side. Then there were two snap locks, one at the top and another near the bottom, and, finally, the original lock at the knob. Still the door opened only a few inches because of a chain hooked to the wall. At this point the eye that had looked on Steely from the peephole now examined him through the three-inch space, scanning also the hallway behind him. The owner of the eye removed it from the space, closed the door while she unhooked the chain, then swung the door open, and said, "Come on in here, Fred boy. My lands, you sho has growed!"

It was an old person's apartment, very neat and very ugly, with pictures of dead relatives on the tables and walls. There was also an old tapestry representing a stoical camel and three Arabs praying to the setting sun, and a faded green rotogravure portrait of Franklin D. Roosevelt. The numbers lady was a thin little cheese-colored woman whose left eye twitched like static. Her short gray hair was curled tightly and held in place by a ragged black net. Steely stared in fascination at the bulging blue veins standing out in a crazy pattern on her scrawny neck and bony arms. Even as the woman talked, he could not remove his eyes from them, expecting that at any moment one of them would burst, and wondering if the blood that squirted out would be blue.

She hardly glanced at the note Steely gave her, for in truth she could scarcely read her name, although she was a genius at simple mathematics. With a varicosed hand she reached into her flat bosom and withdrew a greasy roll of money. Hurriedly counting out the bills, she gave them to the boy and sent him on his way, after which she began the relocking of the door.

Now he was Superman again. The twenty-seven dollars in his pocket gave him a feeling of extraordinary power, too great for an average body to contain. But nobody knew he was Superman. Nobody recognized him because he was traveling incognito. Everybody thought he was just Steely Brown from One Hundred and Sixteenth Street, but in reality he had the strength to beat up every one of them, even if they were all to attack him at the same time. Whenever he desired, he could leap into the air and fly to any place in the wide world.

But as he passed Black Papa he quickened his step. The old man had parked his pushcart near the curb and was searching through a trash can.

His black skin shone in the fading light like an ancient piece of sculptured bronze. He had a tangled stubble of steel-gray beard, a few strands of which seemed pasted at the back of his shining bald head. He wore one small golden earring. None of the boys had ever heard him say anything but the unintelligible words which, all day long, he mumbled over and over.

Cina, cina, cina,
  Dogwé sang, cina lo-gé

So for sport the boys often ran after him and pelted him with stones, chanting

Black Papa, Black Papa,
Can't talk propuh, can't talk propuh.
Black Papa, Black Papa,
Can't talk propuh, can't talk propuh.

The old man would wave his arms at them and chase them away, but he never said anything. Steely always joined in the fun, but when he was alone he hardly dared look at Black Papa. Steely's father had once told him that many years ago Black Papa had been a Haitian seaman who found himself stranded in New York. Having no way to get back home, he had become sick in the mind and taken to collecting junk so that he would have something to eat. Steely had reasoned that if Black Papa were Haitian, he was one of Toussaint's people. He wondered if the great liberator could have looked like this little old man with the pushcart. He tried to picture Black Papa in stately dignity, his arms folded across his chest, epaulets on his shoulders, commanding an army against Napoleon. He did this frequently, but he could never really imagine Black Papa as Toussaint. He never threw stones at Black Papa any more, but he could not very well refuse to take part in the chanting: the fellows would have razzed him and said he was scared.

He forgot about Black Papa as he walked on. He felt again the power that seemed to flow from the smoothly worn bills in his pocket. How wonderful it would be if, just at that moment, he were to meet his father! Then he would ask the question that was bothering him, and surely Paul Brown would give him a good, satisfying answer. Steely looked at all the men he passed on the street, but none of them was Paul Brown. He stopped in front of the Hollywood Bar & Grill where bright red and blue lights darted around the borders of the large plate glass. The jukebox was turned up to full volume.

My baby can't mambo, mambo, mambo
My baby can't mambo, mambo, mambo
My baby can't mambo, mambo, mambo
Gonna put my baby down . . .

A few men were smoking and drinking at the bar, but Paul Brown was not among them. Steely walked away from the glass, depressed now because the thought came to him that he might never see his father again. For several months he had been on an assignment that no one else knew about. Whenever he had a chance he went out of his neighborhood over to Lenox Avenue or Seventh, turning into all the cross streets, looking into every saloon and shoeshine parlor, scanning every face wherever he found men gathered. One day after school he had searched all the way up Amsterdam Avenue above One Hundred and Twenty-fifth Street. He had come home so late that his mother had whipped him with her belt because he would not tell her what he had been doing.

He remembered the day he had given himself the assignment. It was that time when the two detectives had come to the apartment. They were white men, very large, and Steely thought it strange they should look so much alike with their very light blue eyes and clean-shaven reddish faces without even the smallest mustache. Their hard voices seemed jagged in the little room.

"Well, lady, you took your time about getting in touch with us. It's gonna be harder to find him now."

"I figured he'd come back in a few days when he had time to think about it."

"The two of you had a fight, Mrs. Brown?"

"No, not exactly. But we hadn't been getting along too well."

"You say he hasn't been to his job since he left?"

"No, he hasn't. I checked there and got what pay he had coming to him."

"And these names you left at the station, you're sure these are all his friends that you can think of?"

"Yes, that's right."

"Well, don't you worry. If he's still in New York we'll find this Paul Brown for you."

"I just want him to help support these children. They're his as well as mine."

"Yeah, we understand. We'll get in touch with you if anything turns up."

Right then and there Steely had determined to

find Paul Brown first. The police had no business searching for his father. What crime had Paul Brown committed? Steely knew, of course, that something had gone wrong, but it was a family affair and there had been no need to call in these strangers. So for months now he had worked on this assignment, believing he would be the first to find his father. But neither he nor the police had discovered any trace of Paul Brown. As Steely walked toward home, his hand squeezing the roll of bills in his pocket, it occurred to him that his father might be dead. He had never considered this before, nor did he really believe it now. But it was something to think about. His conception of death was such that he felt no sorrow for his father or himself. But there was regret, for if Paul were dead, Steely would never be able to ask his question and he would never hear the answer.

"Hey, pick up on the kid!"

"Yeah, man! Wahooo! What's shaking, Steely?"

If the boy had not been so occupied with his thoughts he would have seen Shotgun, Crazy Mac, Red Louis, and Tommy Morales before they saw him. And he would have found a way to avoid them, probably by crossing the street and waving to them as if he were in a hurry. Better still, he could have retraced his steps to the corner and circled the block altogether. It was not that he had a dislike for these four boys. Indeed, each of them was a person to be admired. But they were so much bigger than he was, and they had the habit of roughing up the Junior Raiders "to make 'em tough." So Steely always avoided them if he could.

These four boys composed the Supreme Council of The Comanche Raiders. Shotgun was a dark brown boy of sixteen who seemed much older. He was squat and fierce-looking. He had acquired his name a couple of years earlier during a gang war when, according to legend, he had fired two blasts of a shotgun from a roof top into the ranks of the enemy and sent them flying. Two of the victims had spent several days in the hospital, but the cops had never been able to find out who had fired the buckshot. The weapon had remained hidden ever since, but its owner had succeeded in giving the impression that on the slightest provocation he would take it from its hiding place and use it. Crazy Mac was so called because of the peculiar way his eyes focused. He was very clever and had the reputation of being able to talk his way out of anything. Red Louis was a tough yellow boy with short red hair and auburn eyebrows and lashes. Tommy Morales had a Puerto Rican mother, spoke Spanish perfectly, and was one of the reasons for the troubled peace that presently existed between The Comanche Raiders and their East Harlem neighbors, The Conquistadores. These four boys determined policy for the Raiders. They had grown up in the neighborhood and were as much a part of the landscape as the red brick of the buildings and the battered trash cans chained to the fences.

"What's happening, kid?"

"Nothing, Shotgun. Same as ever."

"What's shaking with your Juniors?"

"Everything's great. Just great."

Shotgun took a lazy punch at Steely, who ducked his head.

"Crazy, man," said Shotgun, "crazy! This is a quick little kid here. Real fast."

They were gathered under a street light in the middle of the block. The Supreme Council had been discussing different ways to spend their Saturday night. There were a couple of parties in the neighborhood, but these promised to be dull affairs because they already knew all the girls who would probably attend. There was a party in the Bronx to which they had not been invited and at which their appearance would certainly provoke trouble. They had halfway decided on this latter and more dangerous course when Steely arrived; consequently nobody gave the little boy more than distracted attention. But Steely was thoroughly uncomfortable. He could not help thinking of the money clenched in his right hand and of his mother's admonition not to stop for anything.

"Well, see you later," said Steely.

Shotgun said, "Yeah. Later for you, kid."

Steely felt relief. He started toward home. It was Crazy Mac who called him back.

"Hey, Steely. Wait up a minute."

His first thought was to light out for home as fast as his legs could carry him. But he did not want to arouse suspicion. Besides, he was used to doing what the members of the Supreme Council told him. Steely stopped and turned to face Crazy Mac, who now walked toward him.

"What is it?"

"Where're you rushing to?"

"I'm just going home."

Shotgun called, "Hey, Crazy, come on and leave the kid alone. We ain't got all night."

"I will," said Crazy, "just as soon as I see—" He

reached out quickly and gripped Steely's right arm. "—what he's guarding in his pocket there."

"Aw, come on, Crazy," Steely yelled. "My mother told me—" But already his clenched hand was exposed. Steely squeezed the money with all his strength, but the larger boy pressed a thumb into his wrist and he had to let go. Crazy took the money and counted it.

"I knew he was holding something in that pocket," he said with satisfaction.

Now the entire Council was interested. Steely looked furiously from one to the other as they grouped themselves around him and Crazy.

He appealed to Shotgun. "Make him give it back, Shotgun! Please! That's my mother's. Please, Shotgun!"

The Supreme Commander took the money and counted it quickly. He shot a hard look at Steely. "This kid," he said, feigning anger, "is a rat, a stinker, men! Do you hear me?"

The rest of the Council chorused agreement. They winked at one another as their minds were eagerly attempting to divide four into twenty-seven. They were actually fond of Steely in their own peculiar way.

"Imagine," continued the Supreme Commander,

"this little bastard walking around with a fist full of green and holding out on us. After all we've done for him! A rat this kid is! A real rat!"

They grinned. Steely was terrified. The worst thing in the world was happening.

"*Please*, Shotgun!"

"Beat it, kid," said Shotgun with great dignity. "The Council's gonna borrow this loot to cover Certain Emergency Expenses." These last few words were pronounced with relish and pride, as if Shotgun had invented them right there on the spot.

"But it's not mine!"

"I said beat it."

Steely leapt like greased lightning and almost succeeded in snatching the roll from Shotgun's fingers. But he missed, and a blow from the larger boy sent him sprawling onto the sidewalk. He was more outraged and angry than he had ever been in his whole life. He was so angry he literally could hardly see. Like a flash he was on his feet and punching wildly at the Supreme Commander, who held him off with one hand.

"For Chrissakes," laughed Shotgun, "somebody get this little punk off me, will you?"

Just then one of Steely's blows got through Shotgun's guard and struck him flush on the mouth. The gang leader cursed and gave the boy a vicious slap with the back of his hand. Steely was knocked against a building but in an instant he was back, swinging at everyone he could see. A few grown-ups standing nearby had seen the whole thing. They now moved away cautiously. Steely heard a police whistle. The Council of The Comanche Raiders fled down the street. When the police squad car drew up to the sidewalk Steely was the only one there. Exhausted, he sat on the steps trying not to believe in the reality of what had just happened.

"What's going on here, boy?"

He wanted to blurt out everything that had happened to him. He wanted the policemen to take their guns and kill each one of the boys who had robbed him. But he did not believe the cops were any match for Shotgun and the rest of the Council. Also, he knew he would never get his money back, for if the police were to catch the boys they would probably keep the money for themselves. Besides, you were not supposed to tell a cop anything, under any circumstances.

"Nothing," he answered.

When they found out Steely lived in the next

block, one of them, a young man with blond hair, said, "You better get off the street, you little bastard. Next time I catch you in this block after dark I'm gonna run you in."

So Steely walked toward home. His stomach was in a tight little knot and he felt sick. Bitterly he admitted to himself that he was not either Superman, Davy Crockett, Frederick Douglas, or Toussaint L'Ouverture. He was Steely Brown, a little boy who was pushed around by big people. And it would be a long time before he grew large enough to fight them the way he wanted to.

"And if you lose that money, boy, don't you come back at all."

That was the last thing his mother had said before he left home. When Steely reached the place where he lived he stood on the sidewalk and looked fearfully up at the tired old building with its rust-red front. He took a few steps into the hallway, then changed his mind. He had failed in his mission. There was no telling what his mother would do to him. Twenty-seven dollars was a lot of money.

As he walked away he made a vow. He would get another twenty-seven dollars. Somehow, this very night, he would turn his failure into success.

He would come home, give his mother the money, and she would never know the difference. He felt better now, for he was acting like his heroes. None of them would ever admit defeat.

three

Steely was an extremely serious and sensitive boy, but he was not quick-witted. He never took anything lightly. His was really a one-track mind. He searched beneath the surface of everything, even when there was nothing there. His imagination, unusually lively, supplied what was lacking in reality. Completely without guile, when he was faced with a problem he attacked it in the most obvious way, frontally. His dark face was long and thoughtful and was seldom brightened with a smile. His deep brown eyes, which seemed black under certain lights, were so wide and credulous, and yet so uncompromising, that they were disturbing to adults who had learned the ways of the world.

Now, as he walked under the streetlights of One Hundred and Sixteenth Street, his first thoughts were of Mr. Litchstein, who owned a pharmacy in the neighborhood. Steely often cleaned the stock room and the back yard of the store, for which Mr. Litchstein never paid him less than fifty cents and sometimes as much as a dollar.

Two things guided him toward the pharmacy now. Mr. Litchstein was a nice man, and—this was very important—one of the few people who always remembered to call him by his new name. Also, Mr. Litchstein was the only person Steely knew who owned property and he was therefore, to the boy's mind, rich.

Actually the store did not prosper. Its proprietor ignored all the modern methods for attracting people into his place of business. He never turned a salesman away. He would carry any product so long as it did not cost him cash money. Too much stock was displayed, and the store was badly lighted. The fountain had equipment for serving sandwiches, ice cream, and sodas, but there was usually nothing to be had but coffee, which was Mr. Litchstein's favorite beverage.

He was just over fifty years old. His brownish hair was unruly, and had long ago defeated Mr. Litchstein's half-hearted attempts to groom it. What little was left always stood out from the back of his head as if it were being blown by the wind. His quick little eyes, set in a face with large features, looked out on the world with friendly interest and always contained an invitation to exchange views with him. Mr. Litchstein loved to talk, about politics, morality, finance, juvenile delinquency, anything.

The store was, as usual, empty except for a regular customer: a well-dressed, light-complexioned Negro of about the same age, who often dropped in to argue with the pharmacist.

"Jews, Negroes, white folks, race problem," intoned Mr. Litchstein in this conversation, which had begun several weeks before. "That's all I ever hear you talk about. It's a sickness with you. Don't you know anything else to talk about?"

"What are you getting so excited about?" retorted the man. "We're having a civilized conversation. Let's keep it that way."

Mr. Litchstein said, "I always get excited when I hear dangerous ideas. Listen, my friend, there is only one race—" Here he emphasized each word by slowly and insistently striking his palm on the counter. "—and that is the human race!"

"Nuts!" said the customer. Both he and the pharmacist sipped their coffee.

Mr. Litchstein continued. "It is people like you, with your petty frustrations, your petty ambitions, your imagined wrongs—imagined, mind you—that create so much hatred in the world. Oh, hello, Steely." He smiled abruptly at the boy and just as abruptly scowled again as he turned back to the man. "You are blessed and you don't know it. You live in the most wonderful country in the world and you sneer at it. I am not saying everything here is perfect, but at least we can make progress, not like in some countries I could name. You can't deny that the colored people have come a long way. Look at Dr. Ralph Bunche and Marian Anderson and Joe Louis. It's people like that who prove my point."

The man tilted his cup and drained it. "Balls!" he snorted.

Mr. Litchstein flushed red. "Do you know somebody else who was always stirring up race issues?

He was just like you. His name was Adolf Hitler."

The man's coffee went down the wrong pipe and he almost choked. After a spasm of coughing he began to laugh heartily. Mr. Litchstein angrily walked away to the end of the counter, where Steely was standing.

"Do you want something, Steely?"

He smiled and the boy felt reassured, for Mr. Litchstein's smile was as warm as his frown was forbidding. "Yessir," said Steely, "I've got a proposition."

The laughter of the man at the counter still rang inside the store. The pharmacist called to him: "If you find that funny, my friend, you have a very distorted sense of humor." Then he turned back to the boy again. "So you have a proposition, Steely. So let's hear."

"It's like this, Mr. Litchstein . . ." Steely went on to explain that he would clean out the stock room and the back yard of the drugstore and do anything else that needed doing for the next twenty-seven weeks if Mr. Litchstein would advance him the money he needed so badly. The pharmacist was thinking of the next barb he would fire at his laughing adversary. He listened to Steely sympathetically, giving occasional affirmative grunts and nods of his head, but the truth is that he listened with only half an ear. When Steely stopped talking, Mr. Litchstein asked, "And just how much is it you want, Steely?"

The boy eagerly restated the figure. "Twenty-seven dollars."

"Ikes!" cried Mr. Litchstein. The very syllables made him wince as if Steely had pushed a sharp knife between his ribs. Now he gave the boy his full attention, seeing him for the first time.

"Are you serious?"

Steely wagged his head. Mr. Litchstein started to say something but changed his mind. He started to say several things but never got beyond the first word. Finally he sighed and asked, "How old are you, Steely?"

"Ten. I'll be eleven my next birthday."

"Naturally if you're ten you'll be eleven your next birthday," said Mr. Litchstein impatiently. "Steely, don't you know that you should not come to a man who is feeling happy and make him unhappy by asking him for money?"

Steely started to protest. "But I'm gonna—"

Mr. Litchstein held up his hand. "Let me talk, now that you have stated your proposition." Never before had he noticed the boy's eyes. In the black face they seemed almost stark. They accused, they judged, they passed sentence. They were very unfair. Mr. Litchstein swallowed and went on. "Do you know that twenty-seven dollars is more than some people—adult people, mind you—make in a week? That in some countries people don't make twenty-seven dollars a year? And yet you, all of ten years old, come to me and—"

"But I'll work!" Steely blurted out. "Honest. Every week. I promise."

Mr. Litchstein had been leaning on the counter with his elbows. Now he straightened up and gave Steely a wave of his hand. He was more abrupt than was his nature because he felt a cruel joke was being played on him, though he knew that Steely was serious. Certainly, Mr. Litchstein told himself, he had no reason to feel uncomfortable. Who ever heard of lending a kid so much money?

"Go away, Steely," he said. "Be a nice boy and don't bother me." Wearing a very pained expression, he returned to his customer.

The man said, "Now, as I was trying to say before I was interrupted and insulted—"

"And who insulted you?" asked Mr. Litchstein. "Does the truth hurt so much?"

"As I was saying," persisted the man, taking a

new cup of coffee that the druggist poured for him, "the Jews, the Italians, and the Irish run New York, a fact everybody knows, but when I put it to you I am called Adolf Hitler."

Mr. Litchstein said, "And the man who is now Borough President of Manhattan, one of the most important political jobs in the city, elected by the people—if I am not mistaken, he is a colored man like yourself."

"Yes, and we're very proud of him, too," said the man. "But every time a Negro gets a new job, why is it you white folks start patting yourself on the back and saying to us, 'Look at all the wonderful progress you're making'? You exaggerate that one job out of proportion. It's just window dressing and good old dirty politics. The same people are still running the city."

"You," pronounced the pharmacist very distinctly, "are a political slanderer, a hate-mongerer, a race baiter and a rabble-rouser—"

"There you go again with the insults—"

"Worse, you are a cynic who sneers at progress. Your people are better off today than they ever were, who cares for what reasons? But people like you are never satisfied. You grumble from habit; you bite the hand that feeds you."

The Negro laughed again. Mr. Litchstein frowned darkly and glanced quickly toward the end of the counter. He observed, with a sigh of relief, that Steely had gone. Suddenly he put his hand on the man's shoulder and he laughed, too.

"My friend," he said, "you have a very peculiar sense of humor."

Around Harlem and just about any place else he chose to go, Sugar Boy was considered a sharp guy. He wore the latest style clothes and he had a large red stone on his finger. His hair was conked; in other words, it had been straightened with a hot comb, waved, and set in place with a special hair dressing. It is an expensive proposition to maintain a conk that does not grow ragged around the edges, but Sugar Boy always looked as if he had just left the beauty salon. Not the least of his attractions was his long black Chrysler convertible. Of course he rented garage space, but when he found it necessary to park his car near his apartment, he always paid a boy a quarter to watch it until he came back. Very often this boy was Steely.

On two occasions Steely knew of (and on several others that he did not), city detectives had taken Sugar Boy away in handcuffs. As everyone in the block predicted, Sugar Boy was set free within a few hours. Once he sent Steely with a small package to a house just three blocks away, an errand for which he paid the boy a whole dollar. After that he often stopped to chat with Steely on the street. They always talked about baseball, both agreeing that the Brooklyn Dodgers were far and away the best team. Twice Sugar Boy loaded his Chrysler with Steely and his friends and took them to the ball game, where he bought them loads of popcorn and soda and hot dogs. Naturally Steely liked Sugar Boy. He wondered now why he had not thought of his friend at first.

Sugar's apartment was two rooms and a kitchenette, newly painted and decorated, complete with a blond mahogany television set. Sugar smiled when he opened the door to Steely. "Come on in, man." There was a woman in the room whom Steely had sometimes seen in the Chrysler. She was chestnut brown and buxom. She lay on the couch with her fingers laced across her stomach, her eyes closed.

"Whatcha know, man?" Sugar asked. "What can I do you for?" Sugar's smile was bright and toothy and trimmed in gold. It spoke eloquently of a successful and contented young man looking forward to a quiet evening with his lady friend. The smile went well with the new dacron smoking jacket he was wearing.

Without any preliminaries Steely said, "Will you loan me twenty-seven dollars? I promise to pay you back."

"Will I *what?*"

"Loan me twenty-seven dollars."

Sugar Boy's smile vanished from the room without a trace. The woman on the couch gave a short grunt, sat straight up, and exclaimed, "Damn!" as if there was nothing else to be said for a boy like this one.

"Come on, Steely," Sugar Boy said impatiently. "Who sent you? What do you want?"

Steely was annoyed. "Nobody sent me," he shouted. "I want to borrow some money and I'll work and pay you back."

"Okay, okay," said Sugar Boy. He took a handkerchief from the pocket of his dacron jacket and dabbed at his forehead. Then he ran a hand over his smooth wavy hair. He sank into an easy chair and indicated one for Steely, who declined it without word or gesture. The woman was staring at the boy with amusement and sympathy. She was strangely moved by the grim and darkly serious face.

Sugar Boy said, irrelevantly and with a nervous laugh, "What about those Dodgers over the weekend, huh? Man, that was something!"

At the moment Steely did not care about the Dodgers. He sensed that he was going to be betrayed by his friend. He did not answer, and a weighted silence hung between them.

"How old are you?" Sugar Boy asked suddenly.

"I am ten years old," answered Steely in precise syllables that barely hid his conviction that his age had nothing to do with the matter at hand.

Sugar Boy shifted his position in the easy chair and raised his voice as if he had just decided on a new approach. "Look, kid, if you want a buck for the game tomorrow, I can let you have that." He reached his hand into his trousers pocket and brought out a dollar bill. "Go ahead. Take it." Steely's eyes met Sugar Boy's and held them. He had an urge not to take the money, and he reached for it only after habit had won a brief struggle with his sense of dignity. Reluctantly he put it in his pocket, without yielding an inch on the main point.

"The fact is," Sugar Boy continued hurriedly, feeling silly for having to explain something that was obviously impossible, "I can't lay my hands on that much money right now, sport. It's rough out here in these streets, you know what I mean."

"Yeah," Steely said curtly. He turned and went out of the apartment, leaving behind two thoroughly uncomfortable people.

After a moment Sugar Boy mumbled, "A funny kid, huh?"

"Yeah," said the woman, "a funny kid."

Sugar Boy gave a weak little laugh. "Twenty-seven dollars." He shook his head as if to say he would be damned if he understood what the world was coming to. Then he poured himself a stiff drink.

Outside Steely wandered aimlessly with downcast, sullen eyes. Occasionally he took an angry kick at something loose on the sidewalk. A group of junior-high-school girls marched down the street four abreast. Their white socks were heavy and rolled at the tops. The white and brown of their eyes flashed in the neon lights as the taps on the heels of their flat shoes set up a nervous, metallic chatter. All the pedestrians made way for the girls as they swerved by, singing in young strident voices,

My baby can't mambo, mambo, mambo
My baby can't mambo, mambo, mambo
My baby can't mambo, mambo, mambo
Gonna put my baby down . . .

As Steely turned up Lenox Avenue he reflected that people were not what they should be, that is, straightforward and honest. Sugar Boy was the case in point. He had thought Sugar Boy was his friend, but that was not true at all. Friends helped each other when they were in difficulty. It was an almost sacred, though unspoken, understanding that Sugar Boy had violated. Never again, Steely decided, would he allow himself to be friends with anybody. Nor would he stand guard over Sugar's Chrysler or accept another ticket to the ball game.

He remembered now, as he walked along, that first baseball game—so long ago it seemed the first thing that ever happened to him. He remembered his father's eager eyes as he took a customary punch at him, and his own ducking away and quickly bringing up his guard, the father approving with "Oh, boy," the son throwing punch after punch until both his arms were held behind him.

"Hey, hold up, old boy. I don't want to fight," protested Paul. "Tell me something. Did you ever hear of Jackie Robinson?"

Paul said that Jackie Robinson was a Negro ballplayer, the very first one to play in the Big Leagues. "And you know what, young fellow? We're going out to see him tomorrow. We're going to get a demonstration of what a black man can do when he gets the chance."

It was the longest subway ride he had ever taken, that one over to Brooklyn. When they reached Franklin Avenue they walked out of the station and up a long flight of steps, where they took an elevated train out to Ebbets Field. For the entire trip he sat with his nose pressed against the window, staring out at the squared roofs of the dirty gray apartment houses, feeling strange and important because his mother and father were arguing about him.

"Give the boy a chance," his mother said, "and stop filling his head with all that stuff. He'll have enough trouble in his life without you getting him all hotted up over color and race. I been hearing that nonsense all my life and it ain't never did anybody any good as far as I can see."

"What nonsense?" demanded Paul, his voice suddenly so high and outraged that people turned in their seats to look at him. Mae Brown told him to stop shouting, and he continued in a low, intense voice. "The boy's a Negro and he's got to have something to be proud of. They've cheated him of his heroes. They don't give them to him in school, so you and I have got to do it. You can't grow up without your own heroes, Mae. Every white boy has them, but the black boy's got nothing. George Washington . . . Patrick Henry . . . they're white. A black kid's got to have his own heroes because if he can see himself in history he can see himself in the future."

Mae Brown went on in her flat, dry voice as if he had not spoken. "Heroes, smeroes! I just want him to be like every other boy—"

"But he's not every other boy," Paul interrupted. "He's a particular boy."

"—like every other boy and not mixed up and crazy about this race and politics business. Just leave the boy alone, is all I ask. One of my grandfathers was just like that. He hated white folks so much it ate him up inside and drove him crazy. The white folks are on top and he couldn't do anything about that, so naturally it drove him crazy, hating them the way he did. If he read about where a white man did something wrong to a colored man he couldn't eat for three days. He died, just a mean, shriveled-up little old man. I remember thinking he looked like somebody had poisoned him. It was just all that hate inside of him and not having any way to get rid of it."

"Your grandfather just had a little pride, that's all," said Paul, "which is more than I can say for his granddaughter."

"Pride, my foot!" said Mae Brown, and put an end to the conversation by looking out of the window.

At Ebbets Field when Jackie Robinson ran out onto the diamond Steely saw that it was really true: Jackie was really a colored man. Paul Brown slapped his son on the back and yelled, "There he is! There he is!" When Jackie hit a single Paul stood up and yelled louder than anybody in Brooklyn.

Mae said, "Paul Brown, if you don't sit down and stop making a damn fool of yourself, I'm gonna take these kids and go home. You're disgraceful."

Paul smiled broadly at his wife. "Well, can he play or can't he? I ask you, Mae. Can he play or can't he?"

"Well, I hope he can," she said drily. "Ain't that what they pay him for?"

"God, Mae!" Paul exclaimed in disgust. "You're just plain ignorant."

"Well, that's because I haven't spent all my life in college, like you," she said, ending the conversation in that hard, practical way she had: down-to-earth, colorless and unimaginative, and not half so wonderful as Paul Brown.

That summer Paul and Steely went to the ball game often, but Mae Brown never accompanied them again. Usually Paul and Steely sat in the bleachers or in the lower-priced stands. Everything that Jackie Robinson did thrilled Paul; to him Jackie's playing was not just baseball but life itself. He would say to Steely, "Look at him bouncing on third! Keep your eye on him. He'll steal home if he gets half a chance. You see, the thing that makes him great is that he's always outdoing himself. He knows he's under pressure, so he pushes himself beyond what he thinks he's capable of. That's why he's so beautiful to watch. He's black so he knows he can't give in. He reaches harder for the ball, slides harder into the base. The pressure's on him. Remember that, Fred"—here with his arm around the boy's shoulder and their heads close together, both pairs of eyes watching the man on third—"remember that when you're under pressure, you don't give in, you never give in." Suddenly Paul Brown jumps to his feet and shouts, "There he goes!" And thirty thousand people are standing now to watch the action at the plate. There is a scramble of men and a cloud of dust. The man in the black suit spreads his hands horizontally with the palms downward. Sure enough, Jackie Robinson has stolen home, thereby presenting a dramatic demonstration of Paul Brown's faith.

When Steely turned westward on One Hundred and Twenty-fifth Street he realized that he had not eaten his dinner. He knew he ought to be hungry because it was past eight o'clock. Fishing in his pocket, he brought out the dollar Sugar Boy had given him. It was, he concluded, too far away from twenty-seven to be of any real value, so he let himself be swept along by the pedestrian traffic that was alive with voices and activity. He stopped in front of a Chockfull o' Nuts restaurant and watched the people inside being served by the busy counter workers. After a moment he went in and climbed onto a stool.

When the hot dog and orange drink were set before him, his attention was attracted by the purse of the woman who sat directly across the counter. She was a diminutive person with round, almost comic features. Her quick little eyes were magnified several times by thick rimless glasses. In one hand she held a partially consumed egg salad sandwich and in the other a movie magazine. On the counter in front of her lay her purse, a square black imitation-leather container with a brass clasp. Steely wondered idly if it held as much as twenty-seven dollars. At just this moment the mouselike woman looked up from the magazine and her eyes seemed to catch Steely's. A second later she took the purse from the counter and put it on her lap.

These activities were probably unrelated—looking at Steely and removing her purse. But the boy was all too aware of the direction of his thoughts. He became flustered. Hastily he wiped his mouth with a napkin, slid off the stool, and soon lost himself in the stream of people flowing along One Hundred and Twenty-fifth Street.

four

The idea of snatching a purse was not entirely foreign to Steely, for some of the older boys in The Raiders made a regular practice of it. But he had never thought of snatching one himself; the risk had always seemed too great. His father had told him that a whole life could be ruined by a wrong move, even when you were as young as Steely. If he were sent away to the reformatory he would probably never grow up to be like Frederick

Douglas or Toussaint. Besides, a purse could only be snatched from a woman. He believed that whereas anything was fair between males, or between boys and girls, this was not true of grownup ladies. They seemed a race apart and deserved special consideration. So he had never snatched a purse.

But neither had he ever needed twenty-seven dollars before. At his very immature age Steely had now run head-on into a simple but basic truth: that money is hard come by and it is certainly not to be had for the mere asking. Good friends are reluctant to lend it, and it is not found on the street. It is most scarce when the need is greatest. If you don't have it you must get it, because happiness is impossible without it.

He did not now arrive at these conclusions so clearly but he got the general idea. They necessitated a reconsideration of the views he had held up to that time. It was certainly true that purse-snatching was wrong and that, if caught, he could be sent to jail. But he had to have the twenty-seven dollars, and no one would let him work for it. There were boys in his neighborhood who regularly snatched purses and, so far as Steely knew, none of them was the worse for it. They boasted of their speed. Saturday night, they said, was a good night because women were likely to have larger amounts of money with them.

Everything fell nicely into place. Steely could run faster than any of the purse-snatchers in his neighborhood. And this was Saturday night. Besides, he was not going to make a practice of it. He would get what he needed and that would be the end of it.

Steely did not make up his mind right away. Though he had now readjusted his thinking and morals, the performance of the act itself tended to frighten him. He walked along One Hundred and Twenty-fifth Street, near which the snatchers operated. It was nine o'clock. Blumstein's was long since closed, and all its salesgirls and stock clerks had left. The Five-and-Dime store beside Blumstein's was also securely sealed in darkness. From the penny arcade came the clanking of slot-machine games and the erratic crackle of electric rifles blasting away at the bull's-eye stomach of a revolving brown bear. Lucky Millinder was appearing at the Apollo Theater with his all-star revue. Men and women strollers paused under the lights to stare at the life-sized pictures of near-naked Tonya, a brown Polynesian shake dancer from Valdosta, Georgia. Taxis hummed east and west along this main Harlem thoroughfare. Pedestrians stood poised boldly in the middle of the street as the traffic streaked by on both sides, and when they saw an opportunity they dashed for the sidewalk like soldiers deserting a no man's land. A few doors beyond the Apollo five little brown boys, not one more than eight years old, were setting up a fearsome racket with an assortment of bongo drums, tambourines, and kitchen utensils. All were singing in frantic unison while the smallest of them executed twists, somersaults, and pirouettes with agility in the center of the group.

I'm sailing home, island girl, you'll see,
Just sit on the beach and wait for me.
Some bright morning, one fine day,
I'll lay my anchor and be here to stay.
I'm sailing home, island girl, you'll see,
Just sit on the beach and wait for me.

Steely's senses were stung by the frying hot sausage at the stand at Eighth Avenue where the young men congregate on the corner, colorfully togged out in their best, their restless eyes lustfully following the ebony, bronze, and golden girls who stroll by on the arms of their men, murmuring soft and sugared compliments to those without escorts, loudly bragging to one another of small accomplishments, their empty brashness eloquently bespeaking the murdered dreams, the stunted growth. The Baby Grand Bar stingily spilled ever so little of its amber light through the slanted glass front onto the sidewalk. Frank's Steak House stood like a whore with a genteel past, too self-conscious of its lost dignity. When Steely stopped walking he was at St. Nicholas Avenue, where the street prostitutes, pimps, and hack drivers gather for business. Here at the subway station the boy stopped and stood wondering what to do.

Bold action! That was it. Bold action! He remembered now those conversations his father used to have with Lester Bennett, whom he had met in law school. Lester Bennett was a smooth, smiling yellow man who never raised his voice or made an abrupt gesture. Late at night Paul and Mae and Lester would go into the back room and close the door. The only light Steely could see would be the thin white streak that shot from the keyhole and the purplish mist outside the window. Always the talk was of Negroes. No matter where it started, it ended up on the big problem, the big question. Now, as Steely remembered, it was not a particular conversation but all of them, the voices crossing each other in the darkness, lazy laughter often blending with excited speech; and Steely, hearing and trying to fathom every word, feeling himself in the very core of an exciting movement, for he was a Negro and his father was a Negro and it seemed that Negroes were the most important people in the world.

Bold action. That was what Paul Brown talked about all the time. "We're afraid to act boldly. We hesitate and ask ourselves: How will this reflect on our people? What a question! We've been carrying that cross all these years. As if we were on trial! That's the reason I always liked Jack Johnson or at least what little I know about him. He was before my time. But there was one black man who didn't seem to give a damn what the white folks thought, and they still hate him for it."

"From all I ever heard about him," Mae Brown would say, "he was disgraceful."

"That's all you know about it—"

"Why must Paul stand up when he talks? Sit down and we'll listen."

"He's drunk."

"And I'm right. Now, let me finish and see if you can't see it this way, Lester. We've been getting our freedom in drips and drabs—you know that as well as I do. They've made us toe the line by dangling the great American dream in front of our noses. 'Just be a good boy,' they say, 'and don't cause too much trouble and we'll treat you a little more like a human being.' Am I right or am I wrong?"

"You're right. So what?"

"So maybe it was a great dream, but, hell, man, no dream is good forever! Maybe this one is all washed up. Did you ever think of that? All I ever wanted to do was become a full-fledged American, but now I'm not so sure. The full-fledged white Americans, along with the Russians, are the most hated people on earth. And here we Negroes are, begging for a chance to join them. We're arriving on the scene too late; the world may go up in smoke tomorrow. If we're going to get a little taste of that American dream, we'd better get it *now*. Boldness is what we need. Bold politicians, bold lawyers—that's you and me, Les—and bold bank robbers even."

"I never thought of that before! Why don't we have any good black bank robbers?"

"Now you boys are getting ridiculous and I'm getting sleepy."

"Let's let Mae go to bed. Let's march boldly down to the corner bar and boldly order a night-cap, and I'll show you where you're wrong. You've got more spirit than brains. You forget that there're an awful lot of white people in this country."

"How could I forget that?"

"Settle it when you get to the bar. Good night."

The men would say good night to Mae and go through the dark room and out into the hallway, would go past the boy who lay awake trying to digest the meaning of all he had heard. Always there were new ideas or new ways of looking at old ideas. He had no way of understanding the literal meaning of the words; he felt, rather than comprehended.

Steely laid his plans with as much care as his experience allowed. He would have to select a purse that was held only in the woman's hand— one with no strap. He must be certain there were no cops nearby and that the sidewalk over which he would run would not be too crowded. He would not make the grab until the woman was several yards away from the subway exit; thus he could get a good running start and be moving at top speed when he reached for the bag. For the time being there was nothing to do but wait.

A group of hack drivers was gathered near the newsstand. Their faces reflected the yellowish color of their automobiles and the green tint of the subway lamp. All of them looked tired and sleepy, although they talked with animated voices.

"Where's our white brethren?" asked an elderly man with a dark face and a tweed cap. "I pull up here in the daytime and I can't get on the line for the paddies."

A very tall, ashen yellow man with little eyes answered, "You know those paddy boys are scared to come up to Harlem at night."

"Well, I don't much blame 'em," another said. "Damned if Harlem don't go crazy every Saturday night. I swear, it's a wonder anybody's left alive up here come Sunday."

The ashen yellow man mumbled, "White folks' just as bad, probably worse."

"I don't believe that," protested the other. He was a plump young man with a round face and a voice that whined. "White folks drink and fight and shoot and so on, but honest to God, I don't think they raise as much hell as they do up here in Harlem."

"You mean they're just as bad," the yellow man said, "but you don't think they have as good a time."

"You call it a good time if you want to," said the plump one. "I just call it hell-raising."

"The way I look at it, boys," said the older man with the tweed cap, "is that they're all full of crap. But since I'm a spook, I stick up for the spooks, see. I wouldn't give a paddy the time of day because I figure he's the lowest thing God ever made."

"You're right about that," said the yellow one.

The plump man laughed. "You two just got race prejudice in reverse."

"No such thing." For some reason the old man was becoming angry. He had a toothpick in his mouth and he worked it up and down as he talked. "Prejudice means to make up your mind before you know what it's all about, right? I know because one time I looked it up in the dictionary. Well, I'm fifty-seven years old and I've been around white folks all my life, and if I ain't got a right to judge, ain't nobody."

"What'd the paddies ever do to you, Pop?" asked the plump man.

The elderly man answered emphatically, "Not a damn thing 'cause I always try to stay out of their way and I know damned well they'd better stay out of mine."

The yellow man showed interest in the intensity of the old hack driver's words. He lit a cigarette and looked at the other man through narrowed eyes. "Which ones of 'em you reckon is the worse, Pop?"

"The damned cops, naturally," was the quick answer.

"Cops are cops, black or white," said the plump man.

"No, Pop," said the yellow man. "I mean what races?"

"Well, now, son, I'll tell you," the other began as though he had given the question a great deal of thought. "The Italians is rough, the Jews is smart, and the Irish is dumb, but they all manage to get along—"

"The Negroes and the Puerto Ricans must be the dumbest," interrupted the plump man, "because they ain't getting along at all."

The rumble of arriving trains below the surface of the street ended the conversation. The men went to their cars, and soon all of them were employed. Other cabs parked at the curb and another group of drivers formed near the newsstand. This was a younger gathering, and their talk was of women. Steely continued to wait. In the crowd there had been only one purse that had been safe to snatch, but he had hesitated too long.

There was one unescorted woman in the next group that emerged from the subway station. She was short and dumpy and wore a blue flowered dress. In her hand was a small black cloth bag.

Instantly Steely was off. When he passed her he was running as fast as he could. His fingers closed firmly on the bag as he snatched it from her hand.

All she saw was a small dark figure quickly disappearing. Steely had turned the corner and was running westward on One Hundred and Twenty-sixth Street before she realized what had happened. Steely heard the scream, but already he was far away.

"I've got it!" Steely whispered to himself. "I've got it!" he thought over and over again.

There were only a few people on the street in this residential block, and none of them paid any attention to him. He felt exultant. He had acted boldly. He had done a daring deed and now he was safe.

But suddenly there were footsteps behind him. They were heavy, they struck the sidewalk less often than his own, but they came nearer. Steely tried to pull away from them, to widen the gap, but he couldn't. The footsteps seemed right behind him now.

Steely stopped abruptly and jumped off the sidewalk into the street. The man behind him was so large and was moving so fast that he had to go several steps farther before he could stop. He whirled on the boy.

"Come 'ere, boy!" he ordered, holding out one of his hands as if to hypnotize Steely. A huge brown man of middle age, he was breathing heavily. "Gimme that damned purse, y'hear?"

He was panting heavily. The boy was prepared when the man lunged at him suddenly. He ducked back to the sidewalk and ran on in the direction he had been going. Soon the footsteps were after him again, but now they were tired and began to recede in the distance.

Steely cut up Old Broadway, ran a block, then headed back toward Amsterdam Avenue. There he merged with the Saturday night crowd. His heart was thumping loudly. He was safe and the purse was in his pocket, snug against his thigh.

But there was nothing in it! That is, there was nothing like the twenty-seven dollars he needed. There were two one-dollar bills, a stick of lipstick, an eyebrow pencil, and a package of doublemint gum. There were letters, tissues, keys, and identification papers. There were all kinds of things, but there was no twenty-seven dollars.

He had stopped to examine the purse near a dark playground. He pushed the two dollars into his pocket and angrily flung the bag over the fence.

Now Steely had to run again, and he sped as fast as his tired legs could carry him, down the hill eastward into the heart of Harlem, away from the playground and the purse, away from the scene of his sharp disappointment and newly born frustration. It hadn't occurred to him that the purse might not contain the money he wanted. So desperate was his need and so great was the risk he had taken that there hadn't been the slightest doubt that the purse would contain exactly twenty-seven dollars, not a penny more or less. As he ran, his mind churned with wild thoughts and images. He pictured his mother waiting for him impatiently, certainly exasperated by now. He imagined the obstacles he had yet to overcome this night in order to get what he wanted. His body was hotly charged with a growing sense of urgency. When he came to a massive gray-stone church on St. Nicholas Avenue, he sat on the steps and tried to pull himself together.

five

Steely caught a downtown bus and sat next to an open window. He looked out but saw nothing. His mind was turned inward where memories and feelings were stored. His thoughts were not of the great general world because he already had a concrete image of that. The world, as he saw it, was divided into two races, Negroes and white people. Between them there was an exciting contest, and he, Steely, was fortunate enough to have been born on the side of right. The white people were on top now, but this situation was only temporary. Ultimately Negroes would triumph, and Steely expected to make a great contribution to the final victory. It was all very simple; for him the outside world was not complicated at all.

But in personal matters he felt lost and completely adrift. Even now, so many months after Paul's disappearance, Steely was shocked and uncomprehending. Nothing that had happened made any sense to him. He had conjured up a hundred explanations for what had happened, but not one of them could put his searching mind at rest or ease the excruciating sense of loss and hurt. He had even tried to make himself hate Paul, but he was too possessed by a bruised love for his father to admit of any hate. Besides, he could not yet exercise sufficient control over his furious and clashing emotions.

It was wanting to understand so much and yet understanding nothing—this was the salt added to the wound of having suddenly lost the person whom he loved above all others. He asked himself a hundred questions and each unanswered one became a sharp knife that seemed to cut at his soul.

His simple concept of love had not been outraged; it had merely been overridden. No matter how he tried to mold it in his mind, it could not be made to fit the present situation. To him love was the most natural and easy thing, something you could almost take for granted. He loved Paul and Mae Brown for very obvious reasons. He had always loved them and had almost always felt that they loved him. Why should it not be the same between the two of them? Steely had by now discovered that adult love was a different thing entirely, but there was no way in which he could understand why this should be. Nor could he begin to perceive the different forms assumed by such love, or its eternally changing character.

His hurt would not have been so deep had he not felt so much alone. His extreme dependence upon Paul had left him with a void that no other person or activity could fill. He instinctively knew that his mother could be of no help to him, so he did not turn to her. Though there was love, there was really no medium of communication between them. His ideas on almost everything had originated with Paul. He had tried to be like his father and think like him. Never had there been a teacher or a boy on the street who had for even one moment threatened to replace Paul in Steely's esteem. So now, with Paul gone, there was small wonder that he felt so utterly alone.

As he scrambled around in this psychological and emotional state he uncovered something that was to prove very important. Now, for the first time, he began to see contradictions between what people say and what they do. In searching for so many answers, he had shaken his own faith in his father. When Paul Brown had talked about great Negroes, Steely had looked at Paul with wide, credulous eyes and pictured those Negroes in Paul's image. Now, as Steely recalled each little incident, he began to believe that Paul Brown had done some things those heroes would not have done. He felt vaguely disappointed with his father. This embryo stirring of criticism had never been allowed to approach the surface. He even felt a trifle guilty for allowing such thoughts to cross his mind. But once there, they would not go away. Against his wishes he was becoming a sensitive, yet ruthless, observer of the gap between the word and the deed, between the ideal and the accomplished fact. Thus his instant condemnation and banishment, without appeal, of Mr. Litchstein and Sugar Boy from the ever shrinking circle of people whom he liked.

He was disturbed now as he tried to apply the

yardstick to incidents long past. He was remembering those nights when his father would stay away until very late; then he would hear Paul's thudding footsteps on the stairs. Sometimes Paul would trip but he never fell. Steely would hear the squeaking of the banisters and know that his father was holding on while he gathered strength for another try at reaching the fifth floor where they lived. Having gained the hallway and groped his way along the dark passage, Paul would stand outside the door fumbling for his keys, mumbling incoherently. When the door finally swung open the mumbling would cease abruptly as he concentrated on not disturbing the children.

Once in the other room, he would start to take off his clothes. Mae's voice would suddenly drone with dull contempt in the darkness:

"It beats me why you come home at all."

"My God, woman! Don't you ever sleep?" Paul's words would be thick and blurred. With a heavy sigh he would sit on the bed and take off his shoes. Each of them would strike the floor with a dull, inconclusive thud. "Les and I were studying and we stopped for a drink, that's all."

"What are you and Les doing? Drinking your way through law school?"

"Don't worry about it. Don't worry about it."

"What are you trying to be? A playboy like Les?" Her voice would be brittle and trembling. "He's young with no responsibilities. You've got responsibilities—"

"I know. You keep reminding me."

"Well, you shouldn't have to be reminded."

For a moment they would be silent. Then, almost electrically, Mae's tight, trembling words would crackle in the darkness. "Are you running around with women, Paul?"

"Oh, God—"

"Don't 'oh, God' me. What are you doing, buying them, or do you and Les spend all your free time hunting them in bars?"

"Look, Mae—" Paul would shout.

"Don't wake up the kids—"

"Well, cut it out, will you?" Paul's voice would be heavy with disgust. "Jesus, I go out and have a drink—maybe a little too much, so what?—but I come home and get accused of every damned thing that comes into your head. What's the matter with you?"

"I'm sorry, Paul."

"Well, you ought to be."

Another silence would fill the apartment while they both waited.

"Paul."

"What is it?"

"What's the matter? Are you having trouble at school? They say the first year in law school—"

"I'm not having any trouble. At least no more than I'd expect."

"Well, why do you drink so much?"

Paul would not answer.

"What are you doing to us, Paul?"

Silence.

"Good night, Mae. I don't feel like talking. I'm tired and I'm drunk and I'm sleepy. So good night."

"Good night, Paul."

For a long time Steely would lie awake, knowing that both of them were still awake, and wondering what they were thinking.

When he thought of the great Negro leaders, he could not envision them as drunk. He tried very hard, he thought of all kinds of explanations, but the pieces of the picture never seemed to fit together.

There were many such nights and, as he recalled them, they blended together, leaving a single impression of wonder and sadness. But one night stood by itself, stamped indelibly in his memory. It was at the end of Paul's first year in law school. Steely was sound asleep when the voices woke him. They were muffled and distant in the slumbering building.

"Mark, you sure you got him?"

"I've got him. It's just so damned dark out here."

"There ought to be a light."

"The place is at the end of the hallway here."

"Come on, Paulus, old boy. Just a little further."

"Goddamn, he's heavy!"

"Don't you let Paulus fall."

"Vickie, for Christ's sake, keep quiet. Why the hell do we all have to crowd up here anyway? Especially you, Vickie."

"God, it stinks up here."

"This feels like a door."

"This is it."

Steely could remember the heavy knocks at the door. He sat up in bed gasping for breath, realizing only then that he had not breathed since he woke up. Now his heart thumped like the knocks. The light went on in the other room, and after a moment his mother came out, tying the belt of her bathrobe under which her stomach bulged with the baby that was to be Carol Ann. Her eyes were frightened as she rushed to the door crying, "I'm coming, I'm coming!"

Except for his father and Lester Bennett, they were all white. A slight blond man with eyeglasses was helping Lester carry Paul, who hung limply between them, his arms over their shoulders. And there were three women, their white faces whiter in the naked light, their eager eyes darting around the cluttered room, taking in the huddled form of Robby on his cot against the far wall, staring with unconcealed curiosity at Steely, who stared back with open hostility.

Lester said, "We're sorry to bother you at this hour, Mae, but we thought we'd better bring Paul home."

"Paulus," said one of the women. "Not Paul. When did he stop being Paulus?"

Lester groaned. "Oh, for God's sake!"

The blond man spoke sharply. "Shut up, Vickie!"

"Bring him in here," said Mae Brown.

The two men carrying Paul followed her into the other room, where Steely heard them letting his father down onto the bed. Now the three women walked into the room.

"My God, this place is awful. No wonder Paulus—"

"Vickie, don't be as much of a bitch as we know you can be."

The third woman was slender and dark haired. She sat on the arm of the overstuffed chair. She lifted a pale hand with long white fingers to her head. "Jesus, what a party! I won't be able to think straight for a week."

"You're Paulus's little boy, aren't you?"

The woman called Vickie was leaning toward him. Her smile was wide and red-lipped, and her teeth were white and even. But Steely did not like her smile, and it never occurred to him to answer her.

"If I were a sculptor," she said, "I would do your head in bronze. Do you know that?"

He wondered what she was talking about. He stared at her but he still did not speak.

His mother and the two men came out of the other room. "It's our fault, Mae, honestly," Lester was saying. "Honest to God, if I had dreamed something like this would happen . . . well, it's all my fault. Paul kept trying to come home but—well, you know how it is when you've been drinking—we just wouldn't let him."

All the white people voiced their agreement with what Lester was saying. Steely had never heard him talk so loudly before.

"—and the next thing you know," the blond man picked up the story, his voice suddenly high as the words gushed over each other, "poor Paul is out on his feet. But really you can't put him in the doghouse, really, because it was our fault and Paul isn't used to running with us."

"We were trying to cheer Paulus up."

His mother looked at the woman called Vickie. The look was long and strange and hard, as if Mae Brown had always known the woman and had always hated her. So Steely, too, looked at Vickie, a tall woman with shining eyes and soft, neatly clipped black hair. He saw a pretty woman like the movie stars with their clean features and their white skins and that mist of silver and gold that follows them. He had never expected to see such a woman in his home, nor could he have said why he felt afraid of her and why he disliked her so much.

"And what did he have to be cheered up for?" Mae Brown asked in an even voice.

The blond man moved uneasily. He put his hand on Vickie's arm and said, "Come on. Let's go."

Vickie ignored him. "Because he flunked it. You didn't know, did you? Yes, poor Paulus flunked out of school."

"Oh," was all Mae Brown said, but it was hushed and low.

"As a matter of fact," Vickie went on, "we all flunked out. At the end of the first year they have general house cleaning and we got swept out, that's all. But it didn't make that much difference to me because I don't really care. It was just an idea I had. Les, he didn't really care either. He wouldn't have made a good lawyer or a good anything, for that matter." She gave all of her companions a sweeping look that was almost drowsy with scorn. "Neither would any of us. But Paulus—" She shook her head. "You'll never know how much he wanted the law. I know, though. He told me and I listened."

"Well, thank you for telling me," said Mae in the same even tone.

"Any time," Vickie said. She turned and almost stumbled as she walked toward the door. The blond man steadied her.

"I'm sorry about all this, Mae," said Lester, lingering behind the others, who now seemed to be rushing out of the room. "You know how Paul was, how much he wanted to—"

"You talk about him like he was dead, Les," said Mae.

"I'm sorry," Lester said again; then he, too, turned and rushed from the room. Mae Brown closed the door and listened as they stumbled through the hallway.

It was Lester's voice that was heard almost immediately. "Goddamn it, Vickie. I ought to slap your head sideways."

"What did I do?"

"You were just your own sweet self," said one of the women, "and that was what we were afraid of."

Suddenly Vickie began to sing in a loud voice:

"We're six little failures who've lost our way
Bah . . . bah . . . bah . . ."

"Shut her up, for Christ's sake!"

Somebody stumbled. "They ought to put some light in here."

"It stinks to high heaven."

"Thank God for slum clearance," said Vickie.

Then they were feeling their way down the stairs

and their voices faded away. Mae Brown had been standing all this time with her back to the door, her hand over her mouth as if to keep down a scream. Now she became aware that Steely was awake and watching her. She reached quickly for the cord in the center of the room and snapped out the light. But even after Steely heard the switch, in that instant before the light swiftly vanished, he saw her face. The naked light was absorbed by her dark, terrified eyes, the full anguish and the torment written there; and just before she closed the door to the other room Steely heard the sound she made. It was a sudden, weak cry, a whimper, that only half conveyed the hurt she felt.

When Steely reached Ninety-sixth Street he changed buses and rode crosstown through Central Park to the East Side. At Madison Avenue he walked southward into a part of the city that was very different from his Harlem. Here there were small, neat shops, groceries, and delicatessens. In the side streets pretty apartment houses with awnings and trimmed hedges spilled warm light through the blinds of the windows and onto the clean sidewalks. Steely was intimidated by the quiet and reserve of the community. He avoided looking directly into the faces of the people he passed in the street. If he had not been driven by his purpose he would have retraced his steps to Harlem.

It was past ten o'clock. He hardly dared think of his mother and how angry she must be. In his mind he tried to picture whether she was standing up or sitting down as she waited for him. How did she intend to beat him? With the strap or with her hands? He decided that she would use the strap because this would be a long beating and she wouldn't want to hurt her hands. In the same rigid manner with which he judged others, he now judged himself. He was guilty; there was no question of it; and he deserved the worst possible punishment from his mother. Under any circumstances he would have had to submit to the punishment physically, but this admission of his guilt would not allow him to bow to it morally and psychologically. He could not hope to escape the beating, but if he could recover the money, he would, to some extent at least, compensate for his guilt.

Two white boys on bicycles passed him in the street. Both of them pumped laboriously as if they had come a long way and were tired. This was the kind of thing Steely had been waiting for. Keeping to the sidewalk, he followed them, trotting just fast enough to watch them and yet not attract their attention. After several blocks he became tired and wanted to stop. The muscles of his legs trembled, throwing hot and cold waves up his thighs. Then his legs were suddenly numb and his breath came in gasps. He knew he could not run another block. Then the boys turned into Eighty-eighth Street. Steely slowed to a walk. Just as he had hoped, one of the bicycles was in the front areaway of an apartment house. It leaned on its own kickstand just a few feet from the vestibule.

Steely walked past the areaway and glanced at the bicycle. It was a Silver Streak with lots of chromium on it. In the stores it sold for at least fifty dollars.

Steely was surprised and pleased by his own calmness. He did not have the same tightness in his chest that had been there when he snatched the purse. He thought of the guys in the movies who calmly light cigarettes before they pull a big job.

The circumstances seemed favorable. He could see no one sitting out of doors. He walked around the block and then turned back into Eighty-eighth Street. The bicycle was still in the areaway. He put a hand on the gate, pushed it open, and went in.

Holding the bicycle erect by its handle bars, Steely reached down quickly with his other hand and pulled the kickstand quietly into its catch.

Quietly he walked with the bicycle through the gate. Quietly he pushed it over the sidewalk into the street. Then he gave himself a good running start and leaped into the seat. He now owned a bike.

s i x

There was one boy in The Comanche Raiders who was known by everybody for blocks around as the "Bike King." This was fifteen-year-old Junior Robinson, who loved bicycles and seemed to know all about them. His own was thought to be the handsomest outfit in Harlem. It had colored lights, battery-powered horns, fur tails, and an extensive multicolored collection of reflectors. Running across the handle bars were all the flags of the United

Nations, and only recently he had added a portable radio powered by a generator attached to the front wheel.

Once Junior Robinson had put Steely on his cross bar and ridden him down to Ninety-sixth Street. There he had told Steely to take the bike back home by himself, and then he had walked away. As Steely had pedaled homeward the older boy had overtaken him, riding a bike that Steely had never seen before. Then Steely had understood that he had just helped Junior Robinson pull a job. When they reached home Junior had dismantled the new bicycle. He said he always swiped bikes from the "gray" boys because when he walked along their streets he could be sure of finding one that wasn't locked. He confided to Steely that he got a good price for all the bikes he obtained in this manner. He had very good relations with a junk dealer near the East River who dealt in all such merchandise. Junior had cautioned Steely not to try the same thing because the younger boy's legs were too short and he could not pedal fast enough.

Although only a few months had passed since he had received this warning, Steely felt he had grown considerably. He intended to hunt up the Bike

King, who would help him sell the Silver Streak. He did not expect the older boy to refuse, now that the stealing of the bicycle was an accomplished fact.

He wanted to go north on Park Avenue, but he changed his mind when he spotted a police car on the next corner. He decided to ride farther east and turn homeward on Lexington Avenue. He knew he would be in Avenger territory, but he felt he would be relatively safe because he intended riding only along its fringe. If he could ride unmolested for eight short blocks he would be able to cross Ninety-sixth Street. There he would be in the safer neighborhood of The Conquistadores, with whom The Comanche Raiders had recently signed a peace pact. Then he would ride westward into his own territory.

But Steely had no way of knowing of an event of the preceding day that was to have considerable influence on his plans. On the previous morning two boys had fought over a girl at a soda fountain on Ninety-sixth Street. That would have been the end of it had one of the boys not been white and the other Puerto Rican. For almost twenty hours the blocks near Ninety-sixth Street had been the scenes of sporadic but violent clashes between groups of four and five boys. Finally the leaders of both sides had met and agreed to make war on each other this very night. Although the trouble had originated among the older boys, whole neighborhoods of youths were now involved. In an organized war boys down to the age of nine or ten were expected to participate. Girls' groups played an important part in the strategy: they concealed weapons in their clothing and gave them to the boys only when they drew near the scene of the "rumble" that had been agreed upon by both sides.

Thus it happened that when Steely reached Ninety-fifth Street, only a block away from the battle spot, he almost ran into the rear of a large formation of Avengers.

He heard them yelling just before he saw them— a group of boys moving threateningly toward the other corner. Steely braked the Silver Streak and spun around. But the tires screamed over the pavement.

"Hey, lookit the boogie!"

"Where the hell that sonuvabitch come from?"

Ride, Steely, ride!

On foot and bicycle, a group of boys detached themselves from the main body and hurried into the chase. Frantically Steely pushed the Silver

Streak back over the few yards to the corner, where he turned downhill toward Second Avenue. He almost fell off trying to pedal the slack out of the chain, but he managed to stay on. Instantly he had a new plan. He was now pedaling toward the East River. He would turn north at Second Avenue and try to go west across Ninety-sixth Street.

He pedaled furiously down the long block. He knew he had outdistanced those on foot but that the bicycles were still following him.

"Hey, Comancheeeeee!"

"Hey, you black Comancheeee! Hold up!"

"Yeah, we want to talk to you."

For the first time since he had bought it, Steely wished he were not wearing his Comanche jacket. Its luminous green was visible several blocks away.

"Hey, Comancheeee!"

Ride, Steely, ride!

He sped across Ninety-sixth Street and almost collided with the side of a bus. The boys behind him were probably bigger, since they were gaining, but he felt he would be safe because they would not follow him very far into Conquistador territory.

Ride, Steely, ride!

Away he pedaled. Pain dragged at his thigh muscles. He wished he were Superman so that his strength would never give out.

Suddenly he was filled with dismay. He had forgotten that all the buildings had recently been torn down on both sides of Second Avenue to make way for a new housing project. The street was dark and empty except for the cars speeding past. He had no hope of help or protection from grownups who might be on the street. No wonder the Avengers behind him had not given up the chase. He thought of turning toward Lexington Avenue, but he would have to pedal uphill and they would surely catch him. Nor could he turn to First Avenue. Nobody lived over there. He had to keep going forward.

Sweat burned his eyes. He tasted the salt at the edges of his mouth and his chest felt like a hot dry oven. The cobblestones were slowing him down. He heard only the sounds of the bicycles behind him—the clacking of loose lights and horns —and his own heavy breathing.

Keep going, Steely, keep going!

His whole body ached. The bikes behind drew closer. The boys no longer called to him but gave all their strength to their pedaling. He knew he must not give up, as Paul had said, must never give up, but even as he swore this, he knew he would be caught.

One of the Avengers rolled past Steely and came to a sudden halt a few yards ahead, blocking Steely's path. He braked his bike and stood beside it, panting. The other boys rolled up and stopped, too. All of them were two or three years older than Steely. For a full minute nobody said anything because they were all winded.

The boy who had blocked Steely's way seemed to be the leader. He said hoarsely, "Hey, Jack, didn't you hear us calling you?"

Steely did not answer.

"Hey, man, dig that crazy pair of wheels he's riding!"

"Man, that's pretty!"

"Yeah, that's a Silver Streak!"

"That's real pretty, Jack."

"Crazy, man, crazy."

They chanted these words as if they were a part of a ritual. Steely knew that nothing he could say would make any difference, so he kept quiet.

"What did you say, Jack?" asked the leader. "Did I hear you say you're gonna be nice and give us this crazy bike?"

A chubby boy with black curly hair laid his bike

down on the street and walked over to Steely. He gave Steely a stiff shove that separated him from the Silver Streak and landed him on the ground. As he got up, Steely wondered what he could do. The chubby boy was holding his bicycle.

Another boy taunted, "Oh, he's a real little Comanche, he is."

"Oh, I'll bet he's gonna grow up to be real tough."

A slender boy in motorcycle boots laid his bike down. "Come on, let's see how tough Amos 'n' Andy is," he said.

Steely was knocked down and kicked.

He got up and swung at the boy who was closest to him. It was a wild blow, and the boy, the chubby one, struck Steely solidly on the side of his head. Steely was staggered. For a moment he couldn't see. He stood shakily in the center of the ring of Avengers.

"One thing about Little Black Sambo—he don't cry, huh?"

Their voices were almost leisurely, as if they were playing a tiresome game.

"Hey, Peewee, I bet you can't make Sambo cry."

"Let's see about that."

Steely hardly felt the blow, but he was knocked to the cobblestones. He just sat there. He was so weak and dispirited that he had no will to get up.

"Amos 'n' Andy ain't crying yet."

"Shame on you, Peewee."

Suddenly nervousness began to overtake them. Their voices became tense and worried.

"Man, let's clear outa here before some of them spiks come along."

"Yeah, let's hit back across Ninety-sixth."

"Yeah, man."

"Here, Peewee, grab the other handle of this bike."

"Yeah, man!"

"Wahooo!"

"So long, Boogie!"

"Yeah, man!"

"Take it easy, Amos 'n' Andy."

"Wahooo!"

They pedaled away swiftly. Steely did not look after them. He moved to the curbstone and sat there without moving.

He was not angry. In his mind there was not even a thought of the Avengers or of the bruises they had given him. He was thinking of the still-missing twenty-seven dollars, of how long the night was and of how much more of it loomed before him.

seven

Steely knew it would not be easy for him to roll a drunk. He would need both patience and luck. The larger boys could take more chances because they could rely on their strength in case the unexpected developed; that is to say, if the drunk resisted.

Once Steely had seen Shotgun and Red Louis roll a drunk under the One Hundred and Fifteenth Street overpass. The man had come staggering along the street and they had offered to help him get home safely. He had grumbled and tried to wave the boys away. Then he had wobbled on, with them following closely. They had caught up with him under the overpass, gone through his pockets before he knew what had happened, shoved him hard against the large damp stones of the tunnel wall, then run away toward the safety of the crowd on One Hundred and Sixteenth Street.

But of course Steely was too small to try such a thing. There were other ways he had heard of, though he had never seen any of them in practice. Now it was after midnight. Soon the drunks would stagger out of the saloons. Most of them would be able to get home under their own power, but a few would fall to the sidewalk and lie there until the next morning. Others would find shelter and sleep in dark unknown hallways. From the pockets of one or several of these, Steely was determined to obtain the money he needed.

He was in Harlem again. With the new plan his hope and spirit returned. He was tired, for he had never been out so late, but he had no thought of giving up. Tense and excited, he was completely single-minded.

This neighborhood was like his own. Most of the numberless apartments were dark now. But in the windows above the street sat the old people keeping their gray, lonely vigil because they could not sleep. They were exiles in a cramped, busy world that had no time for them.

The street was all shadows and blackness, relieved by the tepid white light from an occasional lamp. Steely searched from block to block. No one walked the street. Were it not for the passing cars, he might have been the only person in the world. It was so still and quiet.

The boy should have been afraid but he was not. It was a new and strange passion that possessed him, and its embrace was almost pleasurable. He was committed to a cause, an objective, and he could not stop himself.

But he stopped suddenly just as he was nearing a street lamp. He had heard the faint creaking of rusty wheels. Then, low and far away, but distinctly:

Cina, cina, cina,
  Dogwé sang, cina lo-gé

Steely had never seen Black Papa at night. As the shriveled old man pushed his cart into the orbit of the lamplight, his dirty gray stubble of beard and matted hair glowed luminously white. His black skin showed ashen, and his eyes seemed darker and deeper than ever they had by daytime. When the old man was directly under the lamp they seemed not to be eyes at all but empty sockets like the two top holes in a grotesque Halloween mask.

Steely held his breath and trembled as Black Papa passed within a few feet, droning his incantation. It was only a simple prayer, Steely's father had told him, a prayer to a Haitian sea god, but the very strangeness of the sounds stirred the boy's imagination. Here in the night, in this strange and empty place, the words seemed full of black foreboding.

Steely hurried away in the opposite direction, suddenly frightened and desperate for a reason he did not know. He was being chased by evil things. Any moment they would snatch out and envelop him in darkness and gloom. Only when he came to a well-lighted avenue did he feel safe.

But for his purpose he had to keep in the dark streets. He forced himself to turn into another dimly lighted block and walk through it.

This was one of those lively Harlem neighborhoods. Here and there men and women languished on steps and in doorways. They were drinking cold beer and cheap wine, relating dirty jokes in loud, uncouth voices, and ribbing one another with explosive, raucous laughter. Steely was passing in front of one such group when a man shouted out of a window several stories overhead.

"For God's sake!" he cried in exasperation, "will you people shut up and go to bed, or at least move down the street and give decent people a chance to sleep?"

A woman in the group got up suddenly. In the faint light Steely could see her twisted, tormented features set in a drunken face, her eyes ablaze like a cat's. She yelled back in a high, hysterical voice:

"You shut up yourself, you old bastard, and mind your own goddamn business!"

In one impulsive sweep of her arm she heaved her bottle up toward the man, losing her balance as she did so, falling among her friends. The bottle crashed against the building and glass fragments began falling into the street. The group of people huddled into the doorway. A man laughed and said, "Damn, woman, ain't no use trying to kill *us* just because you're mad at him."

Steely ran to the corner and across the street. Now he was not very afraid. The sudden noises and the suggested violence of Saturday night created a bizarre, chilling effect, but he clung tenaciously to his purpose.

Then he saw a drunk. The man stumbled from the avenue into the block where Steely was. He wobbled from the steps of the tenements to the parked cars, then back across the sidewalk to the steps again. In order to avoid notice, the boy stood still against a fence. Steely could see the drunk's face. He was of a dark complexion that seemed purple in the wan light. His eyes stared straight ahead as if naked will power alone kept them open. His lips sagged, revealing several gold teeth. He caught sight of Steely and lunged slowly toward the boy with his arms outstretched.

"Hiya, little boy."

He was moving like a figure in a slow-motion picture. Steely darted away and the man fell heavily against the fence where the boy had been standing. He braced himself, groaned and shook his head, not certain that he had seen a little boy at all. Then he lurched forward along the sidewalk again. Steely followed like a frightened animal, waiting anxiously for the man to fall.

But in front of one tenement building the drunk stopped and blinked up at the address. He swayed on his feet and gave a loud, long yawn. Then he seemed to fall toward the doorway and disappear.

Steely felt wild frustration. The man lived in the building! But perhaps this was the wrong house. Maybe he would lie down in the hallway. Steely ran up the steps and into the vestibule. The door to the apartment at the rear of the ground floor hallway was just closing. The man was nowhere in sight.

Out on the street again Steely felt keen disappointment but some relief. He walked along half-heartedly, doubting himself, wondering if he would have shrunk back at the last moment, too afraid to do what had to be done.

"Hello, young fellow."

A white man had pulled his car to the curb and now drove it slowly along beside Steely. He was smiling.

"I said hello, young fellow."

His voice seemed to smile too. Steely had never heard a voice so friendly. But it had come suddenly and it seemed out of place on a dark Harlem street. He quickened his step almost to a run. The car drew up beside him again.

"Come here, little boy. I won't hurt you."

Steely did not stop. The man could not fool him;

he was one of those queers. Steely had heard the boys talk. A queer was a man who acted like a woman and did dirty things. You were not supposed to have anything to do with them. Steely got ready to break into a run.

"What are you afraid of?" the man asked quickly. "I won't hurt you. How would you like to make some money?"

Steely hesitated, then stopped. He turned and looked at the man with mixed fear, hostility, and reluctant interest.

"Come here so I can talk to you. You don't want me to yell all over the street, do you?"

Steely took two steps toward the car but held back as if he might run any minute. He was afraid the man would open the door and grab him. The man was thirtyish. He had a long face that was as friendly as his smile and his voice. Steely was sure he was rich because the car was a long new Cadillac. It had been polished to such a gloss that it sparkled even in the dark. Surely a man who owned such a car could easily afford twenty-seven dollars.

"Now, wouldn't you like to make some money?" the white man asked.

Steely was thinking that he would not have to roll a drunk after all; he would get the money from this queer. Nobody else would know about it. Just once he would do whatever it was this queer man did, and he would never do it again. In answer to the question he nodded his head slowly.

"Of course you would," affirmed the man excitedly, as if to punctuate Steely's unspoken words. "Of course you would."

He let his eyes rest for a long moment on the boy's face. Steely thought he was expected to say something but he didn't know what. He felt uncomfortable and wanted to fidget but he stood still.

"What's your name?"

"Steely."

It was the first word he had spoken in several hours. The sound of his voice surprised him; he could hardly believe he had answered. It was as if the man's warm manner and smile had charmed the word out of him.

"Ah, Steely," breathed the man with satisfaction. He lowered his voice and the next words came out unctuously. "Steely, how would you like to make a whole dollar?"

"I don't want a dollar," Steely said bluntly. "I want twenty-seven dollars."

The smile on the man's face vanished; a frown was there for the quickest moment, then the smile

stole back. "Well, well, you *are* an enterprising little chap, aren't you?" he said. "Ha ha ha," he
laughed. "Well, Steely, if you would like to make
twenty-seven dollars, you just come and take a
little ride with me—"

But already he was speaking to Steely's fleetly
disappearing figure. The boy had seen the troubled
frown and recognized it. In that instant he had
thought of Mr. Litchstein and Sugar Boy and the
violated trust. This man would have been like that,
too. So he ran as fast as he could, though he knew
he was not being followed.

e i g h t

At Central Park Steely walked under the tall trees that at night cast deep shadows and blanket the park with heavy gloom. He moved over the sidewalk just outside the stone wall. Here and there a boy and a girl fumbled with each other in the darkness. Under a street lamp two elderly women sat in stern, animated discussion of family and neighborhood affairs. An occasional car sped through the hush, paused for a red light, then rushed on. The stillness was profound. Steely stepped lightly, as if fearing that a scuffle of his shoe might strike a spark that would explode the highly inflammable night. He sat down when he came to an empty bench tucked away in the shadows.

Now he realized he was tired. He wanted to close his eyes and sleep. He mumbled, "I can't. I've got too much to do." But a few moments later his chin was on his chest and his eyes were closed. The city murmured around him, but he did not hear it.

He was neither asleep nor awake. He was back in that confusing time after the night when they had brought Paul Brown home, remembering how just a few days later Carol Ann was born. Steely was the one who had run down for a taxi. The first two drivers had refused to wait when they found out about the baby because they said they did not want their cars bloodied up. But the third driver was a good guy who had walked up the five flights and helped Paul carry Mae down the stairs. Robby had set up an awful wail, and Paul had told Steely to stay at home and look after his younger brother. Carol Ann had come too soon, they said, and they had to leave her at the hospital for almost a month.

Even then she was the tiniest baby Steely had ever seen.

And all the time his father was so different. It worried Steely no end, the way Paul Brown never talked much any more, just came and went, working two jobs, now that he was not studying law; just came and went with a quiet, subdued look about the eyes that the boy had never seen there before. Paul smiled sometimes, but sadly. Sometimes he laughed, too, but not in the bold, free way he had before, the laughter ringing off the plastered walls, seeming to dominate everything it touched. Nor did he ever put his hand on Steely's shoulder and say all those wonderful and fantastic things, using his hands and arms to draw pictures in the air.

During this period Steely once said, "Let's go out to Ebbets Field next week, Pop, and see Jackie."

"A good idea," Paul said. "If I can find time we'll go."

But of course he forgot all about it. It just never crossed his mind again, and Steely came to know that the Dodgers and Jackie Robinson were not so important any more. Steely told himself he would be like this new Paul Brown and not even think about baseball and such things. He would be quiet like his father, and sad, too, and think the same somber thoughts, even if he did not know what they were.

Steely knew they should have been happy. His mother was no longer working at the laundry. Now she was at home all the time with Carol Ann and Robby. There was plenty to eat, and Steely came home from school for lunch every day. The house was clean because his mother made the place look shining. Steely had never imagined the two rooms could look so nice.

But something was wrong. It was in everything about the house. He had his ways of knowing; they could not fool him. It wasn't only the way his father looked and acted, it was his mother, too. The way she said, "Hi, Paul," when he came in from work, just like that, quiet and polite as if they hardly knew each other. Even when Paul came home late with that red look around his eyes, when Steely could tell that he had been drinking, she would say, "Hi, Paul," and never raise her voice; and he would say, "Hello," and go straight to bed. She would go back to what she had been doing, just as if he had not come in at all. Steely kept thinking it was as if something were dead, but he did not know why he thought this. He would turn his face to the wall, not wanting to look at his mother's face, knowing instinctively that he would not like what he saw there.

Sitting beside the park wall, Steely was not dreaming now, or remembering exactly, but feeling everything just as it had been during those last days.

He had another secret, too, another way of knowing. It was somehow so personal and private that he could never mention it to a soul. He had to keep it shut up inside himself, wrapped in all his senses, bruising and exciting them at the same time; a terrible secret he wished were not his, or, if he must possess it, that he might have just one other person with whom to share it, for it was certainly too much for one little boy to have all by himself. This was a secret telling him so much and yet so little, answering everything but nothing at all.

It had started that night long ago when his mother had screamed. It had waked him and he had climbed out of bed and knocked at the door of their room, calling, "Mama! Mama!" Within the room his mother and father had laughed and told him to go back to bed; everything was all right. But he had not been able to sleep. He had lain awake wondering and listening hard. Only later had he come to understand, had he fitted the pieces of the puzzle together: Red Louis had told The Junior Comanches how he "screwed" the girls in the neighborhood and how one of them, Ruthie Haymes, had once screamed so loud that he had been forced to stop because they were in the hallway of the house where she lived and someone might have heard. Another time Steely and some of his gang had been playing on a roof and had looked down into a room in the back of a lower building. The window had a shade but it had become unhooked, and they could see the man and the woman, naked and sweating like two sleek water animals, locked together, biting, scratching, and rolling, as if they could not let each other go. The other boys had giggled nervously but Steely had crouched as in a trance, his eyes rooted to the feverish, sweat-drenched bodies below. Without wanting to, he had thought of the dogs he and his friends had watched on the street. The comparison had come to his mind instantly and he had wondered at the dirtiness of it all because these two below were not dogs but his own human kind. Horribly fascinated, he had crouched and watched everything, then gone home sick to the stomach, trembling and frightened because he did not know how else to feel.

Then he had come to understand that his mother and father did that too: they lay just that way with their naked bodies. The only thing he could think of was that it was like the dogs on the street. Now he could not help listening for sounds from the other room. And he learned that when they closed the door they did this thing that seemed so nasty to him, and when they left it open they slept as they should, apart from each other, his mother on her side facing the window, his father lying face downward with his head on his arm. Sometimes when they left the door open he would get up late at night and stand long minutes watching them sleep, wondering what determined when they should lie in bed this way or that—and knowing, though he did not want to know, that the strange and violent and naked way was what happened when they were happiest and loved each other and loved the children. He had learned all this by watching their different reactions in the night and the mornings afterward. Steely had gone about obsessed with these thoughts; week after week, month after month, he had given himself to them.

So this was his secret, which seemed so awful to him, his way of knowing they were not happy any more. She said, "Hi, Paul," and he answered, "Hello," and they went into the other room separately, never together as in other times when they used to rush the children to bed before going into the other room together and closing the door. They always left it open now, and Steely could hear nothing but the quiet.

Everything in the house waited; not just his mother and father, but everything: the jet-black gas stove with its two burners, the sink with its cracked porcelain, the fuzzy blue-black flies that sometimes flew through the window and hovered over the pots, Carol Ann's bright yellow painted crib, the two cots on which the boys slept, the big bed in the other room, the green wooden chair. Everything waited as Steely waited, too, knowing that something was to happen, wondering when and what, and knowing that it would be bad.

But when it came, it was in the negative, and so they did not know it had happened until days later. Paul Brown just did not come home, but he might at any moment, and they kept expecting him. Only on the third or fourth day did he know—from the cold hurt look of his mother's eyes and the tight way she held her lips; from this more than anything else—that he should not look for his father from day to day, that Paul had gone away on purpose and would not be back. It struck his mother so deeply she could not cry. It was several months before Steely heard her sobbing in the other room late at night.

In that drowsy state between sleep and consciousness Steely identified the slow, steady creaks of the rusty wheels and was shocked fully awake. He gasped, and stifled his outcry with a tight hand over his own mouth. Black Papa was passing under a street lamp just a few yards away, his white eyes staring straight ahead as if unseeing, his earring catching the light and flinging it back. The mumbled prayer rang softly and clearly in Steely's ears.

Cina, cina, cina,
  Dogwé sang, cina lo-gé

The words seemed to pierce Steely's brain and run around and around there. The old man and his cart passed on into the darkness, his prayer just a murmur now in the balmy night. Steely had not moved since he had raised his head. In his fear his imagination ran wild. Surely it was some kind of omen that he had seen Black Papa twice in one night. The old man was a shadow over all the boy's feelings of love and hope and want, of being alone. In the boy's mind he became the dark symbol of all that had happened: the wrong things he had tried to do and must yet do before the night was over; the terrible secret he had held inside so long; the lost money and the lost father.

Steely got up from the bench and walked away. He did not run this time. He was condemned and afraid, but still determined.

n i n e

Steely walked away from the park at One Hundred and Tenth Street and continued northward on Eighth Avenue. In this early morning hour the rust-red brick buildings drooped their tired dirt-stained jowls of cream-colored window shades as if bored by the monotonous procession of day and night, day and night.

Twice, at different places, Steely passed men who lay on the sidewalk near the curb, but he did not attempt to roll either of them. He could tell, almost from the attitudes of their bodies, that they were derelicts, completely life-wrecked men who had never possessed anything of value. Steely had seen such men all his life and had always been afraid of them, for they were filthy, their smell was nauseating, and their rags of clothing were caked with dirt. They slept troubled but deeply, and seldom bothered to bestir themselves even when their wrecked bodies needed relief. Steely's reaction was one of deep revulsion. He always tried to imagine what their wasted lives had been like but he never could.

In one doorway Steely saw a woman. She was slumped over with her arms around two large shopping bags. She was an old, mustard-colored woman, squat and huge, yet ravaged by time and poor health. All of her features were grotesque, twice as large as they should be, except her eyes, which, closed now, seemed lost in wrinkles of wasted flesh. Her head leaned against the doorway and her toothless mouth gaped open. As Steely hurried past he heard her gruff, sputtering snores and saw the way the wasted flesh of her thick legs seemed to roll down over her shoes. He knew there were men who did not have any money or a place to live, but somehow he had never realized it could happen to a woman. Immediately he thought of his mother and vowed that he would take care of her all his life and never let her grow old and ugly and sick like this gross woman with her great wrinkled arms around the shopping bags.

"Come 'ere, boy!"

Steely jumped. He had not seen the scout car at the curb. Its lights were out and the men within were hardly visible.

"I said come 'ere."

Steely stepped forward hesitantly. He had half a mind to run but was too afraid. He reminded himself that he had not done anything they would know about, but this did not help much. The cop who had spoken was a colored man with a lined brown face in which were set cheerless eyes, glinting coldly in the dim light. The other cop was white, and Steely could not see his face. Steely heard laughter from the far corner and guessed that the two men were spying on the group of people there.

"What's your name, boy?" asked the colored policeman.

"Steely."

"Steely what?"

"Steely Brown."

"Do you know what time it is, Steely Brown?"

"No, sir."

"It's damned near two o'clock in the morning. Did you know that?"

"No, sir."

"Where do you live?"

"A Hundred and Sixteenth Street."

"Well, listen, Steely—that's your name, right?"

Steely nodded.

"Do you want to go to jail?"

Steely shook his head from side to side.

"Well, if you don't want to go to jail . . ." He was looking hard at Steely now and growling in a low voice. ". . . you'd better take some advice I'm gonna give you. I want you to take your little ass and make a beeline for a Hundred and Sixteenth. And if I *ever* catch you out this time of night again, I'm gonna put your little behind in jail and keep you there until you're ninety years old. Do you hear me?" Steely nodded again. "Now beat it, goddamn it, beat it!"

Steely ran toward One Hundred and Sixteenth Street. He wanted to look back but he didn't dare. Remembering the cold eyes, he could almost believe every threatening word. When he had turned down One Hundred and Sixteenth Street and run the whole block to Seventh Avenue, when he was certain the scout car was not following, he turned northward and continued in the direction he had been going.

Now the bars were closing. Some of the emerging men and women laughed and joked on the corners or hurriedly hailed taxis. There were loud, threatening arguments, occasionally resulting in drunken brawls. Steely Brown walked on, turning into first one side street and then another. He knew he must get his mother's twenty-seven dollars at this hour or not at all. He was afraid and excited. The test had come.

The man sat in the doorway with his knees drawn up in front of him. The weight of his body was on one shoulder, pushed against the wall, so the figure seemed like that of a man who had collapsed as he was trying to sit down. The house was set in the darkest part of the street, on one side of which construction was under way, so there was no one to observe Steely from that side. Even though he had been searching he had almost not seen this man, so much a part of the shadows did he seem.

Steely walked by several times to make certain the man was really drunk. Once he walked all the way to the corner to avoid arousing the suspicions of some people who came out of a nearby house. Finally he thought it safe to approach the man, whose position had not changed since Steely had first spotted him.

The wallet was probably in the back pocket of the trousers. Steely would have to lift the tail of the man's jacket, put his hand into the back pocket, and lift out the wallet. It would be almost impossible to perform this operation from the front. Besides, it would be dangerous, for although it was dark, he might be caught in the act by a passer-by. The obvious answer was to step past the man into the vestibule so he could work from behind.

But this Steely hesitated to do. If he had guessed wrong, if the man were not as drunk as Steely hoped, and if he woke up and discovered himself being robbed, Steely would be trapped and unable to run. If luck were against him he would certainly have a better chance to break away if he worked from the front; there would be no chance at all working from behind, for the vestibule would become a narrow prison. He had a vivid picture of the scene: a little boy desperately trying to break out, and a grown man, suddenly awake and angry, blocking the only exit.

But his indecision was short-lived. He *had* to get twenty-seven dollars; and just as he knew he must get it now, so did he know he must get it from this collapsed drunk in the doorway. He would not again be able to summon the strength of purpose, or again submit his mind and body to the same excruciating tension. So he killed all his fear, drowned it in the intense passion eating at him, and gave himself up to this passion—and stepped past the man into the vestibule.

He knelt on one knee and then the other. He paused before lifting the coattail. The back of his intended victim appeared before him as a rounded mass in the general darkness. The man's breath came noisily, as if air were a solid thing that grated on his lungs. Steely put his weight on his knees and one of his hands. With his other he reached forward, slowly, fearing yet anxiously anticipating the thrill of that first second when his fingers would actually touch the fabric of the man's coat. This happened sooner than he expected and he almost jerked his hand away. But he willed down the impulse and kept his fingers resting lightly on the man's back so that the body would become accustomed to his touch. All this he knew to do instinctively, as if the very daring of the act had matured and sharpened his untrained senses. Now his fingers moved quickly as he fought down a panic warning him that every next moment the man would jump up and strike out at him.

The wallet was there! It was in the back pocket where he had hoped it would be, but it was wedged between the buttock and the doorstep where the man slept. He withdrew his hand. He knew what he would have to do: lift the coat, unbutton the pocket, and ease the wallet out as slowly as he could. Any sudden pull at it would be disastrous.

Steely wanted a moment to take a slow deep breath and prepare himself. It seemed as though he had already been in the vestibule for hours. This sense of time pressed in on him, and he could not afford the luxury of the pause he wanted. Taking hold of the coattail, he began to pull slowly and steadily. It was caught between the body and the floor; he knew that, but he must not release it, lest the change wake the sleeping drunk. He continued the pulling pressure, and after a long and terrible moment he felt the coattail begin to move. Slowly . . . slowly . . . little by little . . . it moved.

"Ummm . . ."

The man mumbled and changed his position suddenly. He twisted around so he could sit across the doorway. He lifted his head and let it fall back against the doorsill.

At the first suggestion of movement, Steely had jumped swiftly to his feet and pressed back into the vestibule, quite frozen with sudden terror.

At that moment an automobile passed in the street below and its light illuminated the face of the drunkard. Steely gasped and cried out.

It was the face of his father.

The drunk was Paul Brown.

t e n

In that first moment of recognition he had been unable to stop himself from crying out. Then the car passed and the vestibule was dark again.

Everything swirled before him. His breath had rushed out of him as if he had been struck in the stomach. The shock weakened and paralyzed him.

"Pop! Pop!"

His high, piercing voice did not get through to Paul Brown. Steely knelt and took hold of his father's shoulders. He tried to shake Paul, who fell over into the vestibule with a groan. He lay there sprawled in the cubicle, his arms and legs twisted unnaturally like a great broken doll. His lips were parted, showing the teeth white and prominent. This gave his face an exaggerated, almost comic expression, fixing it in a broad, stupid smile. His breathing was regular and noisy, quite undisturbed by Steely's frantic efforts.

"Pop! Pop!" he screamed. "Paul! Paul Brown!"

The shock and the sudden effort had exhausted Steely. He paused to rest, staring at Paul's blurred face. He saw a drunken buffoon.

Steely was suddenly furious. How could *he,* Paul Brown, lie there like that, drunken and dirty, smelling like any bum in the street? How could anybody who had spoken such beautiful words and inspired such challenging dreams—how could he debase himself and lie in such stupor? The contradiction maddened Steely. He slapped out at the ugliness of the face, landing full on the cheek with the palm of his hand. This blow spent, the others followed without his being able to stop them. *Slap! Slap!* Here were Shotgun and the Council who had taken his money, the boys who had beaten him up and taken the bicycle, the purse with only two dollars in it, the betrayals over and over again; everybody and everything that created unhappiness was all here, and he placed his blows one after the other, his open palm stinging and hurting from the blunt contact with skin and bone. *Slap! Slap!* He wanted to keep striking forever, but then he was exhausted again. He fell over into a corner as the hot breath screamed through his empty lungs.

Paul Brown groaned and moved. He put his hands behind him and pushed himself up to a sitting position. His head hung on his chest and his eyes were closed. Once again he groaned, following it with a deep yawn. He began laboriously to move his head from one side to the other as if he were trying to shake it. Feebly he lifted both hands and buried his face in them. He exhaled loudly and groaned again. Now he uncovered his face and really shook his head. He blinked his eyes open and stared dully into the void. He was conscious.

"It's me, Pop. It's Steely."

Paul painfully turned his head and looked toward the sound.

"It's me, Pop." The boy moved closer. "It's Steely."

"Steely? That you, Fred?"

"That's right, Pop. It's me."

"Really you?"

"Really me."

Paul reached into the darkness and put a heavy hand on the boy's head. He touched the familiar features with the tips of his fingers. Then he made an absurd, crying noise in his throat.

"It's you, Fred," as if he had only just discovered it. After a moment he said, "Is this a Hundred and Twenty-ninth Street, Fred?"

"That's right, Pop."

"See what address this is."

Steely had to strain his eyes to see the numbers. He told his father what they were.

"Well, I got to the right house, anyway." His voice was strangely weak. "This is where I live, Fred. Will you help your old man upstairs?"

"Sure, Pop."

With his arm over Steely's shoulders, Paul got to his feet. Steely took a key from his father's pocket and unlocked the door. Together they went up the stairs.

The room was a very small one on the fourth floor. The cot was spread with an army blanket. A reinforced crate in one corner held a small radio. Near the sink was an electric hot plate. There was no window in the room and it was stuffy with a heavy, musty smell.

Paul had gone to the bathroom on the floor below. Steely sat on the cot waiting for him. He was calmer now, almost peaceful. The room and everything it contained seemed familiar to him; he felt as if he had left home with the intention of coming to this very spot. Every possible path had led him here. He had known his father existed, had believed in him and searched for him, and now Steely had found him.

When Paul returned to the room he looked almost refreshed. His tan skin had lost its drunken pallor. He didn't speak to Steely right away. He plugged in the hot plate and set a small white coffeepot on the burner. Then he sat beside his son on the cot and stared at the wall. His gaze was so intent that Steely, who had so much to say, said nothing at all. Thus they sat in silence, one looking at the other, who looked at the wall, as if there were no medium of communication between them. When the coffee in the pot had come to a boil, Paul poured himself a black cupful. Then he half filled another cup, lightened it with milk, and gave it to

Steely. Paul drank his coffee in two long gulps. Finally he said in a shaky voice, "How are Robby and Carol Ann?"

"They're all right," Steely mumbled.

"And your mother? How is she?"

"She's all right, too, I guess."

"And school? How're you doing in school?"

"School's out," the boy said bluntly.

"Oh," said Paul.

He closed his eyes and turned his head toward the wall again. Steely saw that his father's hands were trembling.

Paul was suddenly exasperated with himself. The words seemed to burst out of him. "I don't know what to say to you! I'm sorry, Steely. That's all I can say and I know that's not enough."

He held up his hands and stared at them. "Look at the way they shake. Look at that!"

Steely was puzzled. He had never heard his father talk this way. He scarcely recognized the thin, high-strung voice.

Suddenly Paul looked at Steely. "What the hell were you doing downstairs?" he demanded. "What time is it?" He looked at his watch. "Well, I'll be damned. What the hell are you doing out at this hour?" Now it was the boy who looked away. "Come on. Tell me."

Steely hesitated. He did not expect a grown person to understand how circumstances sometimes forced you to do things you did not want to do. Hadn't his mother said not to come back if he lost the money? And was it his fault that the big boys had robbed him? He had offered to work and work hard, but nobody would advance him the twenty-seven dollars. His father had once told him you had to guard every minute of your life if you expected to become great; that you could make one little wrong turn and never get back on the right road. Well, how could Steely expect him to understand that sometimes you did a wrong in spite of yourself?

But he told Paul anyway, starting at the very beginning and describing everything that had happened. He did this because all these months, he now realized, he had been feeling alone and had carried so much wrapped up inside himself, and now he wanted to reach out and know Paul again. If Paul could not help, who could?

His words tumbled out in a long stream. When he had finished, Paul Brown put a hand on his shoulder and said, "Steely, if I ever hear of you robbing and stealing—well, you see this?" He held his fist in front of Steely's face. It was a real threat, but a smile followed it and Steely felt everything would be all right after all.

Paul stood up. "Now, let's see," he muttered as he looked around the room. "You've got two dollars and change, which means there are twenty-five more standing between you and the worst whipping you ever heard of." He went to the place on the wall where his clothes hung. He took down an overcoat and a suit.

"There's a fellow down in the basement," he said, "a wonderful individual who makes his living out of other people's miseries."

Steely's heart beat faster to hear his father talk in this fashion, which was the way he remembered.

"As much as we detest such individuals, we must perforce deal with them. These clothes and my watch being worth more than a hundred dollars, he may consent to hold them for a fourth of that amount. What do you think?"

It was like a game that had been interrupted for several months, a wonderful game of word magic. Steely nodded his head eagerly.

Paul was gone only a short while. When he came

back he counted out twenty-five dollars, which he pinned to the inside of Steely's pocket. He sat down on the cot and they were silent again.

A new fear came over Steely. If Paul had given him the money, it meant that he had no intention of returning home with Steely. The boy had thought, had dreamed, had known, that when he found Paul they would go home together. Now the question asserted itself in Steely's mind with an urgency that had been growing for several months.

"Pop, can I ask you something?"

"Sure, Steely."

"You gave in, didn't you? Remember how you said that under pressure we shouldn't ever? But you did. You gave in, Pop, didn't you?"

The repetitive accusation brought a sudden flush of guilt to Paul's face. At first it seemed he would not answer, that he could not; and Steely, sensing the effect of his words, wanted to snatch them back and fill the quiet with soft words that would erase the look on his father's face. But he had not yet learned the language of compromise, of live and let live, of give a little and take a little.

Paul said, "Steely, I've got to talk to you and say things I've never said to you before. And I want you to really listen so you'll understand everything." He shifted his position so they faced each other, their eyes meeting directly. "You remember what I told you about Toussaint and Fred Douglas and all those great black men who lived before you and I were born? Well, you've got to believe in them, Steely, and try your best to make your mark the way they did. You've got to believe in them . . . even if you stop believing in me." Here he paused again and swallowed hard. "Because, you see, you're right. I did give in . . . under pressure, I gave in. I just folded up because I wasn't strong enough. I know you thought I was, and so did I, but I wasn't."

He paused and his eyes took on an excited look. "I discovered something I'd never really thought about before: the biggest job is holding onto your sanity. Sure, life is hard, but the greatest danger is within yourself: the thing or combination of things you carry with you that won't let you triumph."

Paul turned away from his son's wide gaze and went on talking, mumbling now, as if he were alone and were explaining things to himself.

"The worst thing in the world is to come face to face with your own mediocrity . . . to know for certain you possess in abundance all the petty weaknesses and appetites you hate . . . to know you don't have the capacity to measure up to the challenge of your own little dream." He jerked his head around and looked at Steely. "Don't you see, all those things I said, I believe. I couldn't measure up, that's all. So you've got to forget about me. Believe in yourself and the dawning greatness of your people, but forget about me."

Steely's eyes smoldered in their deepness. It was Mr. Litchstein . . . Sugar Boy . . . the queer . . . his father. He heard his mother's voice: "Paul Brown, if words was money you'd be a millionaire." Words . . . words . . . Paul Brown was worse than Mr. Litchstein . . . but the boy loved his father . . .

"Go home now, Steely." Paul put his hand on his son's shoulder. Steely twisted away and stood up. He felt the rage of wild fury. Paul said, "I know how you must feel, Steely, but I can't go back with you. I thought you were a big boy and old enough to understand, but maybe you can't."

People . . . they were always betraying you . . . they said one thing and did the other . . . he hated them.

"You're a goddamn liar!" Steely yelled, the words running out of him just as he had heard them on the street. "You're a dirty goddamn liar!"

Paul slapped Steely hard, but the screaming boy didn't feel it.

"Liars! Just liars! Goddamn liars! I don't believe anything you say, and I don't care if you come back or not, and Mama's right when she says you're no goddamn good, and if it wasn't for you, Carol Ann would have enough to eat and so would Robby, and Mama wouldn't have to cry every night if it wasn't for you. I hate you and I hate every goddamn body!"

Suddenly he was crying. For the first time in a long while he did not try to keep the tears from coming. He sobbed and moaned as if he were in pain. When Paul Brown put his arms around him he fought feebly and finally sought shelter in the huge embrace. He had never felt so weak and unhappy in all his life.

"Please come home, Pop," he heard himself saying. "Please, Pop, please. Mama's mad at you but she'll let you come back. And everybody wants you back. You have to keep trying, Pop . . . you have to give more than you've got. That's what you said, Pop. Remember?"

Paul Brown hugged Steely very tightly so the boy wouldn't see his face. He closed his eyes. He wanted to go back, but how could he face Mae Brown now? He knew, too, that he had given Steely only words. The boy was too young to know the terrible wrong he had done. The boy could never understand the thousand little enemies a man carried within himself that had pulled Paul away from home. Perhaps, if he really tried, he could make the boy believe something high-sounding and noble. But he couldn't fool himself and he couldn't fool Mae Brown. He could hurt her but he couldn't make her believe in what wasn't there. How could he go back?

Yet he was imprisoned by the boy's sensitive love and faith. His mind played with a biblical phrase: *Man* created *God* in his own image. And all the black heroes he had created for the boy were dead and gone to hell if they did not live in Paul Brown.

Later they emerged from the house and walked toward One Hundred and Sixteenth Street. Already the dark of night was passing and the morning winds whipped briskly through the Harlem streets. Paul had bathed and changed his clothes and, in Steely's opinion, had never looked so good. Steely skipped once so that he could walk in step with his father.

When they stopped at a corner the man spoke with mock severity. "You think you're pretty smart, don't you?

"*Oh, boy,*" said Steely, flashing one of his rare smiles as he threw Paul's favorite expression back at him.

Arm in arm they walked through Harlem in the morning. That's the best time of all, morning, because then the air is fresh and clean, and, although the people sleep, there is the sense of awakening.